THE NOVELS OF
RAFAEL SABATINI
UNIFORM EDITION

LOVE-AT-ARMS

LOVE - AT - ARMS

*Being a Narrative excerpted from the Chronicles
of Urbino during the dominion of the high
and mighty Messer Guidobaldo
da Montefeltro*

By

RAFAEL SABATINI

HUTCHINSON & CO. (Publishers), LTD
Paternoster House, LONDON, E.C.4

FIRST PUBLISHED
June 1907

3/6 NET EDITION
April and November 1924, July and November 1925,
July 1926

CHEAP 2/- NET EDITION
October 1917 and February 1921

POPULAR 6d. EDITION
January 1909, February and September 1926,
August 1927

FIRST PRINTED IN UNIFORM EDITION
1927

Printed in Great Britain

" *Le donne, i cavalier', l' arme, gli amori,*
Le cortesie, l' audace imprese io canto."

ARIOSTO

CONTENTS

Love-at-Arms

CHAPTER I

VOX POPULI

FROM the valley, borne aloft on the wings of the evening breeze, rose faintly the tolling of an Angelus bell, and in a goat-herd's hut on the heights above stood six men with heads uncovered and bowed, obeying its summons to evening prayer. A brass lamp, equipped with there beaks, swung from the grimy ceiling, and, with more smoke than flame, shed an indifferent light, and yet a more indifferent smell, throughout the darkening hovel. But it sufficed at least to reveal in the accoutrements. and trappings of that company a richness that was the more striking by contrast with the surrounding squalor.

As the last stroke of the Ave Maria faded on the wind that murmured plaintively through the larches of the hillside, they piously crossed themselves, and, leisurely resuming their head-gear, they looked at one another with questioning glances. Yet before any could voice the inquiry that was in the minds of all, a knock fell upon the rotten timbers of the door.

" At last ! " exclaimed old Fabrizio da Lodi, in a voice charged with relief, whilst a younger man of good shape and gay garments strode to the door in obedience to Fabrizio's glance, and set it wide.

Across the threshold stepped a tall figure under a wide, featherless hat, and wrapped in a cloak, which he loosened as he entered, revealing the very plainest of raiment beneath. A leathern hacketon was tightened at the waist by a girdle of hammered steel, from which depended on his left a long sword with ringed steel quillons, whilst from behind his right hip peeped the hilt of a stout Pistoja dagger.   His hose of red cloth vanished into boots of untanned leather, laced in front and turned down at the knees, and completed in him the general appearance of a mercenary in time of peace, in spite of which the six nobles, in that place of paradoxes, bared their heads anew, and stood in attitudes of deferential attention.

He paused a moment to throw off his cloak, of which the young man who had admitted him hastened to relieve him as readily as if he had been born a servitor.   He next removed his hat, and allowed it to remain slung from his shoulders, displaying, together with a still youthful countenance of surpassing strength and nobility, a mane of jet-black hair coiffed in a broad net of gold thread— the only article of apparel that might have suggested his station to be higher than at first had seemed.

He stepped briskly to the coarse and grease-stained table, about which the company was standing, and his black eyes ran swiftly over the faces that confronted him.

" Sir," he said at last, " I am here.   My horses went lame a half-league beyond Sant' Angelo and I was constrained to end the journey on foot."

" Your Excellency will be tired," cried Fabrizio, with that ready solicitude which is ever at the orders of the great.   A cup of Puglia wine, my lord ?   Here, Fanfulla ! " he called to the young nobleman who had acted as usher. But the new-comer silenced him and put the matter aside with a gesture.

" Let that wait.   Time imports as you little dream. It may well be, illustrious sirs, that had I not come thus I had not come at all."

" How ? " cried one, expressing the wonder that rose in every mind, even as on every countenance some consternation showed.   " Are we betrayed ? "

" If you are in case to fear betraya l, it may well be, my friends.   As I crossed the bridge over the Metauro and took the path that leads hither, my eyes were caught by a crimson light shining from a tangle of bushes by the roadside.   That crimson flame was a reflection of the setting sun flashed from the steel cap of a hidden watcher.

The path took me nearer, and, with my hat so set that it might best conceal my face, I was all eyes. And as I passed the spot where that spy was ambushed, I discerned among the leaves, that might so well have screened him but that the sun had found his helmet out, the evil face of Masuccio Torri."

There was a stir among the listeners, and their consternation increased, whilst one or two changed colour. " For whom did he wait ? That was the question that I asked myself, and I found the answer that it was for me. If I was right, he must also know the distance I had come, so that he would not look to see me afoot, nor yet, perhaps, in garments such as these. And so, thanks to all this and to the hat and cloak in which I closely masked myself, he let me pass unchallenged."

" By the Virgin ! " exclaimed Fabrizio hotly, " I'll swear your conclusions were wrong. In all Italy it was known to no man beyond us six that you were to meet us here, and with my hand upon the Gospels I could swear that not one of us has breathed of it."

He looked around at his companions as if inviting them to bear out his words, and they were not slow to confirm what he had sworn, in terms as vehement as his own, until in the end the new-comer waved them into silence.

" Nor have I breathed it," he assured them, " for I respected your injunction, Messer Fabrizio. Still— what did Masuccio there, hidden like a thief, by the roadside ? Sirs," he continued, in a slightly altered tone, " I know not to what end you have bidden me hither, but if aught of treason lurks in your designs, I cry you beware ! The Duke has knowledge of it, or at least, suspicion. If that spy was not set to watch for me, why, then, he was set to watch for all, that he may anon inform his master what men were present at this meeting."

Fabrizio shrugged his shoulders in a contemptuous indifference which was voiced by his neighbour Ferrabraccio.

" Let him be informed," sneered the latter, a grim smile upon his rugged face. " The knowledge will come to him too late."

The new-comer threw back his head, and a look that was half wonder, half enlightenment, gleamed in the black depths of his imperious eyes. He took a deep breath.

"It would seem, sirs, that I was right," said he, with
a touch of sternness, " and that treason is indeed your
business. "

"My lord of Aquila," Fabrizio answered him, "we
are traitors to a man that we may remain faithful and
loyal to a State."

"What State?" barked the Lord of Aquila contemptuously.

"The Duchy of Babbiano," came the answer.

"You would be false to the Duke that you may be
faithful to the Duchy?" he questioned, scorn running
ever stronger in his voice. "Sirs, it is a riddle I'll not
pretend to solve."

There fell a pause in which they eyed one another, and
their glances were almost as the glances of baffled men.
They had not looked for such a tone from him, and they
questioned with their eyes and minds the wisdom of going
further. At last, with a half-sigh, Fabrizio da Lodi
turned once more to Aquila.

"Lord Count," he began, in a calm, impressive voice,
"I am an old man; the name I bear and the family from
which I spring are honourable alike. You cannot think
so vilely of me as to opine that in my old age I should do
aught to smirch the fair fame of the one or of the other.
To be named a traitor, sir, is to be given a harsh title,
and one, I think, that could fit no man less than it fits me
or any of these my companions. Will you do me the
honour, then, to hear me out, Excellency; and when you
have heard me, judge us. Nay, more than judgment we
ask of you, Lord Count. We ask for guidance that we
may save our country from the ruin that threatens it,
and we promise you that we will take no step that has
not your sanction—that is not urged by you."

Francesco del Falco, Count of Aquila, eyed the old
noble with a glance that had changed whilst he spoke, so
that from scornful that it had been it had now grown full
of mild wonder and inquiry. He slightly inclined his
head in token of acquiescence.

"I beg that you will speak," was all he said, and
Fabrizio would forthwith have spoken but that Ferrabraccio intervened to demand that Aquila should pass

them his knightly word not to betray them in the event of his rejection of the proposals they had to make. When he had given them his promise, and they had seated themselves upon such rude stools as the place afforded, Fabrizio resumed his office of spokesman, and unfolded the business upon which he had invited the Count among them.

In a brief preamble he touched upon the character of Gian Maria Sforza, the reigning Duke of Babbiano—seated upon his throne by his powerful uncle, Lodovico Sforza, Lord of Milan. He exposed the man's reckless extravagances, his continued self-indulgence, his carelessness in matters of statecraft, and his apparent disinclination to fulfil the duties which his high station imposed upon him. On all this Fabrizio touched with most commendable discretion and restraint, as was demanded by the circumstances that in Francesco del Falco he was addressing the Duke's own cousin.

" So far, Excellency," he continued, " you cannot be in ignorance of the general dissatisfaction prevailing among your most illustrious cousin's subjects. There was the conspiracy of Bacolino, a year ago, which, had it succeeded, would have cast us into the hands of Florence. It failed, but another such might not fail again. The increased disfavour of his Highness may bring more adherents to a fresh conspiracy of this character, and we should be lost as an independent State. And the peril that menaces us is the peril of being so lost—not only by defection of our own, but by the force of arms of another. That other is Cæsar Borgia. His dominion is spreading like a plague upon the face of this Italy, which he has threatened to eat up like an artichoke—leaf by leaf. Already his greedy eyes are turned upon us, and what power have we—all unready as we are—wherewith successfully to oppose the overwhelming might of the Duke of Valentinois ? All this his Highness realises, for we have made it more than clear to him, as we have, too, made clear the remedy. Yet does he seem as indifferent to his danger as to his salvation. His time is spent in orgies, in dancing, in hawking and in shameful dalliance, and if we dare throw out a word of warning, threats and curses are the only answer we receive."

Da Lodi paused, as if growing conscious that his manner was becoming over-vehement. But of this his companions, at least, were all unconscious, for they filled the pause with a murmur of angry confirmation. Francesco wrinkled his brow, and sighed.

" I am—alas !—most fully conscious of this danger you speak of. But—what do you expect of *me* ? Why bear me your grievance ? I am no statesman."

" Here is no statesman needed, lord. It is a soldier Babbiano requires ; a martial spirit to organise an army against the invasion that must come—that is coming already. In short, Lord Count, we need such a warrior as are you. What man is there in all Italy—or, indeed, what woman or what child—that has not heard of the prowess of the Lord of Aquila ? Your knightly deeds in the wars 'twixt Pisa and Florence, your feats of arms and generalship in the service of the Venetians are matters for the making of epic song."

" Messer Fabrizio ! " murmured Paolo, seeking to restrain his eulogistic interlocutor, what time a faint tinge crept into his bronze cheeks. But Da Lodi continued, all unheeding

" And shall you, my lord, who have borne yourself so valiantly as a *condottiero* in the service of the stranger, hesitate to employ your skill and valour against the enemies of your own homeland ? Not so, Excellency. We know the patriotic soul of Francesco del Falco, and we count upon it."

" And you do well," he answered firmly. " When the time comes you shall find me ready. But until then, and touching such preparation as must be made—why do you not address his Highness as you do me ? "

A sad smile crossed the noble face of Lodi, whilst Ferrabraccio laughed outright in chill contempt, and with characteristic roughness made answer :

" Shall we speak to him," he cried, " of knightly deeds, of prowess and of valour ? I would as lief enjoin Roderigo Borgia to fulfil the sacred duties of his Vicarship ; I might as profitably sprinkle incense on a dunghill. What we could say to Gian Maria we have said, and since it had been idle to have appealed to him as we have appealed to you, we have shown him yet another way by which Babbiano might be saved and Valentino's onslaught averted."

" Ah ! And this other way ? " inquired the Count, his glance wandering back to Fabrizio.

" An alliance with the house of Urbino," answered Lodi. " Guidobaldo has two nieces. We have sounded him, and we have found him well disposed towards such a marriage as we suggested. Allied thus to the house of Montefeltro, we should receive not only assistance from Guidobaldo, but also from the lords of Bologna, Perugia, Camerino, and some smaller States whose fortunes are linked already to that of Urbino. Thus we should present to Cæsar Borgia a coalition so strong that he would never dare to bring a lance into our territory."

" I heard some talk of it," said Paolo. " It would have been a wise step indeed. Pity that the negotiations came to naught ! "

" But why did they come to naught ? Body of Satan ! —why ? " roared the impetuous Ferrabraccio, as with his mighty fist he smote the table a blow that well-nigh shattered it. " Because Gian Maria was not in a marrying mood ? The girl we proposed to him was beautiful as an angel ; but he would not so much as look. There was a woman in Babbiano who——"

" My lord," cut in Fabrizio hastily, fearing the lengths to which the other might go, " it is as Ferrabraccio says. His Highness would not marry. And this it is has led us to invite you to meet us here to-night. His Highness will do nothing to save the Duchy, and so we turn to you. The people are with us ; in every street of Babbiano are you spoken of openly as the duke they would have govern them and defend their homes. In the sacred name of the people, then," the old man concluded, rising and speaking in a voice shaken by emotion, " and with the people's voice, of which we are but the mouthpiece, we now offer you the crown of Babbiano. Return with us to-night, my lord, and to-morrow, with but twenty spears for escort, we shall ride into Babbiano and proclaim you Duke. Nor need you fear the slightest opposition. One man only of Babbiano—that same Masuccio whom you tell us that you saw to-night—remains faithful to Gian

Maria; faithful because he and the fifty Swiss mercenaries at his heels are paid to be so. Up, my lord! Let your own good sense tell you whether an honest man need scruple to depose a prince whose throne knows no defence beyond the hired protection of fifty foreign spears."

A silence followed that impassioned speech; Lodi remained standing, the others sat, their eager glances turned upon the Count, their ears anxiously alert for his reply. Thus they remained for a brief spell, Aquila himself so still that he scarcely seemed to breathe.

He sat gripping the arms of his chair, his head fallen forward until his chin rested on his breast, a frown darkening his lofty brow. And whilst they waited for his answer, a mighty battle was fought out within his soul. The power so suddenly, so unexpectedly thrust within his reach, and offered him if he would but open his hands to grasp it, dazzled him for one little moment. As in a flash he saw himself Lord of Babbiano. He beheld a proud career of knightly deeds that should cause his name and that of Babbiano to ring throughout the length and breadth of Italy. From the obscure state that it was, his patriotism and his skill as a *condottiero* should render it one of the great Italian powers—the rival of Florence, of Venice or Milan. He had a vision of widened territories and of neighbouring lords becoming vassals to his might. He saw himself wresting Romagna mile by mile from the sway of the ribald Borgia, hunting him to the death as he was wont to hunt the boar in the marshes of Commachio, or driving him into the very Vatican to seek shelter within his father's gates— the last strip of soil that he would leave him to lord it over. He dreamt of a Babbiano courted by the great republics, and the honour of its alliance craved by them that they might withstand the onslaughts of French and Spaniard.

All this he saw in that fleeting vision of his, and Temptation caught his martial spirit in a grip of steel. And then another picture rose before his eyes. What would he do in times of peace? His was a soul that pined in palaces. He was born to the camp and not to the vapid air of courts. In exchange for this power

that was offered him what must he give? His glorious
liberty. Become their lord in many things, to be their
slave in more. Nominally to rule, but actually to
be ruled, until, should he fail to do his rulers' will, there
would be some night another meeting such as this, in
which men would plot to encompass his downfall and to
supplant him as he was invited to supplant Gian Maria.
Lastly, he bethought him of the man whose power he
was bidden to usurp—his own cousin, his father's
sister's son, in whose veins ran the same blood as in
his own.

He raised his head at last and met those anxious
faces on which the fitful light was casting harsh shadows.
The pale ghost of a smile hovered for a second on the
corners of his stern mouth.

"I thank you, sirs, for the honour you have done
me," he made answer slowly, "an honour of which
I fear I am all unworthy."

In strenuous chorus their voices rose to contradict
him.

"At least, then, an honour which I cannot accept."

There was a moment's silence, and their faces, from
eager that they had been, grew downcast to the point
of sullenness.

"But why, my lord?" cried old Fabrizio at last,
his arms outstretched towards the Count, his voice
quivering with intensity. "*Santissima Vergine*!
Why?"

"Because—to give you but one reason out of many—
the man you ask me to overthrow and supplant is of
my own blood." And but that his tone was calm they
might have held that he rebuked them.

"I had thought," hazarded seriously the gay Fanfulla,
"that with such a man as your Excellency, patriotism
and the love of Babbiano would have weighed even
more than the ties of blood."

"And you had thought well, Fanfulla. Did I not
say that the reason I gave you was but one of many?
Tell me, sirs, what cause have you to believe that I
should rule you wisely and well? It so chances that
in the crisis now threatening Babbiano a captain is
needed for its ruler. But let not this delude you,

B

for there may come a season in the fortunes of the State when such a man might be as unfitted for dominion as is the present Duke in this. What then ? A good knight-errant is an indifferent courtier and a bad statesman. Lastly, my friends—since you must know all that is in my heart—there remains the fact that I love myself a little. I love my liberty too well, and I have no mind to stifle in the scented atmosphere of courts. You see I am frank with you. It is my pleasure to roam the world, my harness on my back, free as the blessed wind of heaven. Shall a ducal crown and a cloak of purple——'' He broke off sharply with a laugh. '' There, my friends ! You have had reasons and to spare. Again I thank you, and deplore that, being such as I am, I may not become such as you would have me.''

He sank back in his chair, eyeing them with a glance never so wistful, and after a second's silence Da Lodi's voice implored him, in accents that trembled with pathetic emphasis, to reconsider his resolve. The old man would have proceeded to fresh argument, but Aquila cut him short.

'' I have already so well considered it, Messer Fabrizio,'' he answered resolutely, '' that nothing now could sway me. But this, sirs, I will promise you : I will ride with you to Babbiano, and I will seek to reason with my cousin. More will I do ; I will seek at his hands the office of Gonfalonier, and if he grant it me I will so reorganise our forces and enter into such alliances with our neighbours as shall ensure, at least in some degree, the safety of our State.''

Still they endeavoured to cajole him, but he held firm against their efforts, until in the end, with a sorrowful mien, Da Lodi thanked him for his promise to use his influence with Gian Maria.

'' For this, at least, we thank your Excellency ; and on our part we shall exert such power as we still wield in Babbiano to the end that the high office of Gonfalonier be conferred upon you. We had preferred to see you fill with honour a position higher still, and should you later come to consider——''

'' Dismiss your hopes of that,'' put in the Count,

with a solemn shake of his head. And then, before another word was uttered, young Fanfulla degli Arcipreti leapt of a sudden to his feet, his brows knit, an expression of alarm spreading upon his comely face. A second he remained thus ; then, going swiftly to the door, he opened it, and stood listening, followed by the surprised glances of the assembled company. But it needed not the warning cry with which he turned, to afford them the explanation of his odd behaviour. In the moment's tense silence that had followed his sudden opening of the door they had caught from without the distant fall of marching feet.

CHAPTER II

"Armed men, my lord!" had been Fanfulla's cry. "We are betrayed!"

They looked at one another with stern eyes, and with that grimness that takes the place which fear would hold in meaner souls.

Then Aquila rose slowly to his feet, and with him rose the others, looking to their weapons. He softly breathed a name—"Masuccio Torri."

"Aye," cried Lodi bitterly, "would that we had heeded your warning! Masuccio it will be, and at his heels his fifty mercenaries."

"Not less, I'll swear, by the sound of them," said Ferrabraccio. "And we but six, without our harness."

"Seven," the Count laconically amended, resuming his hat and loosening his sword in its scabbard.

"Not so, my lord," exclaimed Lodi, laying a hand upon the Count's arm. "You must not stay with us. You are our only hope—the only hope of Babbiano. If we are indeed betrayed—though by what infernal means I know not—and they have knowledge that six traitors met here to-night to conspire against the throne of Gian Maria, at least, I'll swear, it is not known that you were to have met us. His Highness may conjecture, but he cannot know for sure, and if you but escape, all may yet be well—saving with us, who matter not. Go, my lord! Remember your promise to seek at your cousin's hand the gonfalon, and may God and His blessed Saints prosper your Excellency."

The old man caught the young man's hand, and

bending his head until his face was hidden in his long white hair, he imprinted a kiss of fealty upon it. But Aquila was not so easily to be dismissed.

" Where are your horses ? " he demanded.

" Tethered at the back. But who would dare ride them at night adown this precipice ? "

" I dare for one," answered the young man steadily, " and so shall you all dare. A broken neck is the worst that can befall us, and I would as lief break mine on the rocks of Sant' Angelo as have it broken by the executioner of Babbiano."

" Bravely said, by the Virgin ! " roared Ferrabraccio. " To horse, sirs ! "

" But the only way is the way by which they come," Fanfulla remonstrated. " The rest is sheer cliff."

" Why, then, my sweet seducer, we'll go to meet them," rejoined Ferrabraccio gaily. " They are on foot, and we'll sweep over them like a mountain torrent. Come, sirs, hasten ! They draw nigh."

" We have but six horses, and we are seven," another objected.

" I have no horse," said Francesco. " I'll follow you afoot."

" What ? " cried Ferrabraccio, who seemed now to have assumed command of the enterprise. " Let our St. Michael bring up the rear ! No, no. You, da Lodi—you are too old for this work."

" Too old ? " blazed the old man, drawing himself up to the full height of what was still a very imposing figure, and his eyes seeming to take fire at this reflection upon his knightly worth. " Were the season other, Ferrabraccio, I could crave leave to show you how much of youth there is still left in me. But——" He paused. His angry eyes had alighted upon the Count, who stood waiting by the door, and the whole expression of his countenance changed. " You are right, Ferra-braccio, I grow old indeed—a dotard. Take you my horse, and begone."

" But you ? " quoth the Count solicitously.

" I shall remain. If you do your duty well by those hirelings they will not trouble me. It will not occur to them that one was left behind. They will think only

of following you after you have cut through them.
Go, sirs; go, or all is lost."

They obeyed him now with a rush that seemed almost
to partake of panic.   In a frenzied haste Fanfulla and
another tore the tetherings loose, and a moment later
they were all mounted and ready for that fearful ride.
The night was dark, yet not too dark.   The sky was
cloudless and thickly starred, whilst a minguant moon
helped to illumine the way by which they were to go.
But on that broken and uncertain mountain-path
the shadows lay thickly enough to make their venture
desperate.

Ferrabraccio, claiming a better knowledge than his
comrades of the way, placed himself at their head,
with the Count beside him.   Behind them, two by
two, came the four others.   They stood on a small ledge
in the shadow of the great cliff that loomed on their
left.   Thence the mountain-side might be scanned—
as well as in such a light it was to be discerned.   The
tramp of feet had now grown louder and nearer, and
with it came the clank of armour.   In front of them
lay the path which sloped, for a hundred yards or more,
to the first corner.   Below them, on the right, the path
again appeared at the point where it jutted out for
some half-dozen yards in its zigzag course, and there
Fanfulla caught the gleam of steel, reflecting the feeble
moonlight.   He drew Ferrabraccio's attention to it,
and the stout warrior at once gave the word to start.
But Francesco interposed.

" If we do so," he objected, " we shall come upon
them past the corner, and at that corner we shall be
forced to slacken speed to avoid being carried over
the edge of the cliff.   Besides, in such a strait our horses
may fail us and refuse the ground.   In any event, we
shall not descend upon them with the same force as
we shall carry if we wait until they come into a straight
line with us.   The shadows here will screen us from
them meanwhile.

" You are right, Lord Count.   We will wait," was
the ready answer.   And what time they waited he
grumbled lustily.

" To be **caught** in such a trap as this !   Body of

Satan ! It was madness to have met in a hut with but one approach."

" We might perhaps have retreated down the cliff behind," said Francesco.

" We might indeed—had we been sparrows or mountain cats. But being men, the way we go is the only way—and a mighty bad way it is. I should like to be buried at Sant' Angelo, Lord Count," he continued whimsically. " It will be conveniently near ; for once I go over the mountain-side, I'll swear naught will stop me until I reach the valley—a parcel of broken bones."

" Steady, my friends," murmured the voice of Aquila. " They come."

And around the fateful corner they were now swinging into view—a company in steel heads and bodies, with partisan on shoulder. A moment they halted now, so that the waiting party almost deemed itself observed. But it soon became clear that the halt was to the end that the stragglers might come up. Masuccio was a man who took no chances ; every knave of his fifty would he have before he ventured the assault.

" Now," murmured the Count, tightening his hat upon his brow, so that it might the better mask his features. Then, rising in his stirrups and raising his sword on high, he let his voice be heard again. But no longer in a whisper. Like a trumpet call it rang, echoed and re-echoed up the mountain-side.

" Forward ! St. Michael and the Virgin ! "

That mighty shout, followed as it was by a thunder of hooves, gave pause to the advancing mercenaries. Masuccio's voice was heard calling to them to stand firm ; bidding them kneel and ward the charge with their pikes ; assuring them with curses that they had but to deal with half a dozen men. But the mountain echoes were delusive, and that thunder of descending hooves seemed to them not of a half-dozen, but a regiment. Despite Masuccio's imprecations, the foremost turned, and in that moment the riders were upon them, through them and over them, like the mighty torrent of which Ferrabraccio had spoken.

A dozen Swiss went down beneath that onslaught,

and another dozen that had been swept aside and over the precipice were half-way to the valley before that calvacade met any check. Masuccio's remaining men strove lustily to stem this human cataract, now that they realised how small was the number of their assailants. They got their partisans to work, and for a few moments the battle raged hot upon the narrow way. The air was charged with the grind and ring of steel, the stamping of men and horses and the shrieks and curses of the maimed.

The Lord of Aquila, ever foremost, fought desperately on. Not only with his sword fought he, but with his horse as well. Rearing the beast on its hind legs, he would swing it round and let it descend when least it was expected, laying about him with his sword at the same time. In vain they sought to bring down his charger with their pikes ; so swift and furious was his action, that before their desire could be accomplished, he was upon those that meditated it, scattering them out of reach to save their skins.

In this ferocious manner he cleared a way before him, and luck served him so well that what blows were wildly aimed at him as he dashed by went wide of striking him. At last he was all but through the press, and but three men now fronted him. Again his charger reared, snorting and pawing the air like a cat, and two of the three knaves before him fled incontinently aside. But the third, who was of braver stuff, dropped on one knee and presented his pike at the horse's belly. Francesco made a wild attempt to save the roan that had served him so gallantly, but he was too late. It came down to impale itself upon the waiting partisan. With a hideous scream the horse sank upon its slayer, crushing him beneath its mighty weight, and hurling its rider forward on to the ground. In an instant he was up and had turned, for all that he was half-stunned by his fall and weakened by the loss of blood from a pike-thrust in the shoulder—of which he had hitherto remained unconscious in the heat of the battle. Two mercenaries were bearing down upon him—the same two that had been the last to fall back before him. He braced himself to meet them, thinking that his last hour was indeed come, when Fanfulla delgi Arcipreti, who had followed him closely through the press, now descended upon his assailants from behind and rode them down. Beside the Count he reigned up and stretched down his hand.

" Mount behind me, Excellency," he urged him.

" There is not time," answered Francesco, who discerned a half-dozen figures hurrying towards him. " I will cling to your stirrup-leather thus. Now spur ! " And without waiting for Fanfulla to obey him, he caught the horse a blow with the flat of his sword across the hams, which sent it boundng forward. They thus continued now that perilous descent, Fanfulla riding and the Count half-running, half-swinging from the stirrup. At last, when they had covered a half-mile in this fashion, and the going had grown easier, they halted that the Count might mount behind his companion, and as they now rode along at an easier pace, Francesco realised that he and Fanfulla were the only two that had come through that ugly place. The gallant Ferrabrassio, hero of a hundred strenuous battles, had gone to the ignoble doom which half in jest he had prophesied himself. His horse had played him false at the outset of the charge, and, taking fright, it had veered aside, despite his efforts to control it, until, losing its foothold, man and beast had gone hurtling over the cliffs. Amerini, Fanfulla had seen slain, whilst the remaining two, being unhorsed, would doubtless be the prisoners of Masuccio.

Some three miles beyond Sant' Angelo, Fanfulla's weary horse splashed across a ford of the Metauro and thus, towards the second hour of night, they gained the territory of Urbino, where for the time they might hold themselves safe from all pursuit.

CHAPTER III

SACKCLOTH AND MOTLEY

THE fool and the friar had fallen a-quarrelling, and—to the shame of the friar and the glory of the fool be it spoken—their subject of contention was a woman. Now, the friar, finding himself no match for the fool in words, and being as broad and stout of girth and limb as the other was puny and misshapen, he had plucked off his sandal that with it he might drive the full force of his arguments through the jester's skull. At that the fool, being a very coward, had fled incontinently through the trees.

Running, like the fool he was, with his head turned to learn whether the good father followed him, he never saw the figure that lay half-hidden in the bracken, and might never have guessed its presence but that, tripping over it, he shot forward, with a tinkle of bells, on to his crooked nose.

He sat up with a groan, which was answered by an oath from the man into whose sides he had dug his flying feet. The two looked at one another in surprise, tempered with anger in the one and dismay in the other.

" A good awakening to you, noble sir," quoth the fool politely ; for by the mien and inches of the man he had roused he thought that courtesy might serve him best.

The other eyed him with interest, as well he might ; for an odder figure it would be hard to find in Italy.

Hunched at back, undersized, and fragile of limb, he was arrayed in doublet, hose and hood, the half of which was black, the other crimson, whilst on his shoulders fell from that same hood—which tightly framed his ugly little face—a foliated cape, from every point of which there hung a tiny silver bell that glimmered in the sunlight and tinkled as he moved. From under bulging brows a pair of bright eyes, set wide as an owl's, took up the mischievous humour of his prodigious mouth.

" A curse on you and him that sent you," was the answering greeting he received. Then the man checked his anger and broke into a laugh at sight of the fear that sprang into the jester's eyes.

" I crave your pardon—most humbly do I crave it, Illustrious," said the fool, still in fear. "I was pursued."

" Pursued ? " echoed the other, in a tone not free from a sudden uneasiness. " And, pray, by whom ? "

" By the very fiend, disguised in the gross flesh and semblance of a Dominican brother."

" Do you jest ? " came the angry queston.

" Jest ? Had you caught his villainous sandal between your shoulders, as did I, you would know how little I have a mind to jest."

" Now answer me a plain question, if you have the wit to answer with," quoth the other, anger ever rising in his voice. " Is there hereabouts a monk ? "

" Aye, is there—may a foul plague rot him—lurking in the bushes yonder. He is over-fat to run, or you had seen him at my heels, arrayed in that panoply of avenging wrath that is the cognisance of the Church Militant."

" Go, bring him hither," was the short answer.

" Gesù ! " gasped the fool, in very real affright. " I'll not go near him till his anger cools—not if you made me straight and bribed me with the Patrimony of St. Peter."

The man turned from him impatiently, and raising his voice, " Fanfulla ! " he called over his shoulder, and then, after a moment's pause, again : " Olà, Fanfulla ! "

" I am here my lord," came an answering voice from behind a clump of bushes on their right, and almost immediately the very splendid youth who had gone to sleep in its shadow stood up and came round to them. At sight of the fool he paused to take stock of him, what time the fool returned the compliment with wonder-stricken interest. For however much Fanfulla's raiment might have suffered in yesternight's affray, it was very gorgeous still, and in the velvet cap upon his head a string of jewels was entwined. Yet not so much by the richness of his trappings was the fool impressed as by the fact that one so manifestly noble should address by such a title, and in a tone of so much deference, this indifferently apparalled fellow over whom he had stumbled. Then his gaze wandered back to the man who lay supported on his elbow, and he noticed now the gold net in which his hair was coiffed, and which was by no means common to mean folk. His little twinkling eyes turned their attention full upon the face before him, and of a sudden a gleam of recognition entered them. His countenance underwent a change, and from grotesque that it had been, it became more grotesque still in its hasty assumption of reverence.

" My Lord of Aquila ! " he murmured, scrambling to his feet.

Scarcely had he got erect when a hand gripped him by the shoulder, and Fanfulla's dagger flashed before his startled eyes.

" Swear on the cross of this never to divulge his Excellency's presence here, or take you the point of it in your foolish heart."

" I swear, I swear ! " he cried, in fearful haste, his hand upon the hilt, which Fanfulla now held towards him.

" Now fetch the priest, good fool," said the Count, with a smile at the hunchback's sudden terror. " You have nothing to fear from us."

When the jester had left them to go upon his errand, Francesco turned to his companion.

" Fanfulla, you are over-cautious," he said, with an easy smile. " What shall it matter that I am recognised ? "

" I would not have it happen for a kingdom while you are so near Sant' Angelo. The six of us who met last night are doomed—those of us who are not dead already. For me, and for Lodi if he was not taken, there may be safety in flight. In the territory of Babbiano I shall never again set foot whilst Gian Maria is Duke, unless I be weary of this world. But of the seventh—yourself—you heard old Lodi swear that the secret could not have transpired. Yet should his Highness come to hear of your presence in these parts and in my company, suspicion might set him on the road that leads to knowledge."

" Ah ! And then ? "

" Then ? " returned the other, eyeing Francesco in surprise. " Why then, the hopes we found on you— the hopes of every man in Babbiano worthy of the name—would be frustrated. But here comes our friend the fool, and, in his wake, the friar."

Fra Domenico—so was he very fitly named, this follower of St. Dominic—approached with a solemnity that proceeded rather from his great girth than from any inflated sense of the dignity of his calling. He bowed before Fanfulla until his great crimson face was hidden and he displayed, instead, a yellow, shaven crown. It was as if the sun had set and the moon had risen in its place.

" Are you skilled in medicine ? " quoth Fanfulla shortly.

" I have some knowledge, Illustrious."

" Then see to this gentleman's wounds."

" Eh ? *Dio mio*! You are wounded, then ? " he began, turning to the Count, and he would have added other questions as pregnant, but that Aquila, drawing aside his hacketon at the shoulder, answered him quickly :

" Here, sir priest."

His lips pursed in solicitude ; the friar would have gone upon his knees but that Francesco, seeing with what labour the movement must be fraught, rose up at once.

" It is not so bad that I cannot stand," said he, submitting himself to the monk's examination.

The latter expressed the opinion that it was nowise dangerous, however much it might be irksome, where- upon the Count invited him to bind it up. To this

Fra Domenico replied that he had neither unguents nor linen, but Fanfulla suggested that he might get these things from the convent of Acquasparta, hard by, and proffered to accompany him thither.

This being determined, they departed, leaving the Count in the company of the jester. Francesco spread his cloak and lay down again, whilst the fool, craving his permission to remain, disposed himself upon his haunches like a Turk.

"Who is your master, fool?" quoth the Count, in an idle spirit.

"There is a man who clothes and feeds me, noble sir, but Folly is my only master."

"To what end does he do this?"

"Because I pretend to be a greater fool than he, so that by contrast with me he seems unto himself wise, which flatters his conceit. Again, perhaps, because I am so much uglier than he that, again by contrast he may account himself a prodigy of beauty."

"Odd, is it not?" the Count humoured him.

"Not half so odd as that the Lord of Aquila should lie here, roughly clad, a wound in his shoulder, talking to a fool."

Francesco eyed him with a smile.

"Give thanks to God that Fanfulla is not here to hear you, or they had been your last words; for pretty though he be, Messer Fanfulla is a very monster of bloodthirstiness. With me it is different. I am a man of very gentle ways, as you may have heard, Messer Buffoon. But see that you forget at once my station and my name, or you may realise how little they need buffoons in the Court of Heaven."

"My lord, forgive. I shall obey you," answered the hunchback, with a stricken manner. And then through the glade came a voice—a woman's voice, wondrous sweet and rich, calling: "Peppino! Peppino!"

"It is my mistress calling me," quoth the fool, leaping to his feet.

"So that you own a mistress, though Folly be your only master," laughed the Count. "It would pleasure me to behold the lady whose property you have the honour to be, Ser Peppino."

"You may behold her if you but turn your head," Peppino whispered.

Idly, with a smile upon his lips that was almost scornful, the Lord of Aquila turned his eyes in the direction in which the fool was already walking. And on the instant his whole expression changed. The amused scorn was swept from his countenance, and in its place there sat now a look of wonder that was almost awe.

Standing there on the edge of the clearing in which he lay, he beheld a woman. He had a vague impression of a slender, shapely height, a fleeting vision of a robe of white damask, a *camorra* of green velvet, and a choicely-wrought girdle of gold. But it was the glory of her peerless face that caught and held his glance in such ecstatic awe ; the miracle of her eyes, which, riveted on his, returned his glance with one of mild surprise. A child she almost seemed, despite her height and womanly proportions, so fresh and youthful was her countenance.

Raised on his elbow, he lay there for a spell and gazed and gazed, his mind running on visions which godly men have had of saints from Paradise.

At last the spell was broken by Peppino's voice addressing her, his back servilely bent. Francesco bethought him of the deference due to one so clearly noble, and, leaping to his feet, his wound forgotten, he bowed profoundly. A second later he gasped for breath, reeled, and swooning, collapsed supine among the bracken.

CHAPTER IV

MONNA VALENTINA

IN after years the Lord of Aquila was wont to aver
in all solemnity that it was the sight of her wondrous
beauty set up such a disorder in his soul that it over-
came his senses, and laid him swooning at her feet.
That he, himself, believed it so, it is not ours to doubt,
for all that, we may be more prone to agree with the
opinion afterwards expressed by Fanfulla and the
friar—and deeply resented by the Count—that in
leaping to his feet in over-violent haste his wound
re-opened, and the pain of this, combining with the
weak condition that resulted from his loss of blood,
had caused his sudden faintness.

"Who is this, Peppe?" she asked the fool, and he,
mindful of the oath he had sworn, answered her brazenly
that he did not know, adding that it was—as she might
see—some poor wounded fellow.

"Wounded?" she echoed, and her glorious eyes
grew very pitiful. "And alone?"

"There was a gentleman here, tending him, Madonna;
but he is gone with Fra Domenico to the Convent
of Acquasparta to seek the necessaries to mend his
shoulder."

"Poor gentleman," she murmured approaching the
fallen figure. "How came he by his hurt?"

"That, Madonna, is more than I can tell."

"Can we do nothing for him until his friends return?"
was her next question, bending over the Count as she
spoke. "Come, Peppino," she cried, "lend me your
aid. Get me water from the brook, yonder."

The fool looked about him for a vessel, and his eye

falling upon the Count's capacious hat, he snatched it up, and went his errand. When he returned, the lady was kneeling with the unconscious man's head in her lap. Into the hatful of water that Peppe brought her she dipped a kerchief, and with this she bathed the brow on which his long black hair lay matted and disordered.

"See how he has bled, Peppe," said she. "His doublet is drenched and he is bleeding still! *Vergine Santa*!" she cried, beholding now the ugly wound that gaped in his shoulder, and turning pale at the sight. "Assuredly he will die of it—and he so young, Peppino, and so comely to behold!"

Francesco stirred and a sigh fluttered through his pallid lips. Then he raised his heavy lids and their glances met and held each other. And so, eyes that were brown and tender looked down into feverish, languid eyes of black, what time her gentle hand held the moist cloth to his aching brow.

"Angel of beauty!" he murmured dreamily, being but half-awake as yet to his position. Then, becoming conscious of her ministrations, "Angel of goodness!" he added, with yet deeper fervour.

She had no answer for him, saving such answer—and it itself it was eloquent enough—as her blushes made, for she was fresh from a convent and all innocent of worldly ways and tricks of gallant speech.

"Do you suffer?" she asked at last.

"Suffer?" quoth he, now waking more and more, and his voice sounding a note of scorn. "Suffer? My head so pillowed and a saint from Heaven ministering to my ills? Nay, I am in no pain, Madonna, but in a joy more sweet than I have ever known.".

"*Gesù* What a nimble tongue!" gibed the fool from the background.

"Are you there, too, Master Buffoon?" quoth Francesco. "And Fanfulla? Is he not here? Why now I bethink me, he went to Acquasparta with the friar." He thrust his elbow under him for more support.

"You must not move," said she, thinking he would essay to rise.

"I would not, lady, if I must," he answered solemnly.

C

And then, with his eyes upon her face, he boldly asked her name.

"My name," she answered readily, "is Valentina dealla Rovere, and I am niece to Guidobaldo of Urbino."

His brows shot up.

"Do I indeed live," he questioned, "or do I but dream the memories of some old romancer's tale, in which a wandering knight is tended thus by a princess?"

"Are you a knight?" she asked, a wonder coming now into her eyes, for even into the seclusion of her convent life had crept strange stories of these mighty men-at-arms.

"Your knight at least, sweet lady," answered he, "and ever your poor champion if you will do me so much honour."

A crimson flush stole now into her cheeks, summoned by his bold words and bolder glances, and her eyes fell. Yet resentment had no part in her confusion. She found no presumption in his speech nor aught that a brave knight might not say to the lady who had succoured him in his distress. Peppe, who stood listening and marking the Count's manner, knowing the knight's station, was filled now with wonder, now with mockery, yet never interfered.

"What is your name, sir knight?" she asked, after a pause.

His eyes looked troubled, and as they shot beyond her to the fool they caught on Peppe's face a grin of sly amusement.

"My name," he said at last, "is Francesco." And then, to prevent that she should further question him—"But tell me, Madonna," he inquired, "how comes a lady of your station here, alone with that poor fraction of a man?" And he indicated the grinning Peppe.

"My people are yonder in the woods, where we have halted for a little space. I am on my way to my uncle's court, from the Convent of Santa Sofia, and for my escort I have Messr Romeo Gonzaga and twenty spears. So that, you see, I am well protected, without counting Ser Peppe here and the saintly Fra Domenico, my confessor."

There was a pause, ended at length by Francesco.

" You will be the younger niece of his Highness of Urbino ? " he said.

" Not so, Messer Francesco," she answered readily " I am the elder."

At that his brows grew of a sudden dark.

" Can you be she whom they would wed to Gian Maria ? " he exclaimed, at which the fool pricked up his ears, whilst she looked at the Count with a gaze that plainly showed how far she was from understanding him.

" You said ? " she asked.

" Why, nothing," he answered, with a sigh, and in that moment a man's voice came ringing through the wood.

" Madonna ! Madonna Valentina ! "

Francesco and the lady turned their eyes in the direction whence the voice proceeded, and they beheld a superbly dazzling figure entering the glade. In beauty of person and richness of apparel he was well worthy of the company of Valentina. His doublet was of grey velvet, set off with scales of beaten gold, and revealing a gold-embroidered vest beneath ; his bonnet matched his doublet, and was decked by a feather that sparkled with costly gems ; his gold-hilted sword was sheathed in a scabbard also of grey velvet set with jewels. His face was comely as a damsel's, his eyes blue and his hair golden.

" Behold," announced Peppino, " Italy's latest translation of the Golden Ass of Apuleius."

Upon seeing the noble niece of Guidobaldo kneeling there with Francesco's head still pillowed in her lap, the new-comer cast up his arms in a gesture of dismay.

" Saints in Heaven ! " he exclaimed, hurrying toward them. " What occupation have you found ? Who is this ugly fellow ? "

" Ugly ? " was all she answered him, in accents of profound surprise.

" Who is he ? " the young man insisted, his tone growing heated. " And what does he here and thus, with you ? *Gesù* ! What would his Highness say ?

How would he deal with me were he to learn of this?
Who is the man, Madonna?"

"Why, as you see, Messer Gonzaga," she answered,
with some heat, "a wounded knight."

"A knight he?" gibed Gonzaga "A thief more
likely, a prowling *masnadiero*. What is your name?"
he roughly asked the Count.

Drawing himself a little away from Valentina, and
reclining entirely upon his elbow, Francesco motioned
him with a wave of the hand to come no nearer.

"I beg, lady, that you will bid your pretty page
stand back a little. I am still faint, and his perfumes
overpower me."

Under the mask of the polite request Gonzaga detected
the mocking, contemptuous note, and it gave fuel to
his anger.

"I am no page, fool," he answered, then, clapping
his hands together, he raised his voice to shout—"Olà
Beltrame! To me!"

"What would you do?" cried the lady, rising to
confront him.

"Carry this ruffian in bonds to Urbino, as is my
duty."

"Sir, you may wound your pretty hands in grasping
me," replied the Count, in chill indifference.

"Ah! You would threaten me with violence,
vassal?" cried the other, retreating some paces farther
as he spoke. "Beltrame!" he called again, "are you
never coming?'

A voice answered him from the thicket, and with
a clank of steel a half-dozen men flung themselves into
the glade.

"Your orders, sir?" craved he that led them, his
eyes wandering to the still prostrate Count.

"Tie me up this dog," Gonzaga bade him. But
before the fellow could move a foot to carry out the
order Valentina barred his way.

"You shall not," she commanded, and so transformed
was she from the ingenuous child that lately had talked
with him, that Francesco gasped in pure astonishment.
"In my uncle's name, I bid you leave this gentleman
where he lies. He is a wounded knight whom I have

been pleased to tend—a matter which seems to have aroused Messer Gonzaga's anger against him."

Beltrame paused, and looked from Valentina to Gonzaga, undecided.

"Madonna," said Gonzaga, with assumed humility, "your word is law with us. But I would have you consider that what I bid Beltrame do is in the interest of his Highness, whose territory is infested by these vagabonding robbers. It is a fact that may not have reached you in your convent retreat, no more than has sufficient knowledge reached you yet—in your incomparable innocence—to distinguish between rogues and honest men. Beltrame, do my bidding."

Valentina's foot tapped the ground impatiently, and into her eyes there came a look of anger that heightened her likeness to her martial uncle. But Peppe it was who spoke.

"For all that there seem to be fools enough, already, meddling in this business," he said, in tones of mock lament, "permit that I join their number, Ser Romeo, and listen to my counsel."

"Out fool," cried Gonzaga, cutting at him with his riding-switch, "we need not your capers."

"No, but you need my wisdom," retorted Ser Peppe, as he leapt beyond Gonzaga's reach. "Hear me, Beltrame! For all that we do not doubt Messer Gonzaga's keen discrimination in judging 'twixt a rogue and an honest man, I do promise you, as surely as though I were Fate herself, that if you obey him now and tie up that gentleman, you will yourself be tied up for it, later on, in a yet uglier fashion."

Beltrame looked alarmed, Gonzaga incredulous. Valentina thanked Peppe with her eyes, thinking that he had but hit upon a subterfuge to serve her wishes, whilst Francesco, who had now risen to his feet, looked on with an amused smile as though the matter concerned him nowise personally. And then, in the very crux of the situation, Fanfulla and Fra Domenico appeared upon the scene.

"You are well-returned, Fanfulla!" the Count called to him. "This pretty gentleman would have had me bound."

" Have you bound ? " echoed Fanfulla in angry
horror " Upon what grounds, pray ? " he demanded
turning fiercely upon Gonzala.

Impressed by Fanfulla's lordly air Romeo Gonzaga
grew amazingly humble for one that but a moment
back had been so overbearing.

" It would seem, sir, that my judgment was at fault
in esteeming his condition," he excused himself.

" Your judgment ? " returned the hot Fanfulla.
" And who bade you judge ? Go cut your milk-teeth,
boy, and meddle not with men if you would live to be
a man yourself some day."

Valentina smiled, Peppe laughed outright, whilst
even Beltrame and his followers grinned, all of which
added not a little to Gonzaga's choler. But scant though
his wisdom might be, it was yet enough to dictate
prudence.

" The presence of Madonna here restrains me," he
answered, with elaborate dignity " But should we
meet again, I shall make bold to show you what manhood
means."

" Perhaps—if by then you shall have come to it."
And with a shrug Fanfulla turned to give his attention
to the Count, whom Fra Domenico was already attending.

Valentina, to relieve the awkwardness of the moment,
proposed to Gonzaga that he should get his escort to
horse, and have her litter in readiness, so that they
might resume their journey as soon as Fra Domenico
should have concluded his ministrations.

Gonzaga bowed, and with a vicious glance at the
strangers and an angry " Follow me ! " to Beltrame and
the others, he departed with the men-at-arms at his
heels.

Valentina remained with Fanfulla and Peppe, whilst
Fra Domenico dressed Francesco's wound, and, presently,
when the task was accomplished, they departed, leaving
Fanfulla and the Count alone. But ere she went she
listened to Francesco's thanks, and suffered him to
touch her ivory fingers with his lips.

There was much he might have said but that the
presence of the other three restrained him. Yet some
little of that much she may have seen reflected in his

eyes, for all that day she rode passive, a fond, wistful smile at the corners of her lips. And although to Gonzaga she manifested no resentment, yet did she twit him, touching that mistake of his. Sore in his dignity, he liked her playful mockery little ; yet he liked the words in which she framed it less.

" How came you into so grievous an error, Ser Romeo ? " she asked him, more than once. How could you deem him a rogue—he with so noble a mien and so beautiful a countenance ? " And, without heeding the sullenness of his answers, she would lapse with a sigh once more into reflection—a thing that galled Gonzaga more, perhaps, than did her gibes.

CHAPTER V

GIAN MARIA

It was a week after the meeting 'twixt the niece of Guidobaldo and the Count of Aquila, when the latter—his wound being well-nigh healed—rode one morning under the great archway that was the main entrance to the city of Babbiano The Captain of the Gate saluted him respectfully as he rode by, and permitted himself to marvel at the pallor of his Excellency's face. And yet, the cause was not very far to seek. It stood upon four spears, among a noisy flock of circling crows, above that very gate—called of San Bacolo—and consisted of four detruncated human heads.

The sight of those dead faces grinning horribly, their long matted hair fluttering like rags in the April breeze, had arrested Francesco's attention as he drew nigh. But when presently he came nearer and looked with more intentness, a shudder of recognition ran through him, and a great horror filled his soul and paled his cheek. The first of those heads was that of the valiant and well-named Ferrabraccio ; the next that of Amerino Amerini ; and the other two, those of his captured companions on that night at Sant' Angelo.

So it would seem that Gian Maria had been busy during the week that was sped, and that there, on the walls of Bibbiano, lay rotting the only fruits which that ill-starred conspiracy was likely to bear.

For a second it entered his mind to turn back. But his stout and fearless nature drove him on, all unattended as he was, and in despite of such vague forebodings as beset him. How much, he wondered, might Gian Maria know of his own share in that mountain meeting, and how would it fare with him if his cousin was aware that it had been proposed to the Count of Aquila to supplant him ?

He was not long, however, in learning that grounds were wanting for such fears as he had entertained. Gian Maria received him with even more than wonted welcome, for he laid much store by Francesco's judgment, and was in sore need of it at present.

Francesco found him at the table, which had been laid for him amidst the treasures of art and learning that enriched the splendid Palace library. It was a place beloved by Gian Maria for the material comforts that it offered him, and so he turned it to a score of vulgar purposes of his own, yet never to that for which it was equipped, being an utter stranger to letters and ignorant as a ploughboy.

Ensconced in a great chair of crimson leather, at a board overladen with choice viands and sparkling with crystal flagons and with vessels and dishes of gold and enamel. Francesco found his cousin, and the air that had been heavy once with the scholarly smell of parchments and musty tomes was saturated now with pungent odours of the table.

In stature Gian Maria was short and inclining, young though he was, to corpulency. His face was round and pale and flabby ; his eyes blue and beady ; his mouth sensual and cruel. He was dressed in a suit of lilac velvet trimmed with lynx fur, and slashed, Spanish fashion, in the sleeves, to show the shirt of fine Rheims linen underneath. About his neck hung a gold chain, bearing an Agnus Dei, which contained a relic of the True Cross—for Gian Maria pushed his devoutness to great lengths.

His welcome of Francesco was more effusive than its wont. He bade the two servants who attended him to lay a plate for his illustrious cousin, and when Aquila shortly yet courteously declined, with the assurance that he had dined already, the Duke insisted that, at least, he should drink a cup of Malvasia. When out of a vessel of beaten gold they had filled a goblet for the Count, his Highness bade the servants go, and relaxed—if, indeed, so much may be said of one who never knew much dignity—before his visitor.

" I hear," said Aquila, when the first compliments
were spent, " strange stories of a conspiracy in your
Duchy, and on the walls of the Gate of San Bacolo I
beheld four heads, of men whom I have known and
honoured."

" And who dishonoured themselves ere their heads
were made a banquet for the crows. There, Francesco ! "
He shuddered, and crossed himself. " It is unlucky to
speak of the dead at table."

" Let us speak, then, of their offence alone," persisted
Francesco subtly. " In what did it lie ? "

" In what ? " returned the Duke amusedly. His
voice was thin and inclining to shrillness. " It is more
than I can say. Masuccio knew. But the dog would
not disclose his secret nor the names of the conspirators
until his task should be accomplished and he had taken
them at the treason he knew they had gathered to ripen.
But," he continued, an olive poised 'twixt thumb and
forefinger, " it seems they were not to be captured as
easily as he thought. He told me the traitors numbered
six, and that they were to meet a seventh there. The
men who returned from the venture tell me, too, and
without shame, that there were but some six or seven
that beset them. Yet they gave the Swiss trouble
enough and killed some nine of them besides a half-score
of more or less grievously wounded, whilst they but
slew two of their assailants and captured another two.
Those were the four heads you saw at the Porta San
Bacolo."

" And Masuccio ? " inquired Francesco. " Has he
not told you since who were those others that escaped ? "

His Highness paused to masticate the olive.

" Why, there lies the difficulty," said he at length.
" The dog is dead. He was killed in the affray. May he
rot in hell for his obstinate reticence ! No, no ! " he
checked himself hastily. " He's dead, and the secret
of this treason, as well as the names of the traitors, have
perished with him. Yet I am a clement man, Francesco,
and sorely though that dog has wronged me by his
silence, I thank Heaven for the grace to say —God rest
his vile soul ! "

The Count flung himself into a chair, as much to

dissemble such signs of relief as might show upon his face, as because he wished to sit.

"But surely Masuccio left you some information!" he exclaimed.

"The very scantiest," returned Gian Maria, in chagrined accents. "It was ever the way of that secretive vassal. Damn him! He frankly told me that if I knew, I would talk. Heard you ever of such insufferable insolence to a prince? All that he would let me learn was that there was a conspiracy afoot to supplant me, and that he was going to capture the conspirators, together with the man whom they were inviting to take my place. Ponder it, Francesco! Such are the murderous plans my loving subjects form, for my undoing—I who rule them with a rod of gold, the most clement, just and generous prince in Italy, *Cristo buono*! Do you marvel that I lost patience and had their hideous heads set upon spears?"

"But did you not say that two of these conspirators were brought back captive?"

The Duke nodded, his mouth too full for words.

Then, at their trial, what transpired?"

"Trial? There was no trial," Gian Maria chewed vigorously for a moment. "I tell you I was so heated with anger at this base ingratitude that I had not even the wit to have the names of their associates tortured out of them. Within a half-hour of their arrival in Babbiano, the heads of these men whom it had pl ased Heaven to deliver up to me were where you saw them to-day."

"You sent them thus to their death?" gasped Francesco, rising to his feet and eyeing his cousin with mingled wonder and anger. "You sent men of such families as these to the headsman, without a trial? I think, Gian Maria, that you must be mad if so rashly you can shed such blood as this."

The Duke sank back in his chair to gape at his impetuous cousin. Then, in sullen anger: "To whom do you speak?" he demanded.

"To a tyrant who calls himself the most clement, just and generous prince in Italy, and who lacks the wisdom to see that he is undermining with his own hands, and by his own rash actions, a throne that is already tottering. Can you not think that this might mean a revolution? It amounts to murder, and though dukes resort to it freely enough in Italy, it is not openly and defiantly wrought, as is this."

Anger there was in the Duke's soul, but there was still more fear—so much, that it shouldered the anger aside.

"I have provided against rebellion," he announced, with an ease that he vainly strove to feel. "I have given the command of my guards to Martino Armstadt, and he has engaged for me a company of five hundred Swiss *lanzknechte* that were lately in the pay of the Baglioni of Perugia."

"And you deem this security?" rejoined Francesco, with a smile of scorn. "To hedge your throne with foreign spears commanded by a foreigner?"

"This and God's grace," was the pious answer.

"Bah!" answered Francesco, impatient at the hypocrisy. "Win the hearts of your people. Let that be your buckler."

"Hush!" whispered Gian Maria. "You blaspheme. Does not every act of my self-sacrificing life point to such an aim? I live for my people. But, by my soul, they ask too much when they ask that I should die for them. If I serve those who plot against my life as I have served these men you speak of, who shall blame me? I tell you, Francesco, I wish I might have those others who escaped, that I might do as much by them. By the living God, I do! And as for the man who was to have supplanted me——" He paused, a deadly smile on his usual sensual mouth completing the sentence more effectively than lay within the power of words. "Who could it have been?" he mused. "I've vowed that if Heaven will grant me that I discover him, I'll burn a candle to Santa Fosca every Saturday for a twelvemonth and go fasting on the Vigil of the Dead. Who—who could it have been, Franceschino?"

"How should I know?" returned Francesco, evading the question.

"You know so much, Checco *mio*. Your mind is so quick to fathom matters of this kind. Think you, now, it might have been the Duca Valentino?"

Francesco shook his head.

"When Cæsar Borgia comes he will know no need to resort to such poor means. He will come in arms to reduce you by his might."

"God and the saints protect me!" gasped the Duke. "You talk of it as if he were already marching."

"Then I talk of it advisedly. The event is none so remote as you would make yourself believe. Listen, Gian Maria! I have not ridden from Aquila for just the pleasure of passing the time of day with you. Fabrizio da Lodi and Fanfulla degli Arcipreti have been with me of late."

"With you?" cried the Duke, his little eyes narrowing themselves as he glanced up at his cousin. "With you—eh?" He shrugged his shoulders and spread his palms before him. "Pish! See into what errors even so clear a mind as mine may fall. Do you know, Francesco, that, marking their absence since that conspiracy was laid, I had a half-suspicion they were connected with it." And he devoted his attention to a honeycomb.

"You have not in all your Duchy two hearts more faithful to Babbiano," was the equivocal reply. "It was on the matter of this very peril that threatens you that they came to me."

"Ah!" Gian Maria's white face grew interested.

And now the Count of Aquila talked to the Duke of Babbiano much as Fabrizio da Lodi had talked to the Count that night at Sant' Angelo. He spoke of the danger that threatened from the Borgia, of the utter lack of preparation, and of Gian Maria's contempt of the counsels given him. He alluded to the discontent rife among his subjects at this state of things, and to the urgent need to set them right. When he had done, the Duke sat silent a while, his eyes bent thoughtfully upon his platter, on which the food lay now unheeded.

"An easy thing is it not, Francesco, to say to a man : this is wrong, and that is wrong. But who is there, pray, to set it right for me?"

"That, if you will say but the word, I will attempt to do."

"You?" cried the Duke, and far from manifesting satisfaction at having one offer himself to undertake

to right this very crooked business, Gian Maria's face
reflected an incredulous anger and some little scorn.
" And how, my marvellous cousin, would you set about
it ? " he inquired, a sneer lurking in his tone.

" I would place such matters as the levying of money
by taxation in the hands of Messer Despuglio, and, at
whatever sacrifice to your own extravagance, I would
see that for months to come the bulk of these moneys
is applied to the levying and arming of suitable men.
I have some skill as a *condottiero*—leastways, so more
than one foregin prince has been forced to acknowledge.
I will lead your army when I have raised it, and I will
enter into alliances for you with our neighbouring States,
who, seeing us armed, will deem us a power worthy
of their alliance. And so, what man can do to stem the
impending flood of this invasion, that will I do to defend
your Duchy. Make me your gonfalonier, and in a month
I will tell you whether it lies in my power or not to save
your State."

The eyes of Gian Maria had narrowed more and more
whilst Francesco spoke, and into his shallow face had
crept an evil, suspicious look. As the Count ceased, he
gave vent to a subdued laugh, bitter with mockery.

" Make you my gonfalonier ? " he muttered in
consummate amusement. " And since when has Babbiano been a republic—or is it your aim to make it
one, and establish yourself as its chief magistrate ? "

" If you misapprehend me so——" began Francesco,
but his cousin interrupted him with heightening scorn.

" Misapprehend you, Messer Franceschino ? No, no.
I understand you but too well." He rose suddenly
from his interrupted meal, and came a step nearer his
cousin. " I hear rumours of this growing love the
people are manifesting for the Count of Aquila, and I
have let them go unheeded That rogue Masuccio
warned me ere he died, and I answered him with my
whip across his face. But I am by no means sure
that I have been proceeding wisely. I had a dream two
nights ago—— But let that be ! When it so happens
that in any State there is man whom the people prefer
to him that rules them, and when it so happens that
this man is of as good blood and high birth as are you,

he becomes a danger to him that sits the throne.   I need
scarce remind you," he added, with a horrid grin, " of
how the Borgias deal with such individuals, nor need
I add that a Sforza may see fit to emulate those very
conclusive measures of precaution.   The family of
Sforza has bred as yet no fools, nor shall I prove myself
the first by placing in another's hands the power to
make himself my master.   You see, my gentle cousin,
how transparent your aims become under my eyes.   I
am keen of vision, Franceschino, keen of vision ! "
He tapped his nose and chuckled a malicious appreciation
of his own acute perceptions.

Francesco regarded him with an eye of stony scorn.
He might have answered, had he been so disposed,
that the Duchy of Babbiano was his to take whenever
he pleased.   He might have told him that, and defied
him.   But he went more slowly than did this man of a
family that bred no fools.

" Do you know me, then, so little, Gian Maria," said
he, not without bitterness, " that you think I hunger
for so empty a thing as this ducal pomp you clutch so
fearfully ?   I tell you, man, that I prefer my liberty
to an imperial throne.   But I waste breath with you.
Yet, some day, when your crown shall have passed from
you and your power have been engulfed in the Borgia's
rapacious maw, remember my offer which might have
saved you and which with insults you disregard, as
you disregarded the advice your older counsellors gave
you."

Gian Maria shrugged his fat shoulders.

" If by that other advice you mean the counsel that
I should take Guidobaldo's niece to wife, you may
give ease unto your patriotic soul.   I have consented
to enter into this alliance.   And now," he ended, with
another of his infernal chuckles, " you see how little
I need dread this terrible son of Pope Alexander.   Allied
with Urbino and the other States that are its friends,
I can defy the might of Cæsar Borgia.   I shall sleep
tranquil of nights beside my beauteous bride, secure in
the protection her uncle's armies will afford me, and
never needing so much as my valiant cousin's aid as my
gonfalonier."

The Count of Aquila changed colour despite himself,
and the Duke's suspicious eyes were as quick to observe
it as was his mind to misinterpret its meaning. He
registered a vow to set a watch on this solicitous cousin
who offered so readily to bear his gonfalon.

"I felicitate you, at least," said Francesco gravely,
"upon the wisdom of that step. Had I known of it
I had not troubled you with other proposals for the
safety of your State. But, may I ask you, Gian Maria,
what influences led you to a course which, hitherto,
you have so obstinately refused to follow?"

The duke shrugged his shoulders.

"They plagued me so," he lamented with a grimace,
"that in the end I consented. I could withstand Lodi
and the others, but when my mother jonied them with
her prayers—I should say, her commands—and pointed
out again my peril to me, I gave way. After all, a man
must wed. And since in my station he need not let
his marriage weigh too much upon him, I resolved on
it for the sake of security and peace."

Since it was the salvation of Babbiano that he aimed
at, the Count of Aquila should have rejoiced at Gian
Maria's wise resolve, and no other consideration should
have tempered so encompassing a thing as that joy
of his should have been. Yet, when later he left his
cousin's presence, the only feeling that he carried with
him was a deep and bitter resentment against the Fate
that willed such things, blent with a sorrowing pity
for the girl that was to wed his cousin and a growing
hatred for the cousin who made him pity her.

CHAPTER VI

THE AMOROUS DUKE

FROM a window of the Palace of Babbiano the Lord of Aquila watched the amazing bustle in the courtyard below, and at his side stood Fanfulla degli Arcipreti, whom he had summoned from Perugia with assurances that, Masuccio being dead, no peril now menaced him.

It was a week after that interview at which Gian Maria had made known his intentions to his cousin, and his Highness was now upon the point of setting out for Urbino to perform the comedy of wooing the Lady Valentina. This was the explanation of that scurrying of servitors and pages, that parading of men-at-arms, and that stamping of horses and mules in the quadrangle below. Francesco watched the scene with a smile of some bitterness, his companion with one of supreme satisfaction.

"Praised be Heaven for having brought his Highness at last to a sense of his duty," remarked the courtier.

"It has often happened to me," said Francesco, disregarding his companion's words, "to malign the Fates for having brought me into the world a count. But in the future I shall give them thanks, for I see how much worse it might have been—I might have been born a prince, with a duchy to rule over. I might have been as that poor man, my cousin, a creature whose life is all pomp and no real dignity, all merrymaking and no real mirth—loveless, isolated and vain."

"But," cried the amazed Fanfulla, "assuredly there are compensations?"

"You see that bustle. You know what it portends. What compensation can there be for that?"

"It is a question you should be the last to ask, my

lord.   You have seen the niece of Guidobaldo, and
having her, can you still ask what compensation does
this marriage offer Gian Maria ? "

"Do   you, then, not   understand ? " returned
Aquila, with a wan smile.   " Do you not see the tragedy
of it ?   Is it nothing that two States, having found that
this marriage would be mutually advantageous, have
determined that it shall take place ?   That meanwhile
the chief actors—the victims, I might almost call them—
have no opportunity of selecting for themselves.   Gian
Maria goes about it resignedly.   He will tell you that he
has always known that some day he must wed and do his
best to beget a son.   He held out long enough against this
alliance, but now that necessity is driving him at last, he
goes about it much as he would go about any other State
affair—a coronation, a banquet or a ball.   Can you wonder now that I could not accept the throne of Babbiano
when it was offered me ?   I tell you, Fanfulla, that were
I at present in my cousin's shoes I would cast crown and
purple at whomsoever had a fancy for them, ere they
crushed the life out of me and left me a poor puppet.
Sooner than endure that hollow mockery of a life I would
become a peasant or a vassal ; I would delve the earth and
lead a humble life, but lead it in my own way, and thank
God for the freedom of it ; choose my own comrades ;
live as I list, where I list ; love as I list, where I list, and
die when God pleases with the knowledge that my life
had not been altogether barren.   And that poor girl,
Fanfulla ! Think of her.   She is to be joined in loveless
union to such a gross, unfeeling clod as Gian Maria.
Have you no pity for her ? "

Fanfulla sighed, his brows clouded.

" I am not so dull but that I can see why you should
reason thus to-day," said he.   " These thoughts have
come to you since you have seen her."

Francesco sighed deeply.

" Who knows ? " he made answer wistfully.   "In the
few moments that we talked together, in the little
time that I beheld her, it may be that she dealt me a
wound far deeper than the one to which she so mercifully
sought to minister."

Now for all that in what the Lord of Aquila said

touching the projected union there was a deal of justice, yet when he asserted that the chief actors were to have no opportunity of selecting for themselves, he said too much. That opportunity they were to have. It occurred three days later at Urbino, when the Duke and Valentina were brought together at the banquet of welcome given by Guidobaldo to his intended nephew-in-law. The sight of her resplendent beauty came as a joyful shock to Gian Maria and filled him with as much impatience to possess her as did his own gross ugliness render him offensive in her eyes. Averse had she been to this wedding from the moment that it had been broached to her. The sight of Gian Maria completed her loathing of the part assigned her, and in her heart she registered a vow that sooner than become the Duchess of Babbiano she would return to her Convent of Santa Sofia and take the veil.

Gian Maria sat beside her at the banquet, and in the intervals of eating—which absorbed him mightily—he whispered compliments at which she shuddered and turned pale. The more strenuously did he strive to please, in his gross and clumsy fashion, the more did he succeed in repelling and disgusting her, until, in the end, with all his fatuousness, he came to deem her oddly cold. Of this, anon he made complaint to that magnificent prince her uncle, but Guidobaldo scoffed at his qualms.

" Do you account my niece a peasant girl ? " he asked. " Would you have her smirk and squirm at every piece of flattery you utter ? So that she weds your Highness what shall the rest signify ? "

" I would she loved me a little," complained Gian Maria foolishly.

Guidobaldo looked him over with an eye that smiled inscrutably, and it may have crossed his mind that this coarse, white-faced Duke was too ambitious.

" I doubt not that she will," he answered, in tones as inscrutable as his glance. " So that you woo with grace and ardour, what woman could withstand your Highness ? Be not put off by such modesty as becomes a maid. "

Those words of Guidobaldo's breathed new courage

into him.   Nor ever after could he think that her coldness
was other than a cloak, a sort of maidenly garment behind
which modesty bade her conceal the inclinations of her
heart.   Reasoning thus, and having in support of it his
wondrous fatuity, it so befell that the more she shunned
and avoided him, the more did he gather conviction of
the intensity of her affection ; the more loathing she betrayed, the more proof did it afford him of the consuming
quality of her passion.   In the end, he went even so far
as to applaud and esteem in her this very maidenly
conduct.

There were hunting-parties, hawking-parties, water-
parties, banquets, comedies, balls, and revels of every
description, and for a week all went well at Urbino.
Then, as suddenly as if a cannon had been fired upon the
Palace, the festivities were interrupted.   The news that
an envoy of Cæsar Borgia's was at Babbiano with a
message from his master came like a cold douche upon
Gian Maria.   It was borne to him in a letter from
Fabrizio da Lodi, imploring his immediate return to treat
with this plenipotentiary of Valentino's.

No longer did he disregard the peril that threatened
him from the all-conquering Borgia, no longer deem exag-
gerated by his advisers the cause for fear.   This sudden
presence of Valentino's messenger, coming, too, at a time
when it would almost seem as if the impending union with
Urbino had spurred the Borgia to act before the alliance
was established, filled him with apprehension.

In one of the princely chambers that had been set aside
for his use during his visit to Urbino he discussed the
tragic news with the two nobles who had accompanied
him—Alvaro de Alvari and Gismondo Santi—and both of
them, whilst urging him to take the advice of Lodi and
return at once, urged him, too, to establish his betrothal
ere he left.

" Bring the matter to an issue at once, your Highness," said Santi, "and thus you will go back to Babbiano
well-armed to meet Duca Valentino's messenger.

Readily accepting this advice, Gian Maria went in
quest of Guidobaldo, and laid before him his proposals,
together with the news which had arrived and which was
the cause of the haste he now manifested.   Guidobaldo

listened gravely. In its way the news affected him as well, for he feared the might of Cæsar Borgia as much as any man in Italy, and he was, by virtue of it, the readier to hasten forward an alliance which should bring another of the neighbouring States into the powerful coalition he was forming.

" It shall be as you wish," answered him the gracious Lord of Urbino, " and the betrothal shall be proclaimed to-day, so that you can bear news of it to Valentino's messenger. When you have heard this envoy, deliver him an answer of such defiance or such caution as you please. Then return in ten days' time to Urbino, and all shall be ready for the nuptials. But first of all, go you and tell Monna Valentina."

Confident of success, Gian Maria obeyed his host, and went in quest of the lady. He gained her ante-chamber, and thence he despatched an idling page to request of her the honour of an audience.

As the youth passed through the door that led to the room beyond, Gian Maria caught for a moment the accent of an exquisite male voice, singing a love-song to the accompaniment of a lute.

" Una donna piu bella assai che 'l sole . . ."

came the words of Petrarch and he heard them still, though muffled, for a moment or two after the boy had gone. Then it ceased abruptly, and a pause followed, at the end of which the page returned. Raising the portiere of blue and gold, he invited Gian Maria to enter.

It was a room that spoke with eloquence of the wealth and refinement of Montefeltro, from the gilding and ultra-marine of the vaulted ceiling with its carved frieze of delicately inlaid woodwork, to the priceless tapestries beneath it. Above a crimson prie-dieu hung a silver cruci-fix, the exquisite workmanship of the famous Anichino of Ferrara. Yonder stood an inlaid cabinet, surmounted by a crystal mirror and some wonders of Murano glass. There was a picture by Mantegna, some costly cameos and delicate enamels, an abundance of books, a dulcimer which a fair-haired page was examining with inquisitive eyes, and by a window on the right stood a very hand-some harp that Guidobaldo had bought his niece in Venice.

In that choice apartment of hers the Duke found Valentina surrounded by her ladies, Peppe the fool, a couple of pages, and a half-dozen gentlemen of her uncle's court. One of these—that same Gonzaga who had escorted her from the Convent of Santa Sofia—most splendidly arrayed in white taby, his vest and doublet rich with gold, sat upon a low stool, idly fingering the lute in his lap, from which Gian Maria inferred that his had been the voice that had reached him in the ante-chamber.

At the Duke's advent they all rose saving Valentina, and received him with a ceremony that somewhat chilled his ardour. He advanced ; then halted clumsily and in a clumsy manner framed a request that he might speak with her alone. In a tired. long-suffering way she dismissed that court of hers, and Gian Maria stood waiting until the last of them had passed out through the tall windows that abutted on to a delightful terrace, where, in the midst of a green square, a marble fountain flashed and glimmered in the sunlight.

" Lady," he said, when they were at last alone, " I have news from Babbiano that demands my instant return." And he approached her by another step.

In truth he was a dull-witted fellow, or else too blinded by fatuity to see and interpret aright the sudden sparkle in her eyes, the sudden, unmistakable expression of relief that spread itself upon her face.

" My lord," she answered, in a low, collected voice, " we shall grieve at your departure."

Fool of a Duke that he was ! Blind, crass and most fatuous of wooers ! Had he been bred in courts and his ears attuned to words that meant nothing, that were but the empty echoes of what should have been meant ; was he so new to courtesies in which the heart had no share, that those words of Valentina's must bring him down upon his knees beside her, to take her dainty fingers in his fat hands, and to become transformed into a boorish lover of the most outrageous type ?

" Shall you so ? " he lisped, his glance growing mighty amorous.

" Shall you indeed grieve ? "

She rose abruptly to her feet.

" I beg that your Highness will rise," she enjoined him

coldly, a coldness which changed swiftly to alarm as her endeavours to release her hand proved vain. For despite her struggles he held on stoutly, This was mere coyness, he assured himself, more maidenly artifice which he must bear with until he had overcome it for all time.

"My lord, I implore you!" she continued. "Bethink you of where you are—of who you are."

"Here will I stay until the crack of doom," he answered! with an odd mixture of humour, ardour and ferocity, "unless you consent to listen to me."

"I am ready to listen, my lord," she answered, without veiling a repugnance that he lacked the wit to see. "But it is not necessary that you should hold my hand, nor fitting that you should kneel."

"Not fitting?" he exclaimed, "Lady, you do not apprehend me rightly. Is it not fitting that all of us—be we princes or vassals—shall kneel sometimes?"

"At your prayers, my lord, yes, most fitting."

"And is not a man at his prayers when he woos? What fitter shrine in all the world than his mistress's feet?"

"Release me," she commanded, still struggling. "Your Highness grows tiresome and ridiculous."

"Ridiculous?"

His great sensual mouth fell open. His white cheeks grew mottled, and his little eyes looked up with a mighty evil gleam in their cruel blue. A moment he stayed so, then he rose up. He released her hands as she had bidden him, but he clutched her arms instead which was yet worse.

"Valentina," he said, in a voice that was far from steady, "why do you use me thus unkindly?"

"But I do not," she protested wearily, drawing back with a shudder from the white face that was so near her own, inspiring her with a loathing she could not repress. "I would not have your Highness look foolish and you cannot conceive how——"

"Can you conceive how deeply, how passionately I love you?" he broke in, his grasp tightening.

"My lord, you are hurting me!"

"And are you not hurting me?" he snarled. "What

is a pinched arm when compared with such wounds as
your eyes are dealing me ?   Are you not——''

She had twisted from his grasp, and in a bound she had
reached the window-door through which her attendants
had passed.

" Valentina ! " he cried, as he sprang after her, and it
was more like the growl of a beast than the cry of a lover.
He caught her, and with scant ceremony he dragged her
back into the room.

At this, her latent loathing, contempt and indignation
rose up in arms.   Never had she heard tell of a woman of
her rank being used in this fashion.   She abhorred him,
yet she had spared him the humiliation of hearing it from
her lips, intending to fight for her liberty with her uncle.
But now, since he handled her as though she had been
a serving-wench ; since he appeared to know nothing of
the deference due to her, nothing of the delicacies of
people well-born and well-bred, she would endure his
odious love-making no further.   Since he elected to
pursue his wooing like a clown, the high-spirited daughter
of Urbino promised herself that in like fashion would
she deal with him.

Swinging herself free from his grasp a second time, she
caught him a stinging buffet on the ducal cheek which—
so greatly did it take him by surprise—all but sent him
sprawling.

" Madonna ! " he panted.   " This indignity to me ! "

" And what indignities have not I suffered at your
hands ? '' she retorted, with a fierceness of glance before
which he recoiled.   And as she now towered before him, a
beautiful embodiment of wrath, he knew not whether he
loved her more than he feared her, yet the desire to
possess her and to tame her was strong within him.

" Am I baggage of your camps," she questioned
furiously," to be so handled by you ?   Do you forget
that I am the niece of Guidobaldo, a lady of the house
of Rovere, and that from my cradle I have known
naught but the respect of all men, be they born never
so high ?   That to such by my birth I have the right ?
Must I tell you in plain words, sir, that though born to
a throne, your manners are those of a groom ?   And
must I tell you, ere you will realise it, that no man,

to whom with my own lips I have not given the right, shall set hands upon me as you have done ? "

Her eyes flashed, her voice rose, and higher raged the storm ; and Gian Maria was so tossed and shattered by it that he could but humbly sue for pardon.

" What shall it signify that I am a Duke," he pleaded timidly, " since I am become a lover ?   What is a Duke then ?   He is but a man, and as the meanest of his subjects his love must take expression.   For what does love know of rank ? "

She was moving towards the window again, and for all that he dared not a second time arrest her by force, he sought by words to do so.

"Madonna," he exclaimed, "I implore you to hear me. In another hour I shall be in the saddle on my way to Babbiano."

" That, sir," she answered him, " is the best news I have heard since your coming."   And without waiting for his reply, she stepped through the open window on to the terrace.

For a second he hesitated, a sense of angry humiliation oppressing his wits.   Then he started to follow her ; but as he reached the window the little crook-backed figure of Ser Peppe stood suddenly before him with a tinkle of bells, and a mocking grin illumining his face.

" Out of the way, fool," growled the angry Duke.   But the odd figure in its motley of red and black continued where it stood.

" If it is Madonna Valentina you seek," said he, " behold her yonder."

And Gian Maria, following the indication of Peppe's lean finger, saw that she had rejoined her ladies and that thus this opportuntiy of speaking with her was at an end. He turned his shoulder upon the jester, and moved ponderously towards the door by which he had originally entered the room.   It had been well for Ser Peppe had he let him go.   But the fool, who loved his mistress dearly, and had many of the instincts of the faithful dog, loving where she loved and hating where she hated, could not repress the desire to send a gibe after the retreating figure and inflict another wound in that much-wounded spirit.

" You find it a hard road to Madonna's heart, Magnificent," he called after him. " Where your wisdom is blind be aided by the keen eyes of folly."

The Duke stood still. A man more dignified would have left that treacherous tongue unheeded. But dignity and Gian Maria were strangers. He turned, and eyed the figure that now followed him into the room.

" You have knowledge to sell," he guessed contemptuously.

" Knowledge I have—vast store—but not for sale, Lord Duke. Such as imports you I will bestow if you ask me, for no more than the joy of beholding you smile."

" Say on," the Duke bade him, without relaxing the grimness that tightened his flabby face.

Peppe bowed.

" It were an easy thing, most High and Mighty, to win the love of Madonna if——" He paused dramatically.

" Yes, yes. *E dunque?* If——? "

" If you had the noble countenance, the splendid height, the shapely limbs, the courtly speech and princely manner of one I wot of."

" Are you deriding me ? " the Duke questioned, unbelievingly.

" Ah no, Highness ! I do but tell you how it were possible that my lady might come to love you. Had you those glorious attributes of him I speak of, and of whom she dreams, it might be easy. But since God fashioned you such as you are—gross of countenance, fat and stunted of shape, boorish of——"

With a roar the infuriated Duke was upon him. But the fool, as nimble of legs as he was of tongue, eluded the vicious grasp of those fat hands, and leaping through the window, ran to the shelter of his mistress's petticoats.

CHAPTER VII

GONZAGA THE INSIDIOUS

WELL indeed had it been for Ser Peppe had he restrained his malicious mood and curbed the mocking speech that had been as vinegar to Gian Maria's wounds For when Gian Maria was sore he was wont to be vindictive, and on the present occasion he was something even more.

There abode with him the memory of the fool's words, and the suggestion that in the heart of Valentina was framed the image of some other man. Now, loving her in his own coarse way, and as he understood love, the rejected Duke waxed furiously jealous of this other at whose existence Peppe had hinted. This unknown stood in his path to Valentina, and to clear that path it suggested itself to Gian Maria that first he must discover it, and to this he thought, with a grim smile, the fool might—willy-nilly—help him.

He returned to his own apartments, and, whilst the preparations for his departure were towards, he bade Alvaro summon Martin Armstadt—the captain of his guard. To the latter his orders were short and secret.

" Take four men," he bade him, " and remain in Urbino after I am gone. Discover the haunts of Peppe the fool. Sieze him, and bring him after me. See that you do it diligently, and let no suspicion of your task arise.'

The bravo—he was little better, for all that he commanded the guards of the Duke of Babbiano—bowed, and answered in his foreign, guttural voice that his Highness should be obeyed.

Thereafter Gian Maria made shift to depart. He took his leave of Guidobaldo, promising to return within a few days for the nuptials, and leaving an impression upon the mind of his host that his interview with Valentina had been very different from the actual.

It was from Valentina herself that Guidobaldo was to learn, after Gian Maria's departure, the true nature of that interview, and what had passed between his niece and his guest. She sought him out in his closet, whither he had repaired, driven thither by the demons of gout that already inhabited his body, and was wont to urge him at times to isolate himself from his court. She found him reclining upon a couch, seeking distraction in a volume of the prose works of Piccinino. He was a handsome man, of excellent shape, scarce thirty years of age. His face was pale, and there were dark circles round his eyes and lines of pain about his strong mouth.

He sat up at her advent, and, setting his book upon the table beside him, he listened to her angry complaints.

At first, the courtly Montefeltro inclined to anger upon learning the roughness with which Gian Maria had borne himself. But presently he smiled.

"When all is said, I see in this no great cause for indignation," he assured her. "I acknowledge that it may lack the formality that should attend the addresses of a man in the Duke's position to a lady in yours. But since he is to wed you, and that soon, why be angered at that he seeks to pay his court like any other man?"

"I have talked in vain, then," she answered petulantly, "and I am misunderstood. I do not intend to wed this ducal clod you have chosen to be my husband."

Guidobaldo stared at her with brows raised, and wonder in his fine eyes. Then he shrugged his shoulders a trifle wearily. This handsome and well-beloved Guidobaldo was very much a prince, so schooled to princely ways as to sometimes forget that he was a man.

"We forgive much to the impetuousness of youth," said he, very coldly. "But there are bounds to the endurance of every one of us. As your uncle and your prince, I claim a double duty from you, and you owe a double allegiance to my wishes. By my twofold authority I have commanded you to wed with Gian Maria."

The princess in her was all forgotten, and it was just the woman who answered him, in a voice of protest :

" But, Highness, I do not love him."

A shade of impatience crossed his lofty face.

" I do not remember," he made answer wearily, " that I loved your aunt. Yet we were wed, and through habit came to love each other and to be happy together."

" I can understand that Monna Elizabetta should have come to love you," she returned. " You are not as Gian Maria. You were not fat and ugly, stupid and cruel, as is he."

It was an appeal that might have won its way to a man's heart through the ever-ready channel of his vanity. But it did not so with Guidobaldo. He only shook his head.

" The matter is not one that I will argue. It were unworthy in us both. Princes, my child, are not as ordinary folk."

" In what are they different ? " she flashed back at him. " Do they not hunger and thirst as ordinary folk ? Are they not subject to the same ills ; do they not experience the same joys ? Are they not born, and do they not die just as ordinary folk ? In what, then, lies this difference that forbids them to mate as ordinary folk ? "

Guidobaldo tossed his arms to Heaven, his eyes full of a consternation that clearly defied utterance. The violence of his gesture drew a gasp of pain from him. At last, when he had mastered it :

" They are different," said he, " in that their lives are not their own to dispose of as they will. They belong to the State which they were born to govern, and in nothing else does this become of so much importance as in their mating. It behoves them to contract such alliances as shall rebound to the advantage of their people." A toss of her auburn head was Valentina's interpolation, but her uncle continued relentlessly in his cold, formal tones—such tones as those in which he might have addressed an assembly of his captains :

" In the present instance we are threatened—Babbiano
and Urbino—by a common foe. And whilst divided,
neither of us could withstand him; united, we shall
combine to his overthrow. Therefore does this alliance
become necessary—imperative."

" I do not apprehend the necessity," she answered
in a voice that breathed defiance. " If such an alliance
as you speak of is desirable, why may it not be made a
purely political one—such a one, for instance, as now
binds Perugia and Camerino to you? What need to
bring me into question? "

" A little knowledge of history would afford you an
answer. Such political alliances are daily made, and
daily broken when more profit offers in another quarter.
But cemented by marriage, the tie, whilst continuing
political, becomes also one of blood. In the case of
Urbino and Babbiano, it enters also into consideration
that I have no son. It might well be, Valentina," he
pursued, with a calculating coldness that revolted her,
" that a son of yours would yet more strongly link
the two duchies. In time both might become united
under him into one great power that might vie successfully with any in Italy. Now leave me, child. As
you see, I am suffering, and when it is thus with me,
and this evil tyrant has me in his clutches, I prefer to
be alone."

There was a pause, and whilst his eyes were upon hers,
hers were upon the ground in avoidance of his glance.
A frown marred her white brow, her lips were set and
her hands clenched. Pity for his physical ills fought
a while with pity for her own mental torment. At last
she threw back her beautiful head, and the manner of
that action was instinct with insubordination.

" It grieves me to harass your Highness in such a
season," she assured him, " but I must beg your indulgence. These things may be as you say. Your
plans may be the noblest that were ever conceived,
since to their consummation would be entailed the
sacrifice of your own flesh and blood—in the person of
your niece. But I will have no part in them. It may
be that I lack a like nobility of soul; it may be that
I am all unworthy of the high station to which I was

born through no fault of my own. And so, my lord,"
she ended, her voice, her face, her gesture all imparting
an irrevocable finality to her words, " I will not wed
this Duke of Babbiano—no, not to cement alliances
with a hundred duchies."

" Valentina ! " he exclaimed, roused out of his
wonted calm. " Do you forget that you are my niece ? "

" Since you appear to have forgotten it."

" These woman's whims——" he began, when she
interrupted him.

" Perhaps they will serve to remind you that I am
a woman, and perhaps if you remember that, you may
consider how very natural it is that, being a woman,
I should refuse to wed for—for political ends."

" To your chamber," he commanded now thoroughly
aroused. " And on your knees beg Heaven's grace to
help you to see your duty, since no words of mine
prevail."

" Oh, that the Duchess were returned from Mantua ! "
she sighed. " The good Monna Elizabetta might melt
you to some pity."

" Monna Elizabetta is too dutiful herself to do aught
but urge you to dutifulness. There, child," he added,
in a more wheedling tone, " set aside this disobedient
mood, which is unlike you and becomes you ill. You
shall be wed with a splendour and magnificence that
will set every princess in Italy green with envy. Your
dowry is set at fifty thousand ducats, and Guiliano della
Rovere shall pronounce the benediction. Already I
have sent orders to Ferrara, to the incomparable Anichino, for the *majestate* girdle ; I will send to Venice
for gold leaf and——"

" But do you not heed me that I will not wed ? " she
broke in with passionate calm, her face white, her
bosom heaving.

He rose, leaning heavily upon a gold-headed cane,
and looked at her a moment without speaking, his
brows contracted. Then :

" Your betrothal to Gian Maria is proclaimed," he
announced in a voice cold with finality. " I have
passed my word to the Duke, and your marriage shall
take place so soon as he returns. Now go. Such

scenes as these are wearisome to a sick man, and they are undignified."

" But, your Highness," she began, an imploring note now taking the place that lately had been held by defiance.

" Go ! " he blazed, stamping his foot, and then to save his dignity—for he feared that she might still remain—he himself turned on his heel and passed from the apartment.

Left to herself, she stood there a moment, allowed a sigh to escape her, and brushed an angry tear from her brown eyes. Then, with a sudden movement that seemed to imply suppression of her mood, she walked to the door by which she entered, and left the chamber.

She went down the long gallery, whose walls glowed with the new frescoes from the wonder-working brush of Andrea Mantegna ; she crossed her ante-chamber and gained the very room where some hours ago she had received the insult of Gian Maria's odious advances. She passed through the now empty room, and stepped out on to the terrace that overlooked the paradise-like gardens of the Palace.

Close by the fountain stood a white marble seat, over which, earlier that day, one of her women had thrown a cloak of crimson velvet. There she now sat herself to think out the monstrous situation that beset her. The air was warm and balmy and heavy with the scent of flowers from the garden below. The splashing of the fountain seemed to soothe her, and for a little while her eyes were upon that gleaming water, which rose high in a crystal column, then broke and fell, a shower of glittering jewels, into the broad marble basin. Then, her eyes growing tired, they strayed to the marble balustrade, where a peacock strode with overweening dignity ; they passed on to the gardens below, gay with early blossoms, in their stately frames of tall boxwood hedges, and flanked by myrtles and tall cypresses standing gaunt and black against the deep saffron of the vesper sky.

Saving the splashing of the fountain, and the occasional harsh scream of the peacock, all was at peace, as if by contrast with the tumult that raged in Valentina's soul.

Then another sound broke the stillness—a soft step, crunching the gravel of the walk. She turned, and behind her stood the magnificent Gonzaga, a smile that at once reflected pleasure and surprise upon his handsome face.

" Alone, Madonna ? " he said, in accents of mild wonder, his fingers softly stirring the strings of the lute he carried, and without which he seldom appeared about the Court.

" As you see," she answered, and her tone was the tone of one whose thoughts are taken up with other things.

Her glance moved away from him again, and in a moment it seemed as if she had forgotten his presence, so absorbed grew the expression of her face.

But Gonzaga was not easily discouraged. Patience was the one virtue that Valentina more than any woman—and there had been many in his young life— had inculcated into a soul that in the main was anything but virtuous. He came a step nearer, and leant lightly against the edge of her seat, his shapely legs crossed, his graceful body inclining ever so slightly towards her.

" You are pensive, Madonna," he murmured, in his rich, caressing voice.

" Why, then," she reproved him, but in a mild tone, " do you intrude upon my thoughts ? "

" Because they seem sad thoughts, Madonna," he answered, glibly, " and I were a poor friend did I not seek to rouse you out of them."

" You are that, Gonzaga ? " she questioned, without looking at him. " You are my friend ? "

He seemed to quiver and then draw himself upright, whilst across his face there swept a shade of something that may have been good or bad or partly both. Then he leant down until his head came very near her own.

" Your friend ? " quoth he. " Ah, more than your friend. Count me your very slave, Madonna."

She looked at him now, and in his countenance she saw a reflection of the ardour that had spoken in his voice. In his eyes there was a glance of burning intensity. She drew away from him, and at first he accounted himself repulsed, but pointing to the space she had left :

" Sit here beside me, Gonzaga," she said quietly, and he, scarce crediting his own good fortune that so much favour should be showered upon him, obeyed her in a half-timid fashion that was at odd variance with his late bold words.

He laughed lightly, perhaps to cover the embarrassment that beset him, and, dropping his jeweled cap, he flung one white-cased leg over the other and took his lute in his lap, his fingers again wandering to the strings.

" I have a new song, Madonna," he announced, with a gaiety that was obviously forced. " It is in *ottava rima*, a faint echo of the immortal Niccolo Correggio, composed in honour of one whose description is beyond the flight of human song."

" Yet you sing of her ? "

" It is no better than an acknowledgment of the impossibility to sing of her. Thus——" And striking a chord or two, he began, *a mezza voce* :

> " Quando sorriderán in ciel
> Gli occhi tuoi ai santi—"

She laid a hand upon his arm to stay him.

" Not now, Gonzaga," she begged, " I am in no humour for your song, sweet though I doubt not that it be."

A shade of disappointment and ruffled vanity crossed his face. Women had been wont to listen greedily to his *strambotti*, enthralled by the cunning of the words and the seductive sweetness of his voice.

" Ah, never look so glum," she cried, smiling now at his crestfallen air. " If I have not hearkened now, I will again. Forgive me, good Gonzaga," she begged him, with a sweetness no man could have resisted. And then a sigh fluttered from her lips ; a sound that was like a sob came after it, and her hand closed upon his arm.

" They are breaking my heart, my friend. Oh that you had left me at peace in the Convent of Santa Sofia ! "

He turned to her, all solicitude and gentleness, to inquire the reason of her outburst.

" It is this odious alliance into which they seek to force me with that man from Babbiano. I have told Guidobaldo that I will not wed this Duke. But as profitably might I tell Fate that I will not die. The one is as unheeding as the other."

Gonzaga sighed profoundly, in sympathy, but said nothing. Here was a grief to which he could not minister, a grievance that he could do nothing to remove. She turned from him with a gesture of impatience.

"You sigh," she exclaimed, "and you bewail the cruelty of the fate in store for me. But you can do nothing for me. You are all words, Gonzaga. You can call yourself more than my friend—my very slave. Yet, when I need your help, what do you offer me ? A sigh ! "

"Madonna, you are unjust," he was quick to answer, with some heat. "I did not dream—I did not dare to dream—that it was my help you sought. My symyathy, I believed, was all that you invited, and so, lest I should seem presumptuous, it was all I offered. But if my help you need or if you seek a means to evade this alliance that you rightly describe as odious, such help as it lies in a man's power to render shall you have from me."

He spoke almost fiercely and with a certain grim confidence, for all that as yet no plan had formed itself in his mind. Indeed, had a course been clear to him there had been perhaps less confidence in his tone, for, after all, he was not by nature a man of action, and his character was the very reverse of valiant. Yet so excellent an actor was he as to deceive even himself by his acting, and in this suggestion of some vague fine deeds that he would do, he felt himself stirred by a sudden martial ardour, and capable of all. He was stirred, too, by the passion with which Valentina's beauty filled him—a passion that went nearer to making a man of him than Nature had succeeded in doing.

That now, in the hour of her need, she should turn so readily to him for assistance, he accepted as proof that she was not deaf to the voice of this great love he bore her, but of which he never yet had dared to show a sign. The passing jealousy that he had entertained for that wounded knight they had met at Acquasparta was laid to rest by her present attitude towards him, the knight himself forgotten.

As for Valentina, she listened to his ready speech and earnest tone with growing wonder both at him and at herself. Her own words had been little more than a petulant outburst. Of actually finding a way to delude her uncle's wishes she had no thought—unless it lay in carrying out that threat of hers to take the veil. Now, however, that Gonzaga spoke so bravely of doing what man could do to help her to evade that marriage, the thought of active resistance took an inviting shape.

A timid hope—a hope that was afraid of being shattered before it grew to any strength—peeped now from the wondering eyes she turned on her companion.

"Is there a way, Gonzaga?" she asked, after a pause.

Now during that pause his mind had been very busy. Something of a poet, he was blessed with wits of a certain quickness, and was a man of very ready fancy. Like an inspiration an idea had come to him; out of this had sprung another, and yet another, until a chain of events by which the frustration of the schemes of Babbiano and Urbino might be accomplished was complete.

"I think," he said slowly, his eyes upon the ground, "that I know a way."

Her glance was now eager, her lip tremulous, and her face a little pale. She leant towards him.

"Tell me," she besought him feverishly.

He set his lute on the seat beside him, and his eyes looked round in apprehensive survey.

"Not here," he muttered. "There are too many ears in the Palace of Urbino. Will it please you to walk in the gardens? I will tell you there."

They rose together, so ready was her assent. They looked at each other for a second. Then, side by side, they passed down the wide marble steps that led from the terrace to the box-flanked walks of the gardens. Here, among the lengthening shadows, they paced in silence for a while, what time Gonzaga sought for words in which to propound his plan. At length, grown impatient, Valentina urged him with a question.

"What I counsel, Madonna," he answered her, "is open defiance."

" Such a course I am already pursuing.   But whither
will it lead me ? "

" I do not mean the mere defiance of words—mere
protestations that you will not wed Gian Maria.   Listen,
Madonna !   The Castle of Roccaleone is your property.
It is perhaps the stoutest fortress in all Italy to-day.
Lightly garrisoned and well-provisioned it might with-
stand a year's siege."

She turned to him, having guessed already the
proposal in his mind, and for all that at first her eyes
looked startled, yet presently they kindled to a light
of daring that augured well for a very stout adventure.
It was a wildly romantic notion, this of Gonzaga's,
worthy of a poet's perfervid brain, and yet it attracted
her by its unprecedented flavour.

" Could it be done ? " she wondered, her eyes sparkling
at the anticipation of such a deed.

" It could, indeed it could," he answered, with an
eagerness no whit less than her own.   " Immure yourself
in Roccaleone, and thence hurl defiance at Urbino and
Babbiano, refusing to surrender until they grant your
terms—that you are to marry as you list."

" And you will help me in this ? " she questioned, her
mind—in its innocence—inclining more and more to the
mad project.

" With all my strength and wit," he answered
readily and gallantly.   " I will so victual the place
that it shall be able to stand siege for a whole year,
should the need arise, and I will find you the men to
arm it—a score will, I should think, be ample for our
needs, since it is mainly upon the natural strength of
the place that we rely."

" And then," said she, " I shall need a captain."

Gonzaga made her a low bow.

" If you will honour me with the office, Madonna, I
shall serve you loyally whilst I have life."

A smile quivered for a second on her lips, but was
gone ere the courtier had straightened himself from his
bow, for far was it from her wishes to wound his spirit.
But the notion of this scented fop in the rôle of captain,
ruling a handful of rough mercenaries, and directing
the operations for the resistance of an assiduous siege,

touched her with its ludicrous note. Yet, if she refused him this, it was more than likely he would deem himself offended and refuse to advance their plans. It crossed her mind—in the full confidence of youth—that if he should fail her when the hour of action came, she was of stout enough heart to aid herself. And so she consented, whereat again he bowed, this time in gratitude. And then a sudden thought occurred to her, and with it came dismay.

"But for all this, Gonzaga—for the men and that victualling—money will be needed."

"If you will let my friendship be proven also in that——" he began.

But she interrupted him, struck suddenly with a solution to the riddle.

"No, no!" she exclaimed. His face fell a little. He had hoped to place her in his debt in every possible way, yet here was one in which she raised a barrier. Upon her head she wore a fret of gold, so richly laced with pearls as to be worth a prince's ransom. This she now made haste to unfasten with fingers that excitement set a-trembling. "There!" she cried holding it out to him. "Turn that to money, my friend. It should yield you ducats enough for this enterprise."

It next occurred to her that she could not go alone into that castle with just Gonzaga and the men he was about to enrol. His answer came with a promptness that showed he had considered, also, that.

"By no means," he answered her. "When the time comes you must select such of your ladies—say three or four—as appear suitable and have your trust. You may take a priest as well, a page or two, and a few servants."

Thus, in the gloaming, amid the shadows of that old Italian garden, was the plot laid by which Valentina was to escape alliance with his Highness of Babbiano. But there was more than that in it, although that was all that Valentina saw. It was, too, a plot by which she might become the wife of Messer Romeo Gonzaga.

He was an exiled member of that famous Mantua family which has bred some scoundrels and one saint.

With the money which, at parting, a doting mother had bestowed upon him, he was cutting a brave figure at the Urbino court, where he was tolerated by virtue of his kinship with Guidobaldo's Duchess, Monna Elizabetta. But his means were running low, and it behoved him to turn his attention to such quarters as might yield him profit. Being poor-spirited, and—since his tastes had not inclined that way—untrained in arms, it would have been futile for him to have sought the career common to adventurers of his age. Yet an adventurer at heart he was, and since the fields of Mars were little suited to his nature, he had long pondered upon the possibilities afforded him by the lists of Cupid. Guidobaldo—purely out of consideration for Monna Elizabetta—had shown him a high degree of favour, and upon this he had been vain enough to found great hopes —for Guidobaldo had two nieces. High had these hopes run when he was chosen to escort the lovely Valentina della Rovere from the Convent of Santa Sofia to her uncle's court. But of late they had withered, since he had learnt what were her uncle's plans for this lady's future. And now, by her own action, and by the plot into which she had entered with him, they rose once more.

To thwart Guidobaldo might prove a dangerous thing, and his life might pay the forfeit if his schemes miscarried—clement and merciful though Guidobaldo was. But if they succeeded, and if by love or by force he could bring Valentina to wed him, he was tolerably confident that Guidobaldo, seeing matters had gone too far—since Gian Maria would certainly refuse to wed Gonzaga's widow—would let them be. To this end no plan could be more propitious than that into which he had lured her. Guidobaldo might besiege them in Roccaleone and might eventually reduce them by force of arms—a circumstance, however, which, despite his words, he deemed extremely remote. But if only he could wed Valentina before they capitulated, he thought that he would have little cause to fear any consequences of Guidobaldo's wrath. After all, in so far as birth and family were concerned, Romeo Gonzaga was nowise the inferior of his Highness of Urbino.

Guidobaldo had yet another niece, and he might cement with her the desired alliance with Babbiano.

Alone in the gardens of the Palace, Gonzaga paced after night had fallen, and with his eyes to the stars that began to fleck the violet sky, he smiled a smile of cunning gratification. He bethought him how well advised had been his suggestion that they should take a priest to Roccaleone. Unless his prophetic sense led him deeply into error, they would find work for that priest before the castle was surrendered.

CHAPTER VIII

AMONG THE DREGS OF WINE

AND so it befell that whilst by Guidobaldo's orders the preparations for Valentina's nuptials went forward with feverish haste—whilst painters, carvers, and artificers in gold and silver applied themselves to their hurried tasks ; whilst messengers raced to Venice for gold leaf and ultramarine for the wedding-chests ; whilst the nuptial bed was being brought from Rome and the chariot from Ferrara ; whilst costly stuffs were being collected and the wedding garments fashioned—the magnificent Romeo Gonzaga was, on his side, as diligently contriving to render vain all that toil of preparation.

On the evening of the third day of his conspiring he sat in the room allotted to him in the Palace of Urbino and matured his plans ; and so well pleased was he with his self-communion that, as he sat at his window, there was a contented smile upon his lips.

He allowed his glance to stray down the slopes of that arid waste of rocks, to the River Metauro, winding its way to the sea, through fertile plains, and gleaming here silver and yonder gold in the evening light. Not quite so complacently would he have smiled had he deemed the enterprise upon which he was engaging to be of that warlike character which he had represented to Valentina. He did not want for cunning, nor for judgment of the working of human minds, and he very reasonably opined that once the Lady Valentina immured herself in Roccaleone and sent word to her uncle that she would not wed Gian Maria nor return to the Count of Urbino until he passed her his ducal word that she should hear no more of the union, the Duke would be the first to capitulate.

He contended that this might not happen at once—
nor did he wish it to ; messages would pass, and
Guidobaldo would seek by cajolery to win back his
niece. This she would resist, and, in the end, her
uncle would see the impossible nature of the situation
and agree to her terms that it might be ended. That
it should come to arms, and that Guidobaldo should
move to besiege Roccaleone, he did not for a moment
believe—for what manner of ridicule would he not
draw upon himself from the neighbouring States ?
At the worst, even if a siege there was, it would never be
carried out with the rigour of ordinary warfare ; there
would be no assaults, no bombarding ; it would be a
simple investment, with the object of intercepting
resources so as to starve the garrison into submission—
for they would never dream of such victualling as
Gonzaga was preparing.

Thus communed Gonzaga with himself, and the smile
enlivening the corners of his weak mouth grew more
thoughtful. He dreamed great dreams that evening ;
he had wondrous visions of a future princely power
that should come to be his own by virtue of this alliance
that he was so skilfully encompassing—a fool in a fool's
paradise, with his folly for only company.

But for all that, his dreams were wondrous sweet to
indulge, and his visions truly alluring to contemplate.
There were plans to be formed and means to be devised
for the flight to Roccaleone. There were calculations
to be made ; the estimating of victuals, arms, and men ;
and, once these calculations were complete, there were
all these things to be obtained. The victuals he had
already provided for, whilst of arms he had no need
to think ; Roccaleone should be well stocked with
them. But the finding of the men gave him some
concern. He had decided to enrol a score, which was
surely the smallest number with which he could make
a fair show of being martially in earnest. But even
though the number was modest, where was he to find
twenty fellows who recked so little of their lives as
to embark upon such an enterprise—even if lured by
generous pay—and thereby incur the ducal displeasure
of Guidobaldo ?

He dressed himself with sober rigour for once in his foppish life, and descended, after night had fallen, to a tavern in a poor street behind the Duomo, hoping that there, among the dregs of wine, he might find what he required.

By great good fortune he chanced upon an old free-booting captain, who once had been a meaner sort of *condottiero*, but who was sorely reduced by bad fortune and bad wine.

The tavern was a dingy, cut-throat place, which the delicate Gonzaga had not entered without a tremor, invoking the saints' protection, and crossing himself ere he set foot across the threshold. Some pieces of goat were being cooked on the embers, in a great fireplace at the end of the room farthest from the door. Before this, Ser Luciano—the taverner—squatted on his heels and fanned so diligently that a cloud of ashes rose ceiling high and spread itself, together with the noisome smoke, throughout the squalid chamber. A brass lamp swung from the ceiling and shone freely through that smoke, as shines the moon through an evening mist. So foully stank the place that at first Gonzaga was moved to get him thence. Only the reflection that nowhere in Urbino was he as likely as here to find the thing he sought, impelled him to stifle his natural squeamishness and remain. He slipped upon some grease, and barely saved himself from measuring his length upon that filthy floor, a matter which provoked a malicious guffaw from a tattered giant who watched with interest his mincing advent.

Perspiring, and with nerves unstrung, the courtier picked his way to a table by the wall, and seated hims lf upon the coarse deal bench before it, praying that he might be left its sole occupant.

On the opposite wall hung a blackened crucifix and a small holy-water stoup that had been dry for a genera-tion, and was now a receptacle for dust and a withered sprig of rosemary. Immediately beneath this—in the company of a couple of tatterdemalions worthy of him—sat the giant who had mocked his escape from falling, and as Gonzaga took his seat he heard the fellow's voice, guttural, bottle-thickened and contentious.

" And this wine, Luciano ? *Sangue della Madonna*!
Will you bring it before dropping dead, pig ? "

Gonzaga shuddered and would have crossed himself
again for protection against what seemed a very devil
incarnate, but that the ruffian's blood-shot eye was set
upon him in a stony stare.

" I come, cavaliere, I come," cried the timid host,
leaping to his feet, and leaving the goat to burn while
he ministered to the giant's unquenchable thirst.

The title caused Gonzaga to start, and he bent his
eyes again on the man's face. He found it villainous
of expression, inflamed and blotched ; the hair hung
matted about a bullet head, and the eyes glared fiercely
from either side of a pendulous nose. Of the knightly
rank by which the taverner addressed him the fellow
bore no outward signs. Arms he carried, it is true ;
a sword and dagger at his belt, whilst beside him on
the table stood a rusty steel-cap. But these warlike
tools served only to give him the appearance of a roving
masnadiero or a cut-throat for hire. Presently abandoning the contemplation of Gonzaga he turned to his
companions, and across to the listener floated a coarse
and boasting tale of a plunderous warfare in Sicily ten
years agone.

Gonzaga became excited. It seemed indeed as if
this were a man who might be useful to him. He
made pretence to sip the wine Luciano had brought
him, and listened avidly to that swashbuckling story,
from which it appeared that this knave had once been
better circumstanced and something of a leader.
Intently he listened, and wondered whether such men
as he boasted he had led in that campaign were still
to be found and could be brought together.

At the end of perhaps a half-hour the two companions
of that thirsty giant rose and took their leave of him.
They cast a passing glance upon Gonzaga, and were gone.

A little while he hesitated. The ruffian seemed to
have lapsed into a reverie, or else he slept with open
eyes. Calling up his courage the gallant rose at last
and moved across the room. All unversed in tavern
ways was the magnificent Gonzaga, and he who at
court, in ballroom or in ante-chamber, was a very mirror

of all the graces of a courtier, felt awkward here and ill
at ease.

At length, summoning his wits to his aid :

" Good sir," said he, with some timidity, " will you
do me the honour to share a flagon with me ? "

The ruffian's eye, which but a moment back had
looked vacuous and melancholy, now quickened until
it seemed ablaze. He raised his bloodshot orbs and
boldly encountered Gonzaga's uneasy glance. His
lips fell apart with an anticipatory smack, his back
stiffened, and his head was raised until his chin took on
so haughty a tilt that Gonzaga feared his proffered
hospitality was on the point of suffering a scornful
rejection.

" Will I share a flagon ? " gasped the fellow, as, being
the sinner that he was and knew himself to be, he might
have gasped : " Will I go to Heaven ? Will I—
will I——? " He paused and pursed his lips. His
eyebrows were puckered and his expression grew mighty
cunning as again he took stock of this pretty fellow who
offered flagons of wine to down-at-heel adventurers
like himself. He had all but asked what was to be
required of him in exchange for this, when suddenly
he bethought him—with the knavish philosophy adver-
sity had taught him—that were he told for what it was
intended that the wine should bribe him, and did the
business suit him not, he should, in the confession of it,
lose the wine ; whilst did he but hold his peace until
he had drunk, it would be his thereafter to please himself
about the business when it came to be proposed.

He composed his rugged features into the rude
semblance of a smile.

" Sweet young sir," he murmured, " sweet, gentle and
most illustrious lord, I would share a hogshead with
such a nobleman as you."

" I am to take it that you will drink ? " quoth Gonzaga, who had scarce known what to make of the man's
last words.

" Body of Bacchus ! Yes. I'll drink with you
gentile signorino, until your purse be empty or the world
run dry." And he leered a mixture of mockery and
satisfaction.

Gonzaga, still half uncertain of his ground, called the taverner and bade him bring a flagon of his best. While Luciano was about the fetching of the wine, constraint sat upon that oddly discordant pair.

"It is a chill night," commented Gonzaga presently, seating himself opposite his swashbuckler.

Young sir, your wits have lost their edge. The night is warm."

"I said," spluttered Gonzaga who was unused to contradiction from his inferiors, and wished now to assert himself, "that the night is chill."

"You lied, then," returned the other, with a fresh leer, "for, as I answered you, the night is warm. *Piaghe di Cristo*! I am an ill man to contradict, my pretty gallant, and if I say the night is warm, warm it shall be though there be snow on Mount Vesuvius."

The courtier turned pink at that, and but for the arrival of the taverner with the wine, it is possible he might have done an unconscionable rashness. At sight of the red liquor the fury died out of the ruffler's face.

"A long life, a long thirst, a long purse, and a short memory!" was his toast, into whose cryptic meaning Gonzaga made no attempt to pry. As the fellow set down his cup, and with his sleeve removed the moisture from his unshorn mouth, "May I not learn," he inquired "whose hospitality I have the honour of enjoying?"

"Heard you ever of Romeo Gonzaga?"

"Of Gonzaga, yes; though of Romeo Gonzaga, never. Are you he?"

Gonzaga bowed his head.

"A noble family yours," returned the swashbuckler, in a tone that implied his own to be as good. "Let me name myself to you. I am Ercole Fortemani," he said, with the proud air of one who announced himself an emperor.

"A formidable name," said Gonzaga, in accents of surprise, "and it bears a noble sound."

The great fellow turned on him in a sudden anger.

"Why that astonishment?" he blazed. "I tell you my name is both noble and formidable, and you shall find me as formidable as I am noble. *Diavolo*! Seems it incredible?"

" Said I so ? " protested Gonzaga.

" You had been dead by now if you had, Messer Gonzaga. But you thought so, and I may take leave to show you how bold a man it needs to think so without suffering."

Ruffled as a turkey-cock, wounded in his pride and in his vanity, Ercole hastened to enlighten Gonzaga on his personality.

" Learn, sir," he announced, " that I am *Captain* Ercole Fortemani. I held that rank in the army of the Pope. I have served the Pisans and the noble Baglioni of Perugia with honour and distinction. I have commanded a hundred lances of Gianoni's famous free-company. I have fought with the French against the Spaniards, and with the Spaniards against the French, and I have served the Borgia who is plotting against both. I have trailed a pike in the emperor's following, and I have held the rank of captain, too, in the army of the King of Naples. Now, young sir, you have learned something of me, and if my name is not written in letters of fire from one end of Italy to the other, it is—Body of God !—because the hands that hired me to the work garnered the glory of my deeds."

" A noble record," said Gonzaga, who had credulously absorbed that catalogue of lies, " a very noble record."

" Not so," the other contradicted, for the lust of contradiction that was part of him. " A great record, if you will, to commend me to hireling service. But you may not call the service of a hireling noble."

" It is a matter we will not quarrel over," said Gonzaga soothingly. The man's ferocity was terrific.

" Who says that we shall not ? " he demanded. " Who will baulk me if I have a mind to quarrel over it ? Answer me ! " and he half rose from his seat, moved by the anger into which he was lashing himself. " But patience ! " he broke off, subsiding on a sudden. " I take it, it was not out of regard for my fine eyes, nor drawn by the elegance of my apparel "—and he raised a corner of his tattered cloak—" nor yet because you wish to throw a main with me, that you have sought my acquaintance, and called for this wine. You require service of me ? "

" You have guessed it."

" A prodigious discernment, by the Host ! " He seemed to incline rather tediously to irony. Then his face grew stern, and he lowered his voice until it was no more than a growling whisper. " Heed me, Messer Gonzaga. If the service you require be the slitting of a gullet or some kindred foul business, which my seeming neediness leads you to suppose me ripe for, let me counsel you, as you value your own skin, to leave the service unmentioned, and get you gone."

In hasty, frantic, fearful protest were Gonzaga's hands outspread.

" Sir, sir—I—I could not have thought it of you," he spluttered, with warmth, much of which was genuine, for it rejoiced him to see some scruples still shining in the foul heap of this man's rascally existence. A knave whose knavery knew no limits would hardly have suited his ends. " I do need a service, but it is no dark-corner work. It is a considerable enterprise, and one in which, I think, you should prove the very man I need."

" Let me know more, quoth Ercole grandiloquently.

" I need first your word that should the undertaking prove unsuited to you or beyond you, you will respect the matter, and keep it secret."

" Body of Satan ! No corpse was ever half so dumb as I shall be."

" Excellent ! Can you find me a score of stout fellows to form a body-guard and a garrison, who, in return for good quarters—perchance for some weeks—and payment at four times the ordinary mercenaries' rate, will be willing to take some risk, and chance even a brush with the Duke's forces ? "

Ercole blew out his mottled cheeks until Gonzaga feared that he would burst them.

" It's outlawry ! " he roared, when he had found his voice. " Outlawry, or I'm a fool."

" Why, yes," confessed Gonzaga. " It is outlaw matter of a kind. But the risk is slender."

" Can you tell me no more ? "

" I dare not."

Ercole emptied his wine-cup at a draught and splashed

the dregs on to the floor. Then, setting down the empty vessel, he sat steeped in thought a while. Growing impatient :

" Well," cried Gonzaga at last, " can you help me ? Can you find the men ? "

" If you were to tell me more of the nature of this service you require, I might find a hundred with ease."

As I have said—I need but a score."

" Ercole looked mighty grave, and thoughtfully rubbed his long nose.

" It might be done," said he, after a pause. " But we shall have to look for desperate knaves ; men who are already under a ban, and to whom it will matter little to have another item added to their indebtedness to the law should they fall into its talons. How soon shall you require this forlorn company ?"'

" By to-morrow night."

" I wonder——" mused Ercole. He was counting on his fingers, and appeared to have lapsed into mental calculations. " I could get half a score or a dozen within a couple of hours. But a score——" Again he paused, and again he fell to thinking. At last, more briskly : " Let us hear what pay you offer me, to thrust myself blindfolded into this business of yours as leader of the company you require ? "he asked suddenly.

Gonzaga's face fell at that. Then he suddenly stiffened, and put on an expression of haughtiness.

" It is my intent to lead this company myself," he loftily informed the ruffler.

" Body of God ! " gasped Ercole, upon whose mind intruded a grotesque picture of such a company as he would assemble being led by this mincing carpet-knight. Then, recollecting himself : " If that be so," said he, " you are best, yourself, enrol it. *Felicissima notte* ! " And he waved him a farewell across the table.

Here was a poser for Gonzaga. How was he to go about such a business as that ? It was beyond his powers. Thus much he protested frankly.

" Now attend to me, young sir," was the other's answer. " The matter stands thus : If I can repair to certain friends of mine with the information that an affair is afoot, the particulars of which I may not give

F

them, but in which I am to lead them myself, sharing such risk as there maybe, I do not doubt that but by this time to-morrow I can have a score of them enrolled—such is their confidence in Ercole Fortemani.   But if I take them to enter a service unknown, under a leader equally unknown, the forming of such a company would be a mighty tedious matter.''

This was an argument to the force of which Gonzaga could not remain insensible. After a moment's considera-tion, he offered Ercole fifty gold florins in earnest of good faith and the promise of pay, thereafter, at the rate of twenty gold florins a month for as long as he should need his services ; and Ercole, who in all his free-lancing days had never earned the tenth of such a sum, was ready to fall upon this most noble gentleman's neck and weep for very joy and brotherly affection.

The matter being settled, Gonzaga produced a heavy bag which gave forth a jangle mighty pleasant to the ears of Fortemani and let it drop with a chink upon the table.

" There are a hundred florins for the equipment of this company.   I do not wish to have a regiment of out-at-elbow tatterdemalions at my heels.''   And his eyes swept in an uncomplimentary manner over Ercole's apparel. " See that you dress them fittingly.''

" It shall be done, Magnificent,'' answered Ercole, with a show of such respect as he had not hitherto manifested " And arms ? ''

" Give them pikes and arquebusses if you will ; but nothing more.   The place we are bound for is well stocked with armour—but even that may not be required.''

" May not be required ? '' echoed the more and more astonished swashbuckler.   Were they to be paid on so lordly a scale, clothed and fed, to induce them upon a business that might carry no fighting with it ?   Surely he had never sold himself into a more likely or promising service, and that night he dreamt in his sleep that he was become a gentleman's steward, and that at his heels marched an endless company of lacqueys in flamboyant liveries.   On the morrow he awoke to the persuasion that at last, of a truth, was his fortune made,

and that hereafter there would be no more pike-trailing
for his war-worn old arms.

Conscientiously he set about enrolling the company,
for, in his way, this Ercole Fortemani was a conscientious
man—boisterous and unruly if you will ; a rogue, in his
way, with scant respect for property ; not above cogging
dice or even filching a purse upon occasion when hard
driven by necessity—for all that he was gently born and
had held honourable employment ; a drunkard by long
habit, and a swaggering brawler upon the merest provo-
cation.   But for all that, riotous and dishonest though
he might be in the general commerce of life, yet to the
hand that hired him he strove—not always successfully,
perhaps, but, at least, always earnestly—to be loyal.

CHAPTER IX

THE " TRATTA DI CORDE "

WHILST the bustle of preparation went on briskly in Urbino, Gian Maria, on his side, was rapidly disposing of affairs in Babbiano, that he might return to the nuptials for which he was impatient.   But he had chanced upon a deeper tangle than he had reckoned with, and more to do than he had looked for.

On the day of his departure from Urbino, he had ridden as far as Cagli and halted at the house of the noble Messer Valdicampo. This had been placed at his disposal and there he proposed to lie the night. They had supped—the Duke de Alveri, Gismondo Santi, Messer Valdicampo, his wife and two daughters, and a couple of friends, potential citizens of Cagli, whom he had invited that they might witness the honour that was being done his house. It waxed late, and the torpor that ensues upon the generous gratification of appetite was settling upon the company when Armstadt—Gian Maria's Swiss captain—entered and approached his master with the air of a man who is the bearer of news.   He halted a pace or two from the Duke's high-backed chair and stood eyeing Gian Maria in stupid patience.

" Well, fool ? " growled the Duke, turning his head.

The Swiss approached another step.   " They have brought him, Highness," he said in a confidential whisper.

" Am I a wizard that I must read your thoughts ? " hectored Gian Maria.   " Who has brought whom ? "

Armstadt eyed the company in hesitation.   Then, stepping close to the Duke, he murmured in his ear :

" The men I left behind have brought the fool—Sere Peppe."

A sudden brightening of the eye showed that Gian

Maria understood. Without apology to the board, he turned and whispered back to his captain to have the fellow taken to his chamber, there to await him. " Let a couple of your knaves be in attendance, and do you come too, Martino."

Martin bowed and withdrew, whereupon Gian Maria found grace to crave his host's pardon, with the explanation that the man had brought him news he had been expecting. Valdicampo, who for the honour of having a duke sleep beneath his roof would have stomached improprieties far more flagrant, belittled the matter and dismissed it. And presently Gian Maria rose with the announcement that he had far to journey on the morrow and so, with his host's good leave, would be abed.

Valdicampo, himself, then played the part of chamberlain, and, taking up one of the large candle branches, he lighted the Duke to his apartments. He would have carried his good offices, and his candles, as far as Gian Maria's very bedchamber, but that in the ante-room his Highness, as politely as might be, bade him set down the lights and leave him.

The Duke remained standing for a moment, deliberating whether to afford knowledge of Alvari and Santi—who had followed him and stood awaiting his commands—of what he was about to do. In the end he decided that he would act alone and upon his sole discretion. So he dismissed them.

When they had gone and he was quite alone, he clapped his hands together, and in answer to that summons the door of his bedroom opened, revealing Martin Armstadt on the threshold.

" He is there ? " inquired the Duke.

" Awaiting your Highness," answered the Swiss, and he held the door for Gian Maria to enter.

The bedchamber apportioned the Duke in the Palazzo Valdicampo was a noble and lofty room, in the midst of which loomed the great carved bed of honour, with its upright pillars and funereal conopy.

On the overmantel stood two five-armed sconces with lighted tapers. Yet Gian Maria did not seem to deem that there was light enough for such purpose as he entertained, for he bade Martin fetch him the candelabra that had been left behind. Then he turned his attention to the group standing by the window, where the light from the overmantel fell full upon it.

This consisted of three men, two being mercenaries of Armstadt's guard, in corselet and morion, and the third who stood captive between, the unfortunate Ser Peppe. The fool's face was paler than its wont, whilst the usual roguery had passed from his eyes and his mouth, fear having taken possession of its room. He met the Duke's cruel glance with one of alarm and piteous entreaty.

Having assured himself that Peppe had no weapons, and that his arms were pinioned behind him, Gian Maria bade the two guards withdraw, but hold themselves in readiness in the antechamber with Armstadt. Then he turned to Peppe with a scowl on his low brow.

" You are not so merry as you were this morning, fool," he scoffed.

Peppino squirmed a little, but his nature, schooled by the long habit of jest, prompted a bold whimsicality in his reply.

" The circumstances are scarcely as propitious—to me. Your Highness, though, seems in excellent good-humour.

Gian Maria looked at him angrily a moment. He was a slow-witted man, and he could devise no ready answer, no such cutting gibe as it would have pleasured him to administer. He walked leisurely to the fireplace and leant his elbow on the overmantel.

" Your humour led you into saying some things for which I should be merciful if I had you whipped."

" And, by the same reasoning, charitable if you had me hanged," returned the fool dryly, a pale smile on his lips.

" Ah ! You acknowledge it ? " cried Gian Maria, never seeing the irony intended. " But I am a very clement prince, fool."

" Proberbially clement," the jester protested, but he did not succeed this time in excluding the sarcasm from his voice.

Gian Maria shot him a furious glance.

" Are you mocking me, animal ? Keep your venomous tongue in bounds, or I'll have you deprived of it."

Peppe's face turned grey at the threat, as well it

might—for what should such a one as he do in the world without a tongue ? "

Seeing him dumb and stricken, the Duke continued.

" Now, for all that you deserve a hanging for your insolence, I am willing that you should come by no hurt so that you answer truthfully such questions as I have for you."

Peppino's grotesque figure was doubled in a bow.

" I await your questions, glorious lord," he answered.

" You spoke——" the Duke hesitated a moment, writhing inwardly at the memory of the exact words in which the fool had spoken. " You spoke this morning of one whom the Lady Valentina had met."

The fear seemed to increase on the jester's face. " Yes," he answered, in a choking voice.

" Where did she meet this knight you spoke of and in such wondrous words of praise described to me ? "

" In the woods at Acquasparta, where the river Metauro is no better than a brook. Some two leagues this side of Sant' Angelo."

" Sant' Angelo ! " echoed Gian Maria, starting at the very mention of the place where the late conspiracy against him had been hatched. " And when was this ? "

" On the Wednesday before Easter, as Monna Valentina was journeying from Santa Sofia to Urbino."

No word spake the Duke in answer. He stood still, his head bowed, and his thoughts running again on that conspiracy. The mountain fight in which Masuccio had been killed had taken place on the Tuesday night, and the conviction—scant though the evidence might be—grew upon him that this man was one of the conspirators who had escaped.

" How came your lady to speak with this man—was he known to her ? " he inquired at last.

" No, Highness ; but he was wounded, and so aroused her compassion. She sought to minister to his hurt."

" Wounded ? " cried Gian Maria, in a shout. " Now by God, it is as I suspected. I'll swear he got that wound the night before at Sant' Angelo. What was his name, fool ? Tell me that, and you shall go free."

For just a second the hunchback seemed to hesitate.

He stood in awesome fear of Gian Maria, of whose cruelties some ghastly tales were told. But in greater fear he stood of the eternal damnation he might earn did he break the oath he had plighted not to divulge that knight's identity.

"Alas!" he sighed ". I would it might be mine to earn my freedom at so light a price; yet it is one that ignorance will not let me pay. I do not know his name."

The Duke looked at him searchingly and suspiciously. Dull though he was by nature, eagerness seemed now to have set a cunning edge upon his wits, and suspicion had led him to observe the fool's momentary hesitation.

"Of what appearance was he? Describe him to me. How was he dressed? What was the manner of his face?"

"Again, Lord Duke, I cannot answer you. I had but the most fleeting glimpse of him."

The Duke's sallow countenance grew very evil-looking, and an ugly smile twisted his lip and laid bare his strong white teeth.

"So fleeting that no memory of him is left you?" quoth he.

"Precisely, Highness."

"You lie, you filth," Gian Maria thundered in a towering rage. "It was but this morning that you said his height was splendid, his countenance noble, his manner princely, his speech courtly, and—I know not what besides. Yet now you tell me—you tell *me*—that your glimpse of him was so fleeting that you cannot describe him. You know his name, rogue, and I will have it from you, or else——"

"Indeed, indeed, most noble lord, be not incensed——" the fool began, in fearful protestation. But the Duke interrupted him.

"Incensed?" he echoed, his eyes dilating in a sort of horror at the notion. "Do you dare impute to me the mortal sin of choler? I am not incensed; there is no anger in me." He crossed himself, as if to exorcise the evil mood if it indeed existed, and devotedly bowing his head and folding his hands—"*Libera me a malo Domine!*" he murmured audibly. Then, with a greater

fierceness than before—" Now," he demanded, " will
you tell me his name ? "

" I would I could," the terrified hunchback began.
But at that the Duke turned from him with a shrug
of angry impatience, and clapping his hands together.

" Ola ! Martino ! " he called. Instantly the door
opened and the Swiss appeared. " Bring in your men
and your rope."

The captain turned on his heel, and simultaneously
the fool cast himself at Gian Maria's feet.

" Mercy, your Highness ! " he wailed. " Do you have
me hanged ? I am——"

" We are not going to hang you," the Duke broke in
coldly. " Dead, you would indeed be dumb and avail
us nothing. We want you alive, Messser Peppino—alive
and talkative ; we find you very reserved for a fool.
But we hope to make you speak."

On his knees, Peppe raised his wild eyes to Heaven.

" Mother of the Afflicted," he prayed, at which the
Duke broke into a contemptuous laugh.

" What has the Heavenly Mother to do with such filth
as you ? Make your appeals to me. I am the more
immediate arbiter of your fate. Tell me the name of that
man you met in the woods, and all may yet be well with
you."

Peppino knelt in silence, a cold sweat gathering on his
pale brow and a horrid fear tightening at his heart and
throat. And yet greater than this horror they were preparing for him was the horror of losing his immortal soul
by a breach of the solemn oath he had sworn. Gian
Maria turned from him, at last, to his *bravi*, who now
entered silently and with the air of men who knew the
work expected of them. Martino mounted the bed, and
swung for an instant from the framework of the canopy.

" It will hold, Highness," he announced.

Gian Maria bade him, since that was so, remove the
velvet hangings, whilst he despatched one of the men to
see that the antechamber door was closed, so that no
cry should penetrate to the apartments of the Valdicampo
household.

In a few seconds all was ready, and Peppino was rudely
lifted from his knees and from the prayers he had been

pattering to the Virgin to lend him strength in this hour of need.

" For the last time, sir fool," quoth the Duke, " will you tell us his name ? "

" Highness, I cannot," answered Peppe, for all that terror was freezing his very blood.

A light of satisfaction gleamed now in Gian Maria's eyes.

" So you know it ! " he exclaimed. " You no longer protest your ignorance, but only that you cannot tell me. Up with him, Martino."

In a last pitiable struggle against the inevitable, the fool broke from his guards and flung himself towards the door. One of the burly Swiss caught him by the neck in a grip that made him cry out with pain. Gian Maria eyed him with a sinister smile, and Martino proceeded to fasten one end of the rope to his pinioned wrists. Then they led him, shivering, to the great bed. The other end of the cord was passed over one of the bared arms of the canopy-frame. This end was grasped by the two men-at-arms. Martino stood beside the prisoner. The Duke flung himself into a great carved chair, an air of relish now investing his round pale face.

" You know what is about to befall you," he said in tones of chilling indifference. " Will you speak before we begin ? "

" My lord," said the fool, in a voice that terror was throttling, " you are a good Christian, a loyal son of Mother Church, and a believer in the eternal fires of hell ? "

A frown settled on Gian Maria's brow. Was the fool to intimidate him with talk of supernatural vengeance ?

" Thus," Peppe continued, " you will perhaps be merciful when I confess my position. I made most solemn oath to the man I met at Acquasparta on that luckless day that I would never reveal his identity. What am I do ? If I keep my oath, you will torture me to death perhaps. If I break it, I shall be damned eternally. Have mercy, noble lord, since now you know how I am placed."

The smile broadened on Gian Maria's face, and the cruelty of his mouth and eyes seemed intensified by it. The fool had told him that which he would have given much to learn. He had told him that this man whose name he sought had so feared that his presence that day at Acquasparta should become known that he had bound the fool by oath not to divulge the secret of it. Of what he had before suspected he was now assured. The man in question was one of the conspirators ; probably the very chief of them. Nothing short of the fool's death under torture would now restrain him from learning the name of that unknown who had done him the double injury of conspiring against him, and—if the fool were to be believed—of capturing the heart of Valentina.

"For the damnation of your soul I shall not be called to answer," he said at last. "Care enough have I to save my own—for temptations are many and this poor flesh is weak. But it is this man's name I need, and —by the five wounds of Lucia of Viterbo !—I will have it. Will you speak ? "

Something like a sob shook the poor fool's deformed frame. But that was all. With bowed head he preserved a stubborn silence. The Duke made a sign to the men, and instantly the two of them threw their weight upon the rope, hoisting Peppe by his wrists until he was at the height of the canopy itself. That done, they paused and turned their eyes upon the Duke for further orders. Again Gian Maria called upon the fool to answer his questions ; but Peppe, a writhing, misshapen mass from which two wriggling legs depended, maintained a stubborn silence.

"Let him go," snarled Gian Maria, out of patience. The men released the rope and allowed some three feet of it to run through their hands. Then they grasped it again, so that Peppe's sudden fall was as suddenly arrested by a jerk that almost wrenched his arms from their sockets. A shriek broke from him at that exquisite torture, and he was dragged once more to the full height of the canopy.

"Will you speak now ? " asked Gian Maria coldly, amusedly almost. But still the fool was silent, his nether lip caught so tightly in his teeth that the blood trickled from it adown his chin. Again the Duke gave the signal, and again they let him go. This time, they allowed him a longer drop so that the wrench with which they arrested it was more severe than had been the first.

Peppe felt his bones starting from their joints, and it was as if a burning iron were searing him at shoulder, elbow and wrist.

" Merciful God ! " he screamed. " Oh, have pity, noble lord."

But the noble lord had him hoisted anew to the canopy. Writhing there in the extremity of his angiush, the poor hunchback poured forth from frothing lips a stream of curses and imprecations, invoking Heaven and hell to strike his tormentors dead.

But the Duke, from whose demeanour it might be inferred that he was inured to the effect produced by this form of torture, looked on with a cruel smile, as of one who watches the progress of events towards the end that he desires and has planned. He was less patient, and his signal came more quickly now. For a third time the fool was dropped and drawn up, now a short three feet from the ground.

This time he did not so much as scream. He hung there, dangling at the rope's end, his mouth all bloody, his face ghastly in its glistening pallor, and of his eyes naught showing save the whites. He hung there, and moaned piteously and incessantly. Martino glanced questioningly at Gian Maria, and his eyes very plailny inquired whether they had not better cease. But Gian Maria paid no heed to him.

" Will that suffice you ? " he asked the fool. " Will you speak now ? "

But the fool's only answer was a moan, whereupon again, at the Duke's relentless signal, he was swung aloft. But at the terror of a fourth drop, more fearful than any of its three predecessors, he awoke very suddenly to the impossible horror of his position. That this agony would endure until he died or fainted he was assured. And, since he seemed incapable of either fainting or dying, suffer more he could not. What was heaven or hell to him then that the thought of either could efface the horror of this torture and strengthen him to continue to endure the agony of it ? He could endure no more— no, not to save a dozen souls if he had had them.

"I'll speak," he screamed   "Let me down, and you shall have his name, Lord Duke."

Pronounce it first, or the manner of your descent shall be as the others."

Peppe passed his tongue over his bleeding lips, hung still and spoke.

"It was your cousin," he panted.   "Francesco de Falco, Count of Aquila."

The Duke stared at him a moment, with startled countenance and mouth agape.

"You are telling me the truth, animal?" he demanded in a quivering voice.   "It was the Count of Aquila who was wounded and whom Monna Valentina tended?"

"I swear it," answered the fool.   "Now in the name of God and His blessed saints, let me down."

For a moment yet he was held there, awaiting Maria's signal.   The Duke continued to eye him with that same astonished look, what time he turned over in his mind the news he had gathered.   Then conviction of the truth sank into his mind.   It was the Lord of Aquila who was the idol of the Babbianians.   What, then, more natural than that the conspirators should have sought to place him on the throne they proposed to wrest from Gian Maria?   He dubbed himself a fool that he had not guessed so much before.

"Let him down," he curtly bade his men.   "Then take him hence and let him go with God.   He has served his purpose."

Gently they lowered him, but when his feet touched the ground he was unable to stand.   His legs doubled under him, and he lay—a little crook-backed heap—upon the rushes of the floor.   His senses had deserted him.

At a sign from Armstadt the two men picked him up and carried him out between them.

Gian Maria moved across the room to a tapestried prie-dieu, and knelt down before an ivory crucifix to render thanks to God for the signal light of grace by which He had vouchsafed to show the Duke his enemy.

Thereafter, drawing from the breast of his doublet, a chaplet of gold and amber beads, he piously discharged his nightly devotions.

CHAPTER X

THE BRAYING OF AN ASS

WHEN on the morrow, towards the twenty-second hour, the High and Mighty Gian Maria Sforza rode into his capital at Babbiano, he found the city in violent turmoil, occasioned, as he rightly guessed, by the ominous presence of Cæsar Borgia's envoy.

A dense and sullen crowd met him at the Porta Romana, and preserved a profound silence as he rode into the city accompanied by Alvari and Santi, and surrounded by his escort of twenty spears in full armour. There was a threat in that silence more ominous than any vociferations, and very white was the Duke's face as he darted scowls of impotent anger this way and that. But there was worse to come. As they rode up the Borgo dell' Annunziata the crowd thickened, and the silence was now replaced by a storm of hooting and angry cries. The people became menacing, and by Armstadt's orders —the Duke was by now too paralysed with fear to issue any—the men-at-arms lowered their pikes in order to open a way, whilst one or two of the populace, who were thrust too near the cavalcade by the surging human tide, went down and were trampled under foot.

Satirical voices asked the Duke derisively was he wed, and where might be his uncle-in-law's spears that were to protect them against the Borgia. Some demanded to know whither the last outrageous levy of taxes was gone, and where was the army it should have served to raise. To this, others replied for the Duke, suggesting a score of vile uses to which the money had been put.

Then, of a sudden, a cry of " Murderer ! " arose, followed by angry demands that he should restore life to the valiant Ferrabraccio, to Amerini, the people's friend, and

94

to those others whom he had lately butchered, or else
follow them in death. Lastly the name of the Count of
Aquila rang wildly in his ears, provoking a storm of
" Evviva ! Live Francesco del Falco ! " and one persistent voice, sounding loudly above the others, styled
him already " il Duca Francesco." At that the blood
mounted to Gian Maria's brain, and a wave of anger
beat back the fear from his heart. He rose in his
stirrups, his eyes ablaze with the jealous wrath that
possessed him.

" Ser Martino ! " he roared hoarsely to his captain.
" Couch lances and go through them at the gallop ! "

The burly Swiss hesitated, brave man though he was.
Alvaro de' Alvari and Gismondo Santi looked at each
other in alarm, and the intrepid old statesman, in whose
heart no pang of fear had been awakened by the rabble's
threatening bay, changed colour as he heard that order
given.

" Highness," he implored the Duke, " you cannot
mean this."

" Not mean it ? " flashed back Gian Maria, his eye
travelling from Santi to the hesitating captain.
" Fool ! " he blazed at the latter. " Brute beast, for
what do you wait ? Did you not hear me ? "

Without a second's delay the captain now raised his
sword, and his deep guttural voice barked an order
to his men which brought their lances below the horizon-
tal. The mob, too, had heard that fierce command, and,
awakening to their peril, those nearest the cavalcade
would have fallen back but that the others, pressing
tightly from behind, held them in the death-ride that now
swept by with clattering arms and hoarse cries.

Shrieks filled the air where lately threats had been
loudly tossed. But some there were in that crowd that
would be no passive witness of this butchery. Half the
stones of the borgo went after that cavalcade and fell
in a persistent shower upon them, rattling like giant hail
upon their armour, dinting many a steel-cap, to its wearer's
sore discomfort. The Duke himself was struck twice,
and on Santi's unprotected scalp an ugly wound was
opened from which the blood flowed in profusion to dve
his snowy locks.

In this undignified manner they reached, at last, the
Palazzo Ducale, leaving a trail of dead and maimed to
mark the way by which they had come.

In a white heat of passion Gian Maria sought his apartments, and came not forth again until, some two hours
later, the presence was announced him of the emissary
from Cæsar Borgia, Duke of Valentinois, who sought an
audience.

Still beside himself, and boiling with wrath at the
indignities he had received, Gian Maria—in no mood for
an interview that would have demanded coolness and
presence of mind from a keener brain than his—received
the envoy, a gloomy, priestly-faced Spaniard, in the
throne-room of the Palace. The Duke was attended by
Alvari, Santi, and Fabrizio da Lodi, while his mother,
Caterina Colonna, occupied a chair of crimson velvet on
which the Sforza lion was wrought in gold.

The interview was brief, and marked by a rudeness at its
close that contrasted sharply with the ceremoniousness of
its inception. It soon became clear that the ambassador's
true mission was to pick a quarrel with Babbiano on
his master's behalf, to the end that the Borgia might be
afforded a sound pretext for invading the Duchy. He
demanded, at first politely and calmly, and later—when
denied—with arrogant insistence, that Gian Maria should
provide the Duke of Valentinois with a hundred lances—
equivalent to five hundred men—as some contribution on
his part towards the stand which Cæsar Borgia meant to
make against the impending French invasion.

Gian Maria never heeded the restraining words which
Lodi whispered in his ear, urging him to temporise
and to put off this messenger until the alliance with the
house of Urbino should be complete and their position
strengthened sufficiently to permit them to brave the
anger of Cæsar Borgia. But neither this nor the wrathful, meaning glances which his cunning mother bent upon
him served to curb him. He obeyed only the voice of
his headstrong mood, never dreaming of the consequences
with which he might be visited.

"You will bear to the Duca Valentino this message from
me," he said, in conclusion. "You will tell him that
what lances I have in Babbiano I intend to keep, that

with them I may defend my own frontiers against his briganding advances. Messer da Lodi," he added, turning to Fabrizio and without so much as waiting to see if the envoy had anything further to say, " let this gentleman be reconducted to his quarters, and see that he has safe conduct hence until he is out of our Duchy."

When the envoy, crimson of face and threatening of eye, had withdrawn under Lodi's escort, Monna Caterina rose, the very incarnation of outraged patience and poured her bitter invective upon her rash son's head.

" Fool ! " she stormed at him. " There goes your Duchy—in the hollow of that man's hand." Then she laughed in bitterness. " After all, in casting it from you perhaps you have chosen the wiser course, for. as truly as there is a God in Heaven, you are utterly unfitted to retain it."

" My lady mother," he answered her, with such dignity as he could muster from the wretched heap in which his wits now seemed to lie, " you will be well advised to devote yourself to your woman's tasks and not to interfere in a man's work."

" Man's work ! " she sneered. " And you perform it like a petulant boy or a peevish woman."

" I perform it, Madonna, as best seems to me, for it happens that I am Duke of Babbiano," he answered sullenly. " I do not fear any Pope's son that ever stepped. The alliance with Urbino is all but completed. Let that be established, and if Valentinɔ shows his teeth —by God ! we'll show ours."

" Aye, but with this difference—that his are a wolf's teeth and yours a lamb's. Besides, this alliance with Urbino is all incomplete as yet. You had been better advised to have sent away the envoy with some indefinite promise that would have afforded you respite enough in which to seal matters with the house of Montefeltro. As it is, your days are numbered. Upon that message you have sent him Cæsar will act at once. For my own part, I have no mind to fall a prey to the invader, and I shall leave Babbiano and seek refuge in Naples. And if a last word of advice I may offer you, it is that you do the same."

Gian Maria rose and came down from the daïs, eyeing

her in a sort of dull amazement. Then he looked as, if for help, to Alvari, to Santi, and lastly to Lodi, who had returned while Caterina was speaking. But no word said any of them, and grave were the eyes of all.

"Poor-spirited are you all!" he sneered. Then his face grew dark and his tone concentrated. "Not so am I," he assured them, "if in the past I may have seemed it sometimes. I am aroused at length, sirs. I heard a voice in the streets of Babbiano to-day, and I saw a sight that has put a fire into my veins. This good tempered, soft, indulgent Duke you knew is gone. The lion is awake at last, and you shall see such things as you had not dreamt of."

They regarded him now with eyes in which the gravity was increased by a light of fearsome wonder and inquiry. Was his mind giving way under the prodigious strain that had been set upon it that day? If not madness, what else did that wild boasting argue?

"Are you all dumb?" he asked them, his eyes feverish. "Or do you deem that I promise more than is mine to fulfil. You shall judge, and soon. To-morrow, my lady mother, whilst you journey south, as you have told us, I go north again, back to Urbino. Not a day will I now waste. Within the week, sirs, by God's grace, I shall be wed. That will give us Urbino for a buckler and with Urbino comes Perugia and Camerino. But more than that. There is a princely dowry comes to us with the Lady Valentina. How, think you, will I spend it? To the last florin it shall go to the arming of men. I will hire me every free *condotta* in Italy. I will raise me such an army as has never before been seen at any time, and with this I shall seek out the Duca Valentino. I'll not sit here at home awaiting the pleasure of his coming, but I'll out to meet him, and with that army I shall descend upon him as a thunderbolt out of Heaven. Aye, my lady mother," he laughed in his madness, " the lamb shall hunt the wolf and rend it so that it shall never stand again to prey on other lambs. This will I do, my friends, and there shall be such fighting as has not been seen since the long-dead days of Castracani."

They stared at him, scarce believing now that he was sane, and marvelling deeply whence had sprung this sudden martial fervour in one whose nature was more indolent than active, more timid than warlike. And yet the reason was not far to seek had they but cared to follow the line of thought to which he himself had given them the clue when he referred to the voice he had heard and the sights he had seen in the streets of Babbiano. The voice was the voice that had acclaimed his cousin Francesco Duke. That it was through that a fierce jealousy had fired him. This man had robbed him at once of the love of his people and of Valentina, and thereby had set in his heart the burning desire to outdo him and to prove wrong in their preference both his people and Valentina. He was like a gamer who risks all on a single throw, and his stake was to be the dowry of his bride, the game a tilt with the forces of the Borgia. If he won he came out covered with glory, and not only the saviour of their liberty, but a glorious figure that all Italy—or, at least, that part of it that had known the iron heel of Valentino—should revere. Thus would he set himself right and thus crush from their minds the memory of his rebellious cousin with whom he was about to deal.

His mother turned to him now, and her words were words of caution, prayers that he should adventure on naught so vast and appalling to her woman's mind, without due thought and argument in council. A servant entered at that moment and approached the Duke.

" Madonna," Gian Maria announced, breaking in upon her earnest words, " I am fully resolved upon my course. If you will but delay a moment and resume your seat you shall witness the first scene of this great drama that I am preparing." Then turning to the waiting servant : " Your message ? " he demanded.

" Captain Armstadt has returned, Highness, and has brought his Excellency."

" Fetch lights and then admit them," he commanded briefly. " To your places, sirs, and you, my mother. I am about to sit in judgment."

Amazed and uncomprehending, they obeyed his wild gestures and resumed their places by the throne even as he walked back to the daïs and sat himself upon the ducal chair. Servants entered, bearing great candelabra of beaten gold which they set on table and overmantel. They withdrew, and when the doors opened again a clank of mail reaching them from without increased the astonishment of the company.

This rose yet higher and left them cold and speechless, when into the chamber stepped the Count of Aquila with a man-at-arms on either side of him, marking him a prisoner With a swift comprehensive glance that took in the entire group about the throne—and without manifesting the slightest surprise at Lodi's presence— Francesco stood still and awaited his cousin's words.

He was elegantly dressed, but without lavishness, and if he had the air of a great lord, it was rather derived from the distinction of his face and carriage. He was without arms, and bareheaded save for the gold coif he always wore which seemed to accentuate the lustrous blackness of his hair. His face was impassive, and the glance as that of a man rather weary of the entertainment provided him.

There was an oppressive silence of some moments, during which his cousin regarded him with an eye that glittered oddly. At last Gian Maria broke into speech, his voice shrill with excitement.

" Know you of any reason," he demanded, " why your head should not be flaunted on a spear among those others on the Gate of San Bacolo ? "

Francesco's eyebrows shot up in justifiable astonishment.

" I know of many," he answered with a smile, an answer which by its simplicity seemed to nonplus the Duke.

" Let us hear some of them," he challenged presently.

" Nay, let us hear, rather, some reason why my poor head should be so harshly dealt with. When a man is rudely taken, as I have been, it is a custom, which perhaps your Highness will follow, to afford him some reason for the outrage."

" You smooth-tongued traitor ! " quoth the Duke, with infinite malice, made angrier by his cousin's dignity. " You choicely-spoken villain ! You would learn why you have been taken ? Tell me, sir, what did you at Acquasparta on the morning of the Wednesday before Easter ? "

The Count's impassive face remained inscrutable, a mask of patient wonder. By the sudden clenching of hands alone did he betray how that thrust had smitten him, and his hands none there remarked. Fabrizio da Lodi, standing behind the Duke, went pale to the lips.

"I do not recall that I did anything there of much account," he answered. "I breathed the good spring air in the woods."

"And nothing else ? " sneered Gian Maria.

"I can bethink me of little else that signifies. I met a lady there with whom I had some talk, a friar, a fool, a popinjay, and some soldiers. But "—he shifted abruptly, his tone growing haughty—" whatever I did, I did as best seemed to me, and I have yet to learn that the Count of Aquila must give account of what he does and where he does it. You have not told me yet, sir, by what right, or fancied right, you hold me prisoner."

"Have I not, indeed ? See you no link between your offence and your presence near Santa Angelo on that day ? "

"If I am to apprehend that you have had me brought here with this indignity to set me riddles for your amusement, I am enlightened and yet amazed. I am no court buffoon."

"Words, words," snapped the Duke. "Do not think to beguile me with them." With a short laugh he turned from Francesco to those upon the daïs. "You will be marvelling, sirs, and you, my lady mother, upon what grounds I have had this traitor seized. You shall learn. On the night of the Tuesday before Easter seven traitors met at Sant' Angelo to plot my overthrow. Of those, the heads of four may be seen on the walls of Babbiano now ; the other three made off, but there stands one of them—the one that was to have occupied this throne after they had unseated me."

The eyes of all were now upon the young Count, whilst his own glance strayed to the face of Lodi, on which there was written a consternation so great that it must have betrayed him had the Duke but chanced to look his way. A pause ensued which none present dared to break. Gian Francesco stood impassively regarding him and made

no sign that he would speak. At length, unable longer
to endure the silence :

"*E dunque* ! " cried the Duke. " Have you no
answer ? "

" I would submit," returned Francesco, " that I have
heard no question. I heard a wild statement, extravag-
ant and mad, the accusation of one demented, a charge
of which no proofs can be forthcoming, else I take it you
had not withheld them. I ask you, sirs, and you, Madonna," he continued, turning to the others, " has his
Highness said anything to which an answer can by any
means be necessary ? "

" Is it proofs you lack ? " cried Gian Maria, but less
confidentially than hitherto, and, so, less fiercely. A
doubt had arisen in his mind born of this strange calm
on the part of Francesco—a calm that to Gian Maria's
perceptions seemed hardly the garb of guilt, but belonged
rather to one who is assured that no peril threatens him.
" Is it proofs you lack ? ' quoth the Duke again, and then
with the air of a man launching an unanswerable question. " How came you by the wound you had that day
in the woods ? "

A smile quivered on Francesco's face, and was gone.

" I asked for proofs, not questions," he protested
wearily. " What shall it prove if I had a hundred
wounds ? "

" Prove ? " echoed the Duke, less and less confident
of his ground, fearing already that he had perhaps gone
too fast and too far upon the road of his suspicions.
" It proves to me, when coupled with your presence there,
that you were in the fight the night before."

Francesco stirred at that. He sighed and smiled at
once. Then assuming a tone of brisk command :

" Bid these men begone," he said, pointing to his
guards. " Then hear me scatter your foul suspicions as
the hurricane scatters the leaves in autumn."

Gian Maria stared at him in stupefaction. That
overwhelming assurance, that lofty, dignified bearing,
which made such a noble contrast with his own coarse
hectoring, were gradually undermining more and
more his confidence. With a wave of his hand he
motioned the soldiers to withdraw, obeying almost

unconsciously the master-mind of his cousin by which he was as unconsciously being swayed.

" Now, Highness," said Francesco, as soon as the men were gone, " before I refute the charge you make, let me clearly understand it.   From the expressions you have used I gather it to be this : A conspiracy was laid a little time ago at Sant' Angelo which had for object to supplant you on the throne of Babbiano and set me in your place.   You charge me with having had in that conspiracy a part—the part assigned to me.   It is so, is it not ? "

Gian Maria nodded.

" You have put it very clearly," he sneered.   " If you can make out your innocence as clearly, I shall be satisfied that I have wronged you."

" That this conspiracy took place we will accept as proven, although to the people of Babbiano the proof may have sensed scant.   A man, since dead, had told your Highness that such a plot was being hatched. Hardly perhaps, in itself, evidence enough to warrant setting the heads of four very valiant gentlemen on spears, but no doubt your Highness had other proofs to which the rest of us had no access."

Gian Maria shivered at the words.   He recalled what Francesco had said on the occasion of their last talk upon this very subject ; he remembered the manner of his own reception that day in Babbiano.

" We must be content that it is so," calmly pursued Francesco.   " Indeed your Highness's action in the matter leaves no doubt.   We will accept, then, that such a plot was laid, but that I had a part in it, that I was the man chosen to take your place—need I prove the idleness of such a charge ? "

" You need, in truth,   By God ! you need, if you would save your head."

The Count stood in an easy posture, his hands clasped behind his back, and smiled up at his cousin's pale face and scowling brow.

" How mysterious are the ways of your justice, cousin," he murmured with infinite relish ; " what a wondrous equity invests your methods !   You have me dragged here by force, and sitting there, you say to me :

" Prove that you have not conspired against me, or the
headman shall have you ! '　By my faith ! Solomon was
a foolish prattler when compared with you."

Gian Maria smote the gilded arm of his chair a blow
for which he was to find his hand blackened on the
morrow.

" Prove it ! " he screamed, like a child in a pet.
" Prove it, prove it, prove it ! "

' And have my words not already proven it ? "
quoth the Count in a voice of such mild wonder and
gentle protest that it left Gian Maria gasping.

Then the Duke made a hasty gesture of impatience.

" Messer Alvari," he said, in a voice of concentrated
rage, " I think you had best recall the guard."

" Wait ! " the Count compelled him, raising his hand.
And now it was seen that the easy insouciance was gone
from his face ; the smile had vanished, and in its place
there was a look of lofty and contemptuous wrath.　" I
will repeat my words.　You have dragged me here before
you by force, and, sitting there on the throne of Babbiano,
you say : ' Prove that you have not conspired against me
if you would save your head.' "　A second he paused, and
noted the puzzled look with which all regarded him.

" Is this a parable ? " sneered the uncomprehending
Duke.

" You have said it," flashed back Francesco.　" A
parable it is.　And if you consider it, does it not afford
you proof enough ? " he asked, a note of triumph in his
voice.　" Do not our relative positions irrefutably show
the baselessness of this your charge ?　Should I stand
here and you sit there if what you allege against me were
true ? " he laughed almost savagely, and his eyes flashed
scornfully upon the Duke.　" If more plainly still you need
it, Gian Maria, I tell you that had I plotted to occupy
your tottering throne, I should be on it now, not standing
here defending myself against a foolish charge.　But can
you doubt it ?　Did you learn no lesson as you rode into
Babbiano to-day ?　Did you not hear them acclaim me
and groan at you.　And yet," he ended, and with a lofty
pity, "you tell me that I plotted.　Why, if I desired your
throne, my only need would be to unfurl my banner in
the streets of your capital, and within the hour Gian

Maria would be Duke no more. Have I proved my innocence, Highness ? " he ended quietly, sadly almost. " Are you convinced how little is my need for plots ? "

But the Duke had no answer for him. Speechless, and in a sort of dazed terror, he sat and scowled before him at his cousin's handsome face, what time the others watched him furtively in silence, trembling for the young man who, here in his grasp, had dared say such things to him. Presently he covered his face with his hands, and sat so, as one deeply in thought, a little while. At last he withdrew them slowly and presented a countenance that passion and chagrin had strangely ravaged in so little time. He turned to Santi, and who stood nearest.

" The guard," he said hoarsely, with a wave of the hand, and Santi went, none daring to utter a word. They waited thus, an odd group, all very grave save one, and he the one that had most cause for gravity. Then the captain re-entered, followed by his two men, and Gian Maria waved a hand towards the prisoner.

" Take him away," he muttered harshly, his face ghastly, and passion shaking him like an aspen. " Take him away, and await my orders in the antechamber."

" If it is farewell, Cousin," said Francesco. " may I hope that you well send a priest to me ? I have lived a faithful Christian."

Gian Maria returned him no answer, but his baleful eye was upon Martino. Reading the significance of that glance, the captain touched Francesco lightly on the arm. A moment the Count stood, looking from the Duke to the soldiers ; a second his glance rested on those assembled there ; then, with a light raising of his shoulders, he turned on his heels, and with his head high passed out of the ducal chamber.

And silence continued after he was gone until Caterina Colonna broke it with a laugh that grated on Gian Maria's now very tender nerves.

" You promised bravely," she mocked him, " to play the lion. But so far we have only heard the braying of an ass."

CHAPTER XI

WANDERING KNIGHTS

THAT taunt of his mother's stirred Gian Maria. He rose from his ducal chair and descended from the daïs on which it stood, possessed by a tempestuous mood that would not brook him to sit still.

"The braying of an ass?" he muttered, facing Caterina. Then he laughed unpleasantly. "The jawbone of an ass did sore execution on one occasion, Madonna, and it may again. A little patience, and you shall see." Next, and with a brisker air, he addressed the four silent courtiers. "You heard him, sirs," he exclaimed. "How do you say that I shall deal with such a traitor?" He waited some seconds for an answer, and it seemed to anger him that none came. "Have you, then, no counsel for me?" he demanded harshly.

"I had not thought" said Lodi hardily, "that this was a case in which your Highness needed counsel. You were drawn to conclude that the Lord of Aquila was a traitor, but from what we have all heard your Highness should now see that he is not."

"Should I so?" the Duke returned, standing still and fixing upon Fabrizio an eye that was dull as a snake's. "Messer da Lodi, your loyalty is a thing that has given signs of wavering of late. Now, if by the grace of God and His blessed saints I have ruled as a merciful prince who errs too much upon the side of clemency, I would enjoin you not to try that clemency too far. I am but a man, after all."

He turned from the fearless front presented by the old statesman, to face the troubled glances of the others.

"Your silence, sirs, tells me that in this matter your

judgment runs parallel with mine. And you are wise, for in such a case there can be but one course. My cousin has uttered words to-day which no man has ever said to a prince and lived. Nor shall we make exception to that rule. My Lord of Aquila's head must pay the price of his temerity."

"My son," cried Caterina, in a voice of horror. Gian Maria faced her in a passion, his countenance grown mottled.

"I have said it," he growled. "I will not sleep until he dies."

"Yet never may you wake again," she answered. And with that preamble she launched upon his head the bitterest criticism he had ever heard. By stinging epithets and contemptuous words, she sought to make him see the folly of what he meditated. Was he indeed tired of ruling Babbiano ? If that were so, she told him he had but to wait for Cæsar Borgia's coming. He need not precipitate matters by a deed that must lead to a revolt, a rising of the people to avenge their idol.

"You have given me but added reasons," he answered her stoutly. "There is no room in my Duchy for a man whose death, if it pleased me to encompass it, would be avenged upon me by my own people."

"Then send him from your dominions," she urged. "Banish him, and all may be well. But if you slay him, I shall not count your life worth a day's purchase."

This advice was sound, and in the end they prevailed upon him to adopt it. But it was not done save at the cost of endless prayers on the part of those courtiers and the persuasions of Caterina's biting scorn and prophecies of the fate that surely awaited him did he touch the life of one so well-beloved. At last, against his will, he suddenly consented that the banishment of his cousin should content him. But it was with infinite bitterness and regret that he passed his word, for his jealousy was of a quality that nothing short of Francesco's death could have appeased. Certain it is that nothing but the fear of the consequences, which his mother had instilled into his heart, could have swayed him to be satisfied that the Count of Aquila should be banished.

He sent for Martino and bade him return the Count

his sword, and he entrusted the message of exile to Fabrizio da Lodi, charging him to apprise Francesco that he was allowed twenty-four hours' grace in which to take himself beyond the dominions of Gian Maria Sforza.

That done—and with an exceedingly ill grace—the Duke turned on his heel, and with a sullen brow he left the ducal chamber and passed, unattended, to his own apartments.

Rejoicing, Fabrizio da Lodi went his errand, which he discharged with certain additions that might have cost him his head had knowledge of them come to Gian Maria. In fact, he seized the opportunity to again press upon Francesco the throne of Babbiano.

" The hour is very ripe," he urged the Count, " and the people love you as surely prince was never loved. It is in their interests that I plead. You are their only hope. Will you not come to them ? "

If for a moment Francesco hesitated, it was rather in consideration of the manner in which the crown was offered than in consequence of any allurement that the offer may have had for him. Once—that night at Sant' Angelo—he had known temptation, and for a moment had listened to the seductions in the voice that invited him to power. But not so now. A thought he gave to the people who had such faith in him, and showered upon him such admiring love, and whom, as a matter of reciprocity, he wished well, and would have served in any capacity but this. He shook his head, and with a smile of regret declined the offer.

" Have patience, old friend," he added. " I am not the stuff that goes to make good princes, although you think it. It is a bondage into which I would not sell myself. A man's life for me, Fabrizio—a free life that is not directed by councillors and at the mercy of the rabble.

Fabrizio's face grew sad. He sighed profoundly, yet since it might not be well for him that he should remain over-long in talk with one who, in the Duke's eyes, was attained with treason, he had not leisure to insist with persuasions, which, after all, he clearly saw must in the end prove barren.

" What was the salvation of the people of Babbiano,"

he murmured, " was also your Excellency's, since did you adopt the course I urge there would be no need to go in banishment."

" Why, this exile suits me excellently well," returned Francesco. " Idle have I been over-long, and the wish to roam is in my veins again. I'll see the world once more, and when I weary of my vagrancy I can withdraw to my lands of Aquila and in that corner of Tuscany, too mean to draw a conqueror's eye, none will molest me, and I shall rest. Babbiano, my friend, shall know me no more after to-night. When I am gone, and the people realise that they may not have what they would, they may rest content perhaps with what they may." And he waved a hand in the direction of the doors leading to the ducal chamber. With that he took his leave of his old friend, and, carrying in his hand the sword and dagger which Captain Armstadt had returned to him, he repaired briskly to the northern wing of the Palace, in which he had his lodging.

In the anteroom he dismissed those of his servants who had been taken from the ranks of the Duke's people, and bade his own Tuscan followers, Zaccaria and Lanciotto, see to the packing of his effects, and make all ready to set out within the hour.

He was no coward, but he had no wish to die just yet if it might be honourably avoided. Life had some sweets to offer Francesco del Falco, and this spurred him to hasten, for he well knew his cousin's unscrupulous ways. He was aware that Gian Maria had been forced by weight of argument to let him go, and he shrewdly feared that did he linger his cousin might veer round again and, without pausing to seek advice a second time, have him disposed of out of hand and reckless of consequences.

Whilst Lanciotto was left busy in the anteroom, the Count passed into his bed-chamber attended by Zaccaria, to make in his raiment such changes as were expedient. But scarce had he began when he was interrupted by the arrival of Fanfulla degli Arcipreti, who Lanciotto ushered in. Francesco's face lighted at sight of his friend, and he held out his hand.

" What is it that has happened ? " cried the young gallant, adding that which showed his question to be unnecessary, for from Fabrizio da Lodi he had had the whole story of what was befallen. He sat himself upon the bed, and—utterly disregarding the presence of Zaccaria, whom he knew to be faithful—he attempted to persuade the Count where Fabrizio had failed. But Paolo cut him short ere he had gone very far.

"Have done with that," he said, and for all that he said it with a laugh, determination sounded sturdy in his accents. "I am a knight-errant, not a prince, and I'll not be converted from one to the other. It were making a helot of a free man, and you do not love me, Fanfulla, if you drive this argument further. Do you think me sad, cast down, at the prospect of this banishment? Why, boy, the blood runs swifter through my veins since I heard the sentence. It frees me from Babbiano in an hour when perhaps my duty— the reciprocation of the people's love—might otherwse have held me here, and it gives me liberty to go forth, my good Fanfulla, in quest of such adventure as I chose to follow." He threw out his arms, and displayed his splendid teeth in a hearty laugh.

Fanfulla eyed him, infected by the boisterous gladness of his mood.

"Why, true indeed, my lord," he acknowledged "you are too fine a bird to sing in a cage. But to go knight-erranting——" He paused, and spread his hands in protest. "There are no longer dragons holding princesses captive."

"Alas! no. But the Venetians are on the eve of war, and they will find work for these hands of mine. I want not for friends among them."

Fanfulla sighed.

"And so we lose you. The stoutest arm in Babbiano leaves us in the hour of need, driven out by that loutish Duke. By my soul, Ser Francesco, I would I might go with you. Here is nothing to be done."

Francesco paused in the act of drawing on a boot, and raised his eyes to stare a moment at his friend.

"But if you wish it, Fanfulla, I shall rejoice to have your company."

And now the idea of it entered Fanfulla's mind in earnest, for his expression had been more or less an idle one. But since Francesco invited him, why not indeed ?

And thus it came to pass that at the third hour of that warm May night a party of four men on horseback and two sumpter mules passed out of Babbiano and took the road that leads to Vinamare, and thence into the territory of Urbino. These riders were the Count of Aquila and Fanfulla degli Arcipreti, followed by Lanciotto leading a mule that bore the arms of those knights-errant and Zaccaria leading another with their general baggage.

All night they rode beneath the stars, and on until some three hours after sunrise, when they made halt in a hollow of the hills not far from Fabriano. They tethered their horses in a grove of peaceful laurel and sheltering mulberry at the foot of a slope that was set with olive trees, grey, gnarled and bent as aged cripples, and beside the river Esino at a spot where it was so narrow that an agile man might leap its width. Here, then, they spread their cloaks and Zaccaria unpacked his victuals, and set before them a simple meal of bread and wine and roasted fowl, which to their hunger made more appeal than a banquet at another season. And when they had eaten they laid them down beside the stream and there beguiled in pleasant talk the time until they fell asleep. They rested them through the heat of the day, and waking some three hours after noon the Count rose up and went some dozen paces down the stream to a spot where it fell into a tiny lake—a pool deep and blue as the cloudless heavens which it mirrored. Here he stripped off his garments and plunged headlong in, to emerge again, some moments later, refreshed and reinvigorated in body and in soul.

As Fanfulla awoke he beheld an apparition coming towards him, a figure lithe and stalwart as a sylvan god, the water shining on the ivory whiteness of his skin and glistening in his sable hair as the sunlight caught it.

" Tell me now, Fanfulla, lives there a man of so depraved a mind that he would prefer a ducal crown to this ? "

And the courtier, seeing Francesco's radiant mien understood perhaps, at last, how sordid was the ambition that could lure a man from such a god-like freedom, and from the holy all-consuming joys it brought him. His thoughts being started upon that course, it was of this they talked what time the Count resumed his garments—his hose of red, his knee-high boots of untanned leather, and his quilted brigandine of plain brown cloth, reputed dagger-proof. He rose at last to buckle on his belt of hammered steel, from which there hung, behind his loins, a stout lengthy dagger, the only weapon that he carried.

At his command the horses were saddled and the sumpters laden once more. Lanciotto held his stirrup, and Zaccaria did like service for Fanfulla, and presently they were cantering out of that fragrant grove on to the elastic sward of broad green pasture-lands. They crossed the stream at a spot where the widened sheet of water scarce went higher than their horses' hocks; then veering to the east they rode away from the hills for a half-league or so until they gained a road. Here they turned northward again and pushed on towards Cagli.

As the bells were ringing the Ave Maria the cavalcade drew up before the Palazzo Valdicampo, where two nights ago Gian Maria had been entertained. Its gates were now as readily thrown wide to welcome the illustrious and glorious Count of Aquila, who was esteemed by Messer Valdicampo no less than his more puissant cousin. Chambers were set at his disposal and at Fanfulla's; servants were bidden to wait upon them; fresh raiment was laid out for them, and a noble supper was prepared to do honour to Francesco. Nor did the generous Valdicampo's manner cool when he learned that Francesco was in disgrace at the Court of Babbiano and banished from the dominions of Duke Gian Maria. He expressed sympathetic regret at so untoward a circumstance and discreetly refrained from passing any opinion thereupon.

Yet later, as they supped, and when perhaps the choice wines had somewhat relaxed his discretion, he permitted himself to speak of Gian Maria's ways in terms that were very far from laudatory.

"Here, in my house," he informed them, "he committed an outrage upon a poor unfortunate, for which an account may yet be asked of me—since it was under my roof that the thing befell, for all that I knew nothing of it."

Upon being pressed by Paolo to tell them more, he parted with the information that the unfortunate in question was Urbino's jester Peppe. At that, Paolo's glance became more intent. The memory of his meeting with the fool and his mistress in the woods a month ago flashed now across his mind, and it came to him that he could rightly guess the source whence his cousin had drawn the information that had led to his own arrest and banishment.

"Of what nature was the outrage?" he inquired.

"From what Peppe himself has told me it would seem that the fool was possessed of some knowledge which Gian Maria sought, but on which Peppe was bound by oath to silence. Gian Maria caused him to be secretly taken and carried off from Urbino. His *sbirri* brought the fellow here, and to make him speak the Duke improvised in his bed-chamber a *tratti di corde*, which had the desired result."

The Count's face grew dark with anger. "The coward!" he muttered. "The dastardly craven!"

"But bethink you, sir Count," exclaimed Valdicampo, "that this poor Peppe is a frail and deformed creature, lacking the strength of an ordinary man, and do not judge him over-harshly."

"It was not of him I spoke," replied Francesco, "but of my cousin, that cowardly tyrant, Gian Maria Sforza. Tell me, Messer Valdicampo, what has become of Ser Peppe?"

"He is still here. I have had him tended, and his condition is already much improved. It will not be long ere he is recovered, but for a few days yet his arms will remain almost useless. They were all but torn from his body."

When the meal was done Francesco begged his host to conduct him to Peppe's chamber. This Valdicampo did, and, leaving Fanfulla in the company of the ladies of his house, he escorted the Count to the room where the poor ill-used hunchback was abed tended by one of the women of Valdicampo's household.

H

"Here is a visitor to see you, Ser Peppe," the old gentleman announced, setting down his candle on a table by the bed. The jester turned his great head towards the newcomer's, and sought with melancholy eyes the face of his visitor. At sight of him a look of terror spread itself upon his countenance.

"My lord," he cried, struggling into a sitting posture, "my noble, gracious lord, have mercy on me. I could tear out this craven tongue of mine. But did you know what agonies I suffered, and to what a torture they submitted me to render me unfaithful, it may be that you, yourself, would pity me."

"Why, that I do," answered Francesco gently. "Indeed, could I have seen the consequences that oath would have for you, I had not bound you by it."

The fear in Peppe's face gave place to unbelief.

"And you forgive me, lord?" he cried. "I dreaded when you entered that you were come to punish me for what wrong I may have done you in speaking. But if you forgive me it may be that Heaven will forgive me also, and that I may not be damned. And that were a thousand pities, for what, my lord, should I do in hell?"

"Deride the agonies of Gian Maria," answered Francesco, with a laugh.

"It were almost worth burning for," mused Peppe putting forth a hand, whose lacerated, swollen wrist bore evidence to the torture he had suffered. At sight of it the Count made an exclamation of angry horror and hastened to inquire into the poor fool's condition.

"It is not so bad now," Peppe answered him, "and it is only in consequence of Messer Valdicampo's insistence that I have kept my bed. I can scarce use my arms, it is true, but they are improving. To-morrow I shall be up, and I hope to set out for Urbino, where my dear mistress must be distressed with fears for my absence, for she is a very kind and tender-hearted lady."

This resolve of Peppe's prompted the Count to offer to conduct him to Urbino on the morrow, since he, himself, would be journeying that way—an offer which the fool accepted without hesitation and with lively gratitude.

CHAPTER XII

In the morning Francesco set out once more, accompanied by his servants, Fanfulla, and the fool. The latter was now so far restored as to be able to sit a mule, but lest the riding should over-tire him they proceeded at little more than an ambling pace along the lovely valleys of the Metauro. Thus it befell that when the night descended it found them still journeying and some two leagues distant from Urbino. Another league they travelled in the moonlight, and the fool was beguiling the time for them with a droll story culled from the bright pages of Messer Boccaccio, when of a sudden his sharp ears caught a sound that struck him dumb in the middle of a sentence.

" Are you faint ? " asked Francesco, turning quickly towards him, and mindful of the fellow's sore condition.

" No, no," answered the fool, with a readiness that dispelled the Count's alarm on that score. " I thought I heard a sound of marching in the distance."

" The wind in the trees, Peppino," explained Fanfulla.

" I do not think——" He stopped short and listened ; and now they all heard it, for it came wafted to them on a gust of the fitful breeze that smote their faces.

" You are right," said Francesco. " It is the tramp of men. But what of that, Peppe ? Men will march in Italy. Let us hear the end of your story."

" But who should march in Urbino, and by night ? " the fool persisted.

" Do I know or do I care ? " quoth the Count. " Your story, man."

For all that he was far from satisfied, the fool resumed his narrative. But he no longer told it with his former

irresistible humour. His mind was occupied with that
sound of marching, which came steadily nearer. At
length he could endure it no longer, and the apathy of
his companions fired him openly to rebel.

"My lord," he cried, turning to the Count, and again
leaving his story interrupted, "they are all but upon
us."

"True!" agreed Francesco indifferently "The next
turn yonder should bring us into them."

"Then I beg you, Lord Count, to step inside. Let
us pause here under the trees until they have passed.
I am full of fears. Perhaps I am a coward, but I mislike
these roving night-bands. It may be a company of
masnadieri."

"What then?" returned the Count, without slack-
ening speed. "What cause have we to fear a party
of robbers?"

But Fanfulla and the servants joined their advice
to Peppe's and prevailed at last upon Francesco to
take cover until this company should have passed. He
consented, to pacify them, and wheeling to the right
they entered the border of the forest, drawing rein well
in the shadow, whence they could survey the road
and see who passed across the patch of moonlight that
illumined it. And presently the company came along
and swung into that revealing flood of light. To the
astonishment of the watchers they beheld no marauding
party such as they had been led to expect, but a very
orderly company of some twenty men, soberly arrayed in
leather, hacketons and salades of bright steel, marching
sword on thigh and pike on shoulder. At the head of
this company rode a powerfully-built man on a great
sorrel horse, at sight of whom the fool swore softly
in astonishment. In the middle of the party came four
litters borne by mules, and at the side of one of them
rode a slender, graceful figure that provoked from
Peppe a second oath. But the profoundest objurgation
of all was wrung from him at sight of a portly bulk in
the black habit of the Dominicans ambling in the rear,
who just then was in angry altercation with a fellow
that was urging his mule along with the butt of his
partisan.

"May you be roasted on a gridiron like Saint Lawrence," gasped the irate priest. "Would you break my neck, brute beast that you are ? Do you but wait until we reach Roccaleone, and by St. Dominic, I'll get your ruffianly commander to hang you for this ill-seasoned jest."

But his tormentor laughed for answer and smote the mule again, a blow this time that almost caused it to rear up. The friar cried out in angry alarm, and then, still storming and threatening his persecutor, he passed on. After him came six heavily-laden carts, each drawn by a pair of bullocks, and the rear of the procession was brought up by a flock of a dozen bleating sheep, herded by a blasphemant man-at-arms. They passed the astonished watchers who remained concealed until that odd company had melted away into the night.

"I could swear," said Fanfulla "that that friar and I have met before."

"Nor would you do a perjury," answered him the fool. "For it is that fat hog Fra Domenico—he that went with you to the Convent of Acquasparta to fetch unguents for his Excellency."

"What does he in that company, and who are they ?" asked the Count turning to the fool as they rode out of their ambush.

"Ask me where the devil keeps his lures," quoth the fool, "and I'll make some shift to answer you. But as for what does Fra Domenico in that galley, it is more than I can hazard a guess on. He is not the only one known to me," Peppino added. "There was Ercole Fortemani, a great, dirty, blustering ruffian whom I never saw in aught but rags, riding at their head in garments of most unwonted wholeness ; and there was Romeo Gonzaga, whom I never knew to stir by night save to an assignation. Strange things must be happening in Urbino."

"And the litters ?" inquired Francesco "Can you hazard no guess as to their meaning ?"

"None," said he, "saving that they may account for the presence of Messer Gonzaga. For litters argue women."

"It seems, fool, that not even your wisdom shall

avail us. But you heard the friar say they were bound for Roccaleone?"

"Yes, I heard that. And by means of it we shall probably learn the rest at the end of our journey."

And being a man of extremely inquisitive mind, the fool set his inquiries on foot the moment they entered the gates of Urbino in the morning—for they had reached the city over-late to gain admittance that same night, and were forced to seek shelter in one of the houses by the river. It was of the Captain of the Gate that he sought information.

"Can you tell me, Ser Capitan," he inquired, "what company was that that travelled yesternight to Roccaleone?"

The captain looked at him a moment.

"There was none that I know of," said he. "Certainly none from Urbino."

"You keep a marvellous watch," said the fool dryly. "I tell you that a company of men-at-arms some twenty strong went last night from Urbino to Roccaleone."

"To Roccaleone?" echoed the captain, with a musing air, more attentively than before, as if the repetition of that name had suggested something to his mind. "Why, it is the castle of Monna Valentina."

"True, sapient sir. But what of the company, and why was it travelling so, by night?"

"How know you it proceeded from Urbino?" quoth the captain earnestly.

"Because at its head I recognised the roaring warrior Ercole Fortemani, in the middle rode Romeo Gonzaga, in the rear came Fra Domenico Madonna's confessor—men of Urbino all."

The officer's face grew purple at the news.

"Were there any women in the party?" he cried.

"I saw none," replied the fool, in whom this sudden eagerness of the captain's awakened caution and reflection.

"But there were four litters," put in Francesco whose nature was less suspicious and alert than the wise fool's.

Too late Peppe scowled caution at him. The captain swore a great oath.

"It is she," he cried, with assurance. "And this
company was travelling to Roccaleone, you say? How
know you that?"

"We heard it from the friar," answered Francesco
readily.

"Then, by the Virgin! we have them. Olà!"
He turned from them and ran shouting into the gate-
house, to re-emerge a moment later with half a dozen
soldiers at his heels.

"To the Palace," he commanded, and as his men
surrounded Francesco's party, "Come, sir," he said
to the Count, "You must go with us, and tell your
story to the Duke."

"There is no need for all this force," answered
Francesco coldly. "In any case I could not pass
through Urbino without seeing Duke Guidobaldo. I
am the Count of Aquila."

At once the captain's bearing grew respectful. He
made his apologies for the violent measures of his zeal
and bade his men fall behind. Ordering them to
follow him, he mounted a horse that was brought him
and rode briskly through the borgo at the Count's
side. And as he rode he told them what the jester's
quick intuition had already whispered to him. The
lady Valentina was fled from Urbino in the night and
in her company were gone three of her ladies, and—it
was also supposed, since they had disappeared—Fra
Domenico and Romeo Gonzaga.

Aghast at what he heard, Francesco pressed his
informer for more news. But there was little more that
the captain could tell him, beyond the fact that it was
believed she had been driven to it to escape her impending marriage with the Duke of Babbiano. Guidobaldo was distraught at what had happened and anxious
to bring the lady back before news of her behaviour
should reach the ears of Gian Maria. It was, therefore,
a matter of no little satisfaction to the captain that
the task should be his to bear Guidobaldo this news
of her whereabouts which from Francesco and the
jester he had derived.

Peppe looked glum and sullen. Had he but bridled
his cursed curiosity, and had the Count but taken the

alarm in time and held his peace, all might have been
well with his beloved *patrona*. As it was, he—the one
man ready to die that he might serve her—had been
the very one to betray her refuge. He heard the Count's
laugh, and the sound of it was fuel to his anger. But
Francesco only thought of the splendid daring of the
lady's action.

"But these men-at-arms that she had with her?" he
cried. "For what purpose so numerous a bodyguard?"

The captain looked at him a moment.

"Can you not guess?" he inquired. "Perhaps you
do not know the Castle of Roccaleone."

"It were odd if I did not know the most impregnable
fortress in Italy."

"Why, then, does it not become clear? She has
taken this company for a garrison, and in Roccaleone
she clearly intends to resist in rebel fashion the wishes
of his Highness."

At that the Count threw back his head, and scared
the passers-by with as hearty a peal of laughter as ever
crossed his lips.

"By the Host!" he gasped, laughter still choking
his utterance. "There is a maid for you? Do you
hear what the captain says, Fanfulla? She means to
resist this wedding by armed force if needs be. Now, on
my soul, if Guidobaldo insists upon the union after
this, why, then he has no heart, no feeling. As I live
she is a kinswoman that such a warlike prince might
well be proud of. Small wonder that they do not fear
the Borgia in Urbino." And he laughed again. But
the captain scowled at him, and Peppe frowned.

"She is a rebellious jade," quoth the captain sourly.

"Nay, softly," returned Francesco; for all that he
still laughed. "If you were of knightly rank I'd break
a lance with you on that score. As it is——" he paused,
his laughter ceased, and his dark eyes took the captain's
measure in a curious way. "Best leave her uncensured,
Ser Capitano. She is of the house of Rovere, and
closely allied to that of Montefeltro."

The officer felt the rebuke, and silence reigned between
them after that.

It was whilst Francesco, Fanfulla and Peppe waited

in the antechamber for admittance to the Duke that
the jester vented some of the bitterness he felt at their
babbling. The splendid room was thronged with a
courtly crowd. There were magnificent nobles and
envoys, dark ecclesiastics and purple prelates, captains
in steel and court officers in silk and velvet. Yet,
heedless of who might hear him, Peppe voiced his
rebuke, and the terms he employed were neither as
measured nor as respectful as the Count's rank dictated.
Yet with that fairness of mind that made him so univer-
sally beloved, Francesco offered no resentment to the
fool's reproof. He saw that it was deserved, for it threw
upon the matter a light that was new and more searching.
But he presently saw further than did the fool, and he
smiled at the other's scowls.

" Not so loud, Peppe," said he. " You over-estimate
the harm. At worst, we have but anticipated by a
little what the Duke must have learnt from other
sources."

" But it is just that little—the few hours or days—
that will do the mischief," snapped the jester testily,
for all that he lowered his voice. " In a few days Gian
Maria will be back. If he were met with the news
that the lady Valentina were missing, that she had run
away with Romeo Gonzaga—for that, you'll see, will
presently be the tale—do you think he would linger here
or further care to pursue his wooing ? Not he. These
alliances that are for State purposes alone, in which the
heart plays no part, demand, at least, that on the lady's
side there shall be a record unblemished by the breath
of scandal. His Highness would have returned him
home, and Madonna would have been rid of him."

" But at a strange price, Peppe," answered Francesco gravely. " Still," he added, " I agree that I would
have served her purpose better by keeping silent. But
that such an affair will cool the ardour of my cousin I
do not think. You are wrong in placing this among the
alliances in which the heart has no part. On my
cousin's side—if all they say be true—the heart plays
a very considerable part indeed. But, for the rest—
what harm have we done ? "

" Time will show," said the hunchback.

"It will show, then, that I have done no hurt whatever to her interests. By now she is safe in Roccaleone. What, then, can befall her? Guidobaldo, no doubt, will repair to her, and across the moat he will entreat her to be a dutiful niece and to return. She will offer to do so on condition that he pass her his princely word not to further molest her with the matter of this marriage. And then——"

"Well?" growled the fool. "And then? Who shall say what may befall then? Let us say that his Highness reduces her by force."

"A siege?" laughed the Count. "Pooh! Where is your wisdom, fool? Do you think the splendid Guidobaldo is eager to become the sport of Italy and go down to posterity as the duke who besieged his niece because she resisted his ordainings touching the matter of her wedding?"

"Guidobaldo da Montefeltro can be a violent man upon occasion," the fool was answering, when the officer who had left them appeared with the announcement that his Highness waited them.

They found the Prince in a very gloomy mood, and after greeting Francesco with cool ceremony he questioned him on the matter of the company they had met yesternight. These inquiries he conducted with characteristic dignity and no more show of concern than if it had been an affair of a strayed falcon. He thanked Francesco for his information, and gave orders that the seneschal should place apartments at his and Fanfulla's disposal for as long as it should please them to grace his court. With that he dismissed them, bidding the officer remain to receive his orders.

"And that," said Francesco to Peppe as they crossed the antechamber in the wake of a servant, "is the man who would lay siege to his niece's castle? For once, sir fool, your wisdom is at fault."

"You do not know the Duke, Excellency," answered the fool. "Beneath that frozen exterior burns a furnace, and there is no madness he would not commit."

But Francesco only laughed as, linking arms with Fanfulla, he passed down the gallery on his way to the apartments to which the servant was conducting them.

CHAPTER XIII

In a measure the events that followed would almost
tend to show that the fool was right. For even if the
notion of besieging Valentina and reducing her by
force of arms was not Guidobaldo's own in the first
place, yet he lent a very willing ear to the counsel that
they should thus proceed when angrily urged two days
thereafter by the Duke of Babbiano.

Upon hearing the news Gian Maria had abandoned
himself to such a licence of rage as made those about
him tremble from the highest to the meanest. The
disappointment of his passion was in itself justification
enough for this; but, in addition, Gian Maria beheld
in the flight of Valentina the frustration of those bold
schemes of which he had talked so loudly to his counsellors and his mother. It was his confidence in those
same schemes that had induced him to send that defiant
answer to Cæsar Borgia. As a consequence of this there
was haste—most desperate haste—that he should wed,
since wedding was to lend him the power to carry out
his brave promises of protecting his crown from the
Duke of Valentinois, not to speak of the utter routing
of the Borgia which he had wildly undertaken to
accomplish.

That the destinies of States should be tossed to the
winds of Heaven by a slip of a girl was to him something
as insufferable as it had been unexpected.

" She must be brought back ! " he had screeched in
his towering passion. " She must be brought back at
once."

" True ! " answered Guidobaldo, in his serene way ;
" she must be brought back. So far, I agree with

you entirely. Tell me, now, how the thing is to be accomplished." And there was sarcasm in his voice.

" What difficulties does it present ? " inquired Gian Maria.

" No difficulties," was the ironical reply. " She has shut herself up in the stoutest castle in Italy and tells me that she will not come forth until I promise her freedom of choice in the matter of marriage. Clearly, there are no difficulties attached to her being brought back."

Gian Maria showed his teeth.

" Do you give me leave to go about it in my own way ? " he asked.

" Not only do I give you leave, but I'll render you all the assistance in my power, if you can devise a means for luring her from Roccaleone."

" I hesitate no longer. Your niece, Lord Duke, is a rebel, and as a rebel is she to be treated. She has garrisoned a castle, and hurled defiance at the ruler of the land. It is a declaration of war, Highness, and war we shall have.

" You would resort to force ? " asked Guidobaldo disapproval lurking in his voice.

" To the force of arms, your Highness," answered Gian Maria, with prompt fierceness. " I will lay siege to this castle of hers, and I shall tear stone from stone. Oh, I would have wooed her nicely had she let me, with gentle words and mincing ways that maidens love. But since she defies us, I'll woo her with arquebuse and cannon, and seek by starvation to make her surrender to my suit. My love shall put on armour to subject her, and I vow to God that I shall not shave my beard until I am inside her castle."

Guidobaldo looked grave.

" I should counsel gentler measures," said he. " Besiege her if you will, but do not resort to too much violence. Cut off their resources and let hunger be your advocate. Even so, I fear me, you will be laughed at by all Italy," he added bluntly.

" A fig for that ! Let the fools laugh if they be minded to. What forces has she at Roccaleone ? "

At the question Guidobaldo's brow grew dark. It

was as if he had recalled some circumstance that had lain forgotten.

"Some twenty knaves led by a notorious ruffian of the name of Fortemani. The company was enrolled, they tell me, by a gentleman of my court, a kinsman of my Duchess, Messer Romeo Gonzaga."

"Is he with her now?" gasped Gian Maria.

"It would seem he is."

"By the Virgin's Ring of Perugia!" spluttered Gian Maria in increased dismay. "Do you suggest that they fled together?"

"My lord!" Guidobaldo's voice rang sharp and threatening. "It is of my niece that you are speaking. She took this gentleman with her just as she took three of her ladies and a page or two, to form such attendance as befits her birth."

Gian Maria took a turn in the apartment, a frown wrinkling his brow and his lips pressed tight. Guidobaldo's proud words by no means convinced him. But the one preponderating desire in his heart just then was to humble the girl who had dared to flout him, to make her bend her stubborn neck. At last:

"I may indeed become the laughing-stock of Italy," he muttered, in a concentrated voice, "but I shall carry my resolve through, and my first act upon entering Roccaleone will be to hang this knave Gonzaga from its highest turret."

That very day Gian Maria began his preparations for the expedition against Roccaleone, and word of it was carried by Fanfulla to Francesco—for the latter had left his quarters at the palace upon hearing of Gian Maria's coming, and was now lodging at the sign of the "Sun."

Upon hearing the news he swore a mighty oath in which he consigned his cousin to the devil, by whom, in that moment, he pronounced him begotten.

"Do you think," he asked, when he was calmer, "that this man Gonzaga is her lover?"

"It is more than I can say," answered Fanfulla. "There is the fact that she fled with him. Though when I questioned Peppe on this subject he first laughed the notion to scorn, and then grew grave. 'She

loves him not, the popinjay,' he said; 'but he
loves her, or I am blind else, and he's a villain, I
know.' ''

Francesco stood up, his face mighty serious and his
dark eyes full of uneasy thought.

"By the Host! It is a shameful thing," he cried
out at last. " This poor lady so beset on every hand by
a parcel of villains, each more unscrupulous than the
other. Fanfulla, send for Peppe. We must despatch
the fool to her with warning of Gian Maria's coming,
and warning, too, against this man of Mantua she has
fled with."

"Too late," answered Fanfulla. " The fool departed
this morning for Roccaleone to join his *patrona*."

Francesco looked his dismay.

"She will be undone," he groaned. " Thus between
the upper and the nether stone—between Gian Maria
and Romeo Gonzaga. *Gesù*! she will be undone!
And she so brave and so high-spirited! "

He moved slowly to the casement and stood staring
at the windows across the street, on which the setting
sun fell in a ruddy glow. But it was not the windows
that he saw. It was a scene in the woods of Acquasparta on that morning after the mountain fight; a man
lying wounded in the bracken, and over him a gentle
lady bending with eyes of pity and solicitude. Often
since had his thoughts revisited that scene, sometimes
with a smile, sometimes with a sigh, and sometimes
with both at once.

He turned suddenly upon Fanfulla. "I will go
myself," he announced.

"You?" echoed Fanfulla. " But the Venetians?"

By a gesture the Count signified how little the
Venetians weighed with him when compared with the
fortunes of this lady.

"I am going to Roccaleone," he insisted, " now—at
once." And striding to the door he beat his hands
together and called Lanciotto.

"You said, Fanfulla, that in these days there are no
longer maidens held in bondage to whom a knight-
errant may lend aid. You were at fault, for in Monna
Valentina we have the captive maiden, in my cousin

the dragon, in Gonzaga another, and in me the errant
knight who is destined—I hope—to save her."

"You will save her from Gian Maria?" questioned
Fanfulla incredulously.

"I will attempt it."

He turned to his servant, who entered as he spoke.

"We set out in a quarter of an hour, Lanciotto," said
he. "Saddle for me and for yourself. You are to go
with me. Zaccaria may remain with Messer degli
Arcipreti. You will care for him, Fanfulla, and he will
serve you well."

"But what of me?" cried Fanfulla. "Do I not
accompany you?"

"If you will; yes. But you might serve me better
by returning to Babbiano and watching the events
there, sending me word of what befalls—for great things
will befall soon if my cousin returns not and the Borgia
advances. It is upon this that I am founding such
hopes as I have."

"But whither shall I send you word? To Roccaleone?"

Francesco reflected a moment. "If you do not hear
from me, then send your news to Roccaleone, for if I
should linger there and we are besieged it will perhaps
be impossible to send a message to you. But if—as
I hope—I go to Aquila, I will send you word of it."

"To Aquila?"

"Yes. It may be that I shall be at Aquila before the
week is out. But keep it secret, Fanfulla, and I'll
fool these dukes to the very top of their unhealthy
bent."

A half-hour later the Count of Aquila, mounted on
a stout Calabrian horse, and attended by Lanciotto
on a mule, rode gently down towards the valley. They
went unnoticed, for what cared for them the peasants
that sang at their labours in the *contado*?

They met a merchant, whose servant was urging
his laden sumpters up the hilly road to the city on their
heights, and they passed him with a courteous greeting.
Farther they came upon a mounted company of nobles
and ladies returning from a hawking party and
followed by attendants bearing their hooded falcons,

and their gay laughter still rang in Francesco's ears
after he had passed from their sight and vanished
in the purple mists of eventide that came up to meet
him from the river.

They turned westward towards the Apennines and
pushed on after night had fallen, until the fourth hour,
when, at Francesco's suggestion, they drew rein before
a sleepy wayside *locanda* and awoke the host to demand
shelter. There they slept no longer than until matins,
so that the grey light of dawn saw them once more
upon their way, and by the time the sun had struck with
its first golden shaft the grey crest of the old hills, they
drew rein on the brink of the roaring torrent at the foot
of the mighty crag that was crowned by the Castle of
Roccaleone.

Grim and gaunt it loomed above the fertile vale,
with that torrent circling it in a natural moat, like a
giant sentinel of the Apennines that were its background.
And now the sunlight raced down the slopes of the old
mountains like a tide. It smote the square tower of the
keep, then flowed down the wall, setting the old grey
stone a-gleaming and flashing back from a mullioned
window placed high up. Lower it came, revealing
grotesque gargoyles, flooding the crenellated battlements
and turning green the ivy and lichen that but a moment
back had blackened the stout projecting buttresses.
Thence it leapt to the ground and drove the shadow
before it down the grassy slope until it reached the
stream and sparkled on its foaming, tumbling waters,
scattering a hundred colours through the flying spray.

And all that time, until the sun had reached him and
included him in the picture it was awakening, the Count
of Aquila sat in his saddle with thoughtful eyes uplifted
to the fortress.

Then, Lanciotto following him, he walked his horse
round the western side, where the torrent was replaced
by a smooth arm of water, for which a cutting had been
made to complete the isolation of the crag of Roccaleone.
But here, where the castle might more easily have
become vulnerable, a blank wall greeted him, broken
by no more than a narrow slit or two midway between
the battlements. He rode on towards the northern

side, crossing a footbridge that spanned the river, and at last coming to a halt before the entrance tower. Here again the moat was formed by the torrential waters of the mountain stream.

He bade his servant rouse the inmates, and Lanciotto hallooed in a voice that nature had made deep and powerful. The echo of it went booming up to scare the birds on the hillside, but evoked no answer from the silent castle.

"They keep a zealous watch," laughed the Count. "Again, Lanciotto."

The man obeyed him, and again and again his deep voice rang out like a trumpet-call before sign was made from within that it had been heard. At length above the parapet of the tower appeared a stunted figure with head unkempt, as grotesque almost as any of the gargoyles beneath, and an owlish face peered at them from one of the crenels of the battlement and demanded in surly croaking tones their business. Instantly the Count recognised Peppe.

"Good morrow, fool," he bade him.

"You, my lord!" exclaimed the jester.

"You sleep soundly at Roccaleone," quoth Francesco. "Bestir that knavish garrison of yours and bid the lazy dogs let down the bridge. I have news for Monna Valentina."

"At once, Excellency," the fool replied, and would have gone upon the instant but that Francesco recalled him.

"Say, Peppe, a knight—the knight she met at Acquasparta, if you will. But leave my name unspoken."

With the assurance that he would obey his wishes Peppe went his errand. A slight delay ensued, and then upon the battlements appeared Gonzaga, sleepy and contentious, attended by a couple of Fortemani's knaves, who came to ask the nature of Francesco's business.

"It is with Monna Valentina," answered him Francesco, raising head and voice, so that Gonzaga recognised him for the wounded knight of Acquasparta, remembered and scowled.

"I am Monna Valentina's captain here," he announced with arrogance. "And you may deliver to me such messages as you bear."

There followed a contention conducted ill-humouredly on the part of Gonzaga and scarcely less so on the Count's, Francesco stoutly refusing to communicate his business to any but Valentina, and Gonzaga as stoutly refusing to disturb the lady at that hour, or to lower the bridge. Words flew between them across the waters of the moat, and grew hotter at each fresh exchange, till in the end they were abruptly terminated by the appearance of Valentina herself, attended by Peppino.

"What is this, Gonzaga?" she inquired, her manner excited, for the fool had told her that it was the knight Francesco who sought admittance, and at the very mention of the name she had flushed, then paled, then started for the ramparts. "Why is this knight denied admittance since he bears a message for me?" And from where she stood she sought with admiring eyes the graceful shape of the Count of Aquila—the knight-errant of her dreams. Francesco bared his head, and bent to the withers of his horse in courteous greeting. She turned to Gonzaga impatiently.

"For what do you wait?" she cried. "Have you not understood my wishes? Let the bridge be lowered."

"Bethink you, Madonna," he remonstrated. "You do not know this man. He may be a spy of Gian Maria's—a hireling paid to betray us."

"You fool," she answered sharply. "Do you not see that it is the wounded knight we met that day you were escorting me to Urbino?"

"What shall that signify?" demanded he. "Is it proof of his honesty of purpose or loyalty to you? Be advised, Madonna, and let him deliver his message from where he is. He is safer there."

She measured him with a determined eye.

"Messer Gonzaga, order them to lower the bridge," she bade him.

"But, lady, bethink you of your peril."

"Peril?" she echoed. "Peril from two men, and we a garrison of over twenty? Surely the man is a coward who talks so readily of perils. Have the drawbridge lowered."

"But if——" he began, with a desperate vehemence, when again she cut him short.

"Am I to be obeyed? Am I mistress, and will you bid them lower the bridge, or must I, myself, go see to it?"

With a look of despairing anger and a shrug of the shoulders he turned from her and despatched one of his men with an order. A few moments later, with a creaking of hinges and a clanking of chains, the great bridge swung down and dropped with a thud to span the gulf. Instantly the Count spurred his horse forward, and, followed by Lanciotto, rode across the plank and under the archway of the entrance tower into the first courtyard.

Now, scarcely had he drawn rein there when through a door at the far end appeared the gigantic figure of Fortemani, half-clad and sword in hand. At sight of Francesco the fellow leaped down a half-dozen steps and advanced towards him with a burst of oaths.

"To me!" he shouted, in a voice that might have waked the dead. "Olá! Olá! What devil's work is this? How come you here? By whose orders was the bridge let down?"

"By the orders of Monna Valentina's captain," answered Francesco, wondering what madman might be this.

"Captain?" cried the other, coming to a standstill and his face turning purple "Body of Satan! What captain? I am captain here."

The Count looked him over in surprise.

"Why, then," said he, "you are the very man I seek. I congratulate you on the watch you keep, Messer Capitano. Your castle is so excellently patrolled that had I been minded for a climb I had scaled your walls and got within your gates without arousing any of your slumbering sentries."

Fortemani eyed him with a lowering glance. The prosperity of the past four days had increased the insolence inherent in the man.

"Is that your affair?" he growled menacingly.

"You are over-bold, sir stranger, to seek a quarrel with me, and over-pert to tell me how I shall discharge my captaincy. By the Passion! You shall be punished."

"Punished—I?" echoed Francesco, on whose brow there now descended a scowl as black as Ercole's own.

"Aye, punished, young sir. Ercole Fortemani is my name."

"I have heard of you," answered the Count contemptuously, "and of how you belie that name of yours, for they tell me that a more drunken, cowardly, good-for-nothing rogue is not to be found in Italy—no, not even in the Pope's dominions. And have a care how you cast the word 'punishment" at your betters, animal. The moat is none so distant, and the immersion may profit it. For I'll swear you've not been washed since they baptised you—if, indeed, you be a son of Mother Church at all."

"*Sangue di Cristo*!" spluttered the enraged bully, his face mottled. "This to me? Come down from that horse."

He laid hold of Francesco's leg to drag him to the ground, but the Count wrenched it free by a quick motion that left a gash from his spur upon the captain's hands. Simultaneously he raised his whip, and would have laid the lash of it across the broad of Fortemani's back—for it had angered him beyond words to have a ruffian of this fellow's quality seeking to ruffle it with him—but at that moment a female voice, stern and imperative, bade them hold in their quarrel.

Fortemani fell back nursing his lacerated hand and muttering curses, whilst Francesco turned in the direction whence that voice had come. Midway on the flight of stone steps he beheld Valentina, followed by Gonzaga, Peppe, and a couple of men-at-arms, descending from the battlements.

Calm and queenly she stood, dressed in a camorra of grey velvet with black sleeves, which excellently set off her handsome height. Gonzaga was leaning forward speaking into her ear, and for all that his voice was subdued, some of his words travelled down to Francesco on the still morning air.

" Was I not wise, Madonna, in that I hesitated to admit him ? You see what manner of man he is."

The blood flamed in Francesco's cheeks, nor did it soften his chagrin to note the look which Valentina flashed down at him.

Instantly he leapt to the ground, and flinging his reins to Lanciotto he went forward to the foot of that stone staircase, his broad hat slung back upon his shoulders, to meet that descending company.

" Is this seemly, sir ? " she questioned angrily. " Does it become you to brawl with my garrison the moment you are admitted ? "

The blood rose higher in Francesco's face, and now suffused his temples and reached his hair. Yet his voice was well restrained as he made answer:

" Madonna, this knave was insolent."

" An insolence that you, no doubt, provoked," put in Gonzaga, a dimple showing on his woman's cheek. But the sterner rebuke fell from the lips of Valentina.

" Knave ? " she questioned, with flushed countenance. ' If you would not have me regret your admittance, Messer Francesco, I pray you curb your words. Here are no knaves. That, sir, is the captain of my soldiers."

Francesco bowed submissively, as patient under her reproof as he had been hasty under Fortemani's.

" It was on the matter of this captaincy that we fell to words," he answered with more humility. " By his own announcement I understood this nobleman "— and his eyes turned to Gonzaga—" to be your captain."

" He is the captain of my castle," she informed him.

" As you see, Ser Francesco," put in Peppe, who had perched himself upon the balustrade, " we suffer from no lack of captains here. We have also Fra Domenico, who is captain of our souls and of the kitchen ; myself am captain of——"

" Devil take you, fool," snapped Gonzaga, thrusting him roughly from his perch. Then turning abruptly to the Count : " You bear a message for us, sir ? " he questioned loftily.

Swallowing the cavalier tone, and overlooking the pronoun Gonzaga employed, Francesco inclined his head again to the lady.

" I should prefer to deliver it in more privacy than this." And his eye travelled round the court and up the steps behind, where was now collected the entire company of Fortemani. Gonzaga sneered and tossed his golden curls, but Valentina saw naught unreasonable in the request, and bidding Romeo attend her and Francesco follow, she led the way.

They crossed the quadrangle, and, mounting the steps down which Fortemani had dashed to meet the Count, they passed into the banqueting-hall, which opened directly upon the south side of the courtyard. The Count, following in her wake, ran the gauntlet of scowls of the assembled mercenaries. He stalked past them unmoved, taking their measure as he went, and estimating their true value with the unerring eye of the practised *condottiero* who has had to do with the enrolling of men and the handling of them. So little did he like their looks that on the threshold of the hall he paused and stayed Gonzaga.

" I am loath to leave my servant at the mercy of those ruffians, sir. May I beg that you will warn them against offering him violence ? "

" Ruffians ? " cried the lady angrily, before Gonzaga could offer a reply. " They are my soldiers."

Again he bowed, and there was a cold politeness in the tones in which he answered her :

" I crave your pardon, and I will say no more—unless it be to deplore that I may not felicitate you on your choice."

It was Gonzaga's turn to wax angry, for the choice had been his.

" Your message will have need to be a weighty one, sir, to earn our patience for your impertinence."

Francesco returned the look of those blue eyes which vainly sought to flash ferociously, and he made little attempt to keep his scorn from showing in his glance. He permitted himself even to shrug his shoulders, a trifle impatiently.

" Indeed, indeed, I think that I had best begone," he answered regretfully, " for it is a place whose inmates seem all bent on quarrelling with me. First your captain Fortemani greets me with an insolence hard

to leave unpunished.   You yourself, Madonna, resent
that I should crave protection for my man against
those fellows whose looks give rise for my solicitation.
You are angry that I should dub them ruffians, as if I
had followed the calling of arms these ten years without
acquiring knowledge of the quality of a man however
much you may disguise him.   And lastly, to crown all,
this *cicisbeo* "—and he spread a hand contemptuously
towards Gonzaga—" speaks of my impertinences."

"Madonna," cried Gonzaga, "I beg that you will let
me deal with him."

Unwittingly, unwillingly, Gonzaga saved the situation
by that prayer.   The anger that was fast rising in
Madonna's heart, stirred by the proud bearing of the
Count, was scattered before the unconscious humour
of her captain's appeal, in such ludicrous contrast was
his mincing speech and slender figure with Francesco's
firm tones and lean, active height.   She did not laugh,
for that would have been to have spoilt all, but she
looked from one to the other with quiet relish, noting
the glance of surprise and raised eyebrows with which
the Count received the courtier's request to be let deal
with him.   And thus, being turned from anger, the
balance of her mind was quick to adjust itself, and
she bethought her that perhaps there was reason in what
this knight advanced and that his reception had lacked
the courtesy that was his due.   In a moment, with
incomparable grace and skill, she had soothed Gonzaga's
ruffled vanity and appeased the Count's more sturdy
resentment

"And now, Messer Francesco," she concluded, "let
us be friends, and let me hear your business.   I beg that
you will sit."

They had passed into the banqueting-hall—a noble
apartment, whose walls were frescoed with hunting and
pastoral scenes, one or two of which were the work of
Pisaniello.   There were, too, some stray trophies of the
chase, and, here and there, a suit of costly armour that
caught the sunlight pouring through the tall mullioned
windows.   At the far end stood a richly carved screen
of cedar, and above this appeared the twisted railing
of the minstrels' gallery.   In a tall arm-chair of untanned

leather, at the head of the capacious board, Monna
Valentina sat herself, Gonzaga taking his stand at her
elbow, and Francesco fronting her leaning lightly
against the table.

"The news I bear you, lady, is soon told," said the
Count. "I would its quality were better. Your suitor
Gian Maria, returning to Guidobaldo's court, eager for
the nuptials that were promised him, has learnt of your
flight to Roccaleone and is raising—indeed will have
raised by now—an army to invest and reduce your
fortress."

Gonzaga turned as pale as the vest of white silk that
gleamed beneath his doublet of pear-coloured velvet at
this realisation of the prophecies he had uttered without
believing. A sickly fear possessed his soul. What
fate would they mete out to him who had been the
leading spirit of Valentina's rebellion? He could have
groaned aloud at this miscarriage of all his fine plans.
Where, now, would be the time to talk of love, to press
and carry his suit with Valentina and render himself
her husband? There would be war in the air and
bloody work that made his skin creep and turn cold
to ponder on. And the irony of it all was keenly cruel.
It was the very contingency that he had prophesied,
assured that neither Guidobaldo nor Gian Maria would
be so mad as to court ridicule by engaging upon it.

For a second Francesco's eyes rested on the courtier's
face and saw the fear written there for all to read. The
shadow of a smile quivered on his lips as his glance
moved on to meet the eyes of Valentina sparkling as
sparkles frost beneath the sun.

"Why, let them come!" she exclaimed, almost in
exultation. "This ducal oaf shall find me very ready for
him. We are armed at all points. We have victuals
to last us three months, if need be, and we have no
lack of weapons. Let Gian Maria come, and he will
find Valentina della Rovere none so easy to reduce.
To you, sir," she continued, with more calm, "to you on
whom I have no claim, I am more than grateful for your
chivalrous act in riding here to warn me."

Francesco sighed; a look of regret crossed his face.
"Alas!" he said. "When I rode hither, Madonna,

I had hoped to serve you to a better purpose. I had advice to offer and assistance if you should need it ; but the sight of those men-at-arms of yours makes me fear that it is not advice upon which it would be wise to act. For the plan I had in mind, it would be of the first importance that your soldiers should be trustworthy, and this, I fear me, they are not."

"Nevertheless," put in Gonzaga, feverishly clinging to a slender hope, "let us hear it."

"I beg that you will," said Valentina.

Thus enjoined, Francesco pondered a moment.

"Are you acquainted with the politics of Babbiano ? " he inquired.

"I know something of them."

"I will make the position quite clear to you, Madonna," he rejoined. And with that he told her of the threatened descent of Cæsar Borgia upon Gian Maria's duchy, and hence of the little time at her suitor's disposal ; so that if he could but be held in check before the walls of Roccaleone for a little while, all might be well. "But seeing in what haste he is," he ended, "his methods are likely to be rough and desperate, and I had thought that meanwhile you need not remain here, Madonna."

"Not remain ? " she cried, scorn of the notion in her voice.

"Not remain ? " quoth Gonzaga timorously, hope sounding in his.

"Precisely, Madonna. I would have proposed that you leave Gian Maria an empty nest, so that even if the castle should fall into his hands he would gain nothing."

"You would advise me to fly ? " she demanded.

"I came prepared to do so, but the sight of your men restrains me. They are not trustworthy, and to save their dirty skins they might throw Roccaleone open to the besiegers, and thus your flight would be discovered while yet there might be time to render it futile."

Before she could frame an answer there was Gonzaga feverishly urging her to act upon so wise and timely a suggestion and seek safety in flight from a place that Gian Maria would tear stone from stone. His words pattered quickly and piteously in entreaty, till in the end, facing him squarely :

" Are you afraid, Gonzaga ? " she asked him.

" I am—afraid for you, Madonna," he answered readily.

" Then let your fears have peace. For whether I stay or whether I go, one thing is certain : Gian Maria never shall set hands upon me." She turned again to Francesco. " I see a certain wisdom in the counsel of flight you would have offered me, no less than in what I take to be your advice that I should remain. But did I but consult my humour I should stay and deliver battle when this tyrant shows himself. But prudence, too, must be consulted, and I will give the matter thought." And now she thanked him with a generous charm for having come to her with this news and proffered his assistance, asking what motives brought him.

" Such motives as must ever impel a knight to serve a lady in distress," said he, " and perhaps, too, the memory of the charity with which you tended my wounds that day at Acquasparta."

For a second their glances met, quivered in the meeting, and fell apart again, an odd confusion in the breast of each, all of which Gonzaga, sunk in moody rumination, observed not. To lighten the awkward silence that was fallen, she asked him how it had transpired so soon that it was to Roccaleone she had fled.

" Do you not know ? " he cried. " Has not Peppe told you ? "

" I have had no speech with him. He but reached the castle, himself, late last night, and I first saw him this morning when he came to announce your presence."

And then, before more could be said, there arose a din of shouting from without. The door was pushed suddenly open, and Peppe darted into the room.

" Your man, Ser Francesco ! " he cried, his face white with excitement. " Come quickly, or they will kill him."

CHAPTER XIV

FORTEMANI DRINKS WATER

THE thing had begun with the lowering glances that Francesco had observed, and had grown to gibes and insults after he had disappeared. But Lanciotto had preserved an unruffled front, being a man schooled in the Count of Aquila's service to silence and a wondrous patience. This insensibility those hinds translated into cowardice, and emboldened by it—like the mongrels that they were—their offensiveness grew more direct and gradually more threatening. Lanciotto's patience was slowly oozing away, and, indeed, it was no longer anything but the fear of provoking his master's anger that restrained him. At length one burly ruffian, who had bidden him remove his head-piece in the company of gentlemen, and whose request had been by Lanciotto as disregarded as the rest, advanced menacingly towards him and caught him by the leg as Ercole had caught his master. Exasperated at that, Lanciotto had swung his leg free and caught the rash fellow a vicious kick in the face that had felled him, stunned and bleeding.

The roar from the man's companions told Lanciot to what to expect. In an instant they were upon him, clamouring for his blood. He sought to draw his master's sword, which, together with the Count's other armour, was slung across his saddle bow; but before he could extricate it he was seized by a dozen hands and cropped, fighting, from the saddle. On the ground they overpowered him, and a mailed hand was set upon his mouth, crushing back into his throat the cry for help he would have raised.

On the west side of the courtyard a fountain issuing from the wall had once poured its water through a lion's head into a vast tank of moss-grown granite. But it had

been disused for some time, and the pipe in the lion's
mouth was dry.   The tank, however, was more than half
full of water, which, during the late untenanting of the
castle, had turned foul and stagnant.   To drown Lanciotto in this was the amiable suggestion that emanated from
Fortemani himself—a suggestion uproariously received
by his knaves, who set themselves to act upon it.   They
roughly dragged the bleeding and frantically-struggling
Lanciotto across the yard and gained the border of the
tank, intending fully to sink him into it and hold him
under, to drown there like a rat.

But in that instant a something burst upon him like
a bolt from out of Heaven.   In one or two, and presently
in more, the cruel laughter turned to sudden howls of pain
as a lash of bullock-hide caught them about head and
face and shoulders.

" Back there, you beasts, you animals, back ! " roared
a voice of thunder, and back they went unquestioning
before that pitiless lash, like the pack of craven hounds
they were.

It was Francesco who, single-handed, and armed with
no more than a whip, was scattering them from about his
maltreated servant as the hawk scatters a flight of noisy
sparrows.   And now between him and Lanciotto there
stood no more than the broad bulk of Ercole Fortemani,
his back to the Count ; for, as yet, he had not realised the
interruption.

Francesco dropped his whip, and setting one hand at
the captain's girdle, and the other at his dirty neck, he
hoisted him up with a strength incredible and hurled him
from his path and into the slimy water of the tank.

There was a mighty roar drowned in a mightier splash
as Fortemani, spread-eagled, struck the surface and sank
from sight, whilst with the flying spray there came a
fetid odour to tell of the unsavouriness of that unexpected bath.

Without pausing to see the completion of his work,
Francesco stooped over his prostrate servant.

" Have the beasts hurt you, Lanciotto ? " he questioned ? "   But before the fellow could reply, one of
those hinds had sprung upon the stooping Count and
struck him with a dagger between the shoulder blades.

A woman's alarmed cry rang out, for Valentina was watching the affray from the steps of the hall, with Gonzaga at her elbow.

But Francesco's quilted brigandine had stood the test of steel, and the point of that assassin's dagger glanced harmlessly aside, doing no worse hurt than a rent in the silk surface of the garment. A second later the fellow found himself caught as in a bond of steel. The dagger was wrenched from his grasp and the point of it laid against his breast even as the Count forced him down upon his knees. In a flash was the thing done, yet to the wretched man who saw himself upon the threshold of Eternity, and who—like a true son of the Church—had a wholesome fear of hell, it seemed an hour whilst, with livid cheeks and eyes starting from his head, he waited for that poniard to sink into his heart as it was aimed. But not in his heart did the blow fall. With a sudden snort of angry amusement the Count pitched the dagger from him and brought down his clenched fist with a crushing force into the ruffian's face. The fellow sank unconscious beneath that mighty blow, and Francesco, regaining the whip that lay almost at his feet, rose up to confront what others there might be.

From the tank, standing breast-deep in that stinking water, his head and face grotesquely masked in a vile green slime of putrid vegetation, Ercole Fortemani bellowed with horrid blasphemy that he would have his aggressor's blood, but stirred never a foot to take it. Not that he was by nature wholly a coward; but, inspired by a wholesome fear of the man who could perform such a miracle of strength, he remained out of Francesco's reach, well in the middle of that square basin, and lustily roared orders to his men to tear the fellow to pieces. But his men had seen enough of the Count's methods, and made no advance upon that stalwart, dauntless figure that stood waiting for them with a whip which several had already tasted. Huddled together, more like a flock of frightened sheep than a body of men of war, they stood near the entrance tower, the mock of Peppe, who from the stone-gallery above—much to the amusement of Valentina's ladies and two pert pages that were with them—applauded in high-flown terms their wondrous valour.

They stirred at last, but it was at Valentina's bidding.
She had been conferring with Gonzaga, who—giving it for
his reason that she, herself, might need protection—had
remained beside her, well out of the fray.   She had been
urging him to do something, and at last he had obeyed her
and moved down the short flight of steps into the court;
but so reluctantly and slowly that, with an exclamation
of impatience, she suddenly brushed past him herself to
do the task she had begged of him.   Past Francesco she
went with a word of such commendation of his valour and
a look of such deep admiration that the blood sprang
responsive to his cheek.   She paused with a solicitous
inquiry for the now risen but sorely bruised Lanciotto.
She flashed an angry look and an angry command of
silence at the great Ercole, still bellowing from his tank,
and then, within ten paces of his followers, she halted,
and with wrathful mien, and hand outstretched towards
their captain, she bade them arrest him.

That sudden, unexpected order struck dumb the voci-
ferous Fortemani.   He ceased, and gaped at his men,
who eyed one another now in doubt ; but the doubt was
quickly dispelled by the lady's own words :

" You will make him prisoner, and conduct him to the
guardroom, or I will have you and him swept out of my
castle," she informed them, as confidently as though
she had a hundred men-at-arms to do her bidding on
them.

A pace or so behind her stood the lily-cheeked Gonzaga,
gnawing his lip, timid and conjecturing.   Behind him
again loomed the stalwart height of Francesco del Falco
with, at his side, Lanciotto, of mien almost as resolute
as his own.

That was the full force with which the lady spoke of
sweeping them—as if they had been so much foulness—
trom Roccaleone, unless they did her bidding. They were
still hesitating, when the Count advanced to Valentina's
side.

" You have heard the choice our lady gives you," he
said sternly.   " Let us know whether you will obey or
disobey.   This choice that is yours now may not be
yours again.   But if you elect to disobey Madonna, the
gate is behind you, the bridge still down.   Get you gone ! "

Furtively, from under lowering brows, Gonzaga darted a look of impotent malice at the Count. Whatever issue had the affair, this man must not remain in Roccaleone. He was too strong, too dominant, and he would render himself master of the place by no other title than that strength of his and that manner of command which Gonzaga accounted a coarse, swashbuckling bully's gift, but would have given much to be possessed of. Of how strong and dominant indeed he was never had Francesco offered a more signal proof. Those men, bruised and maltreated by him, would beyond doubt have massed together and made short work of one less dauntless ; but when a mighty courage such as his goes hand-in-hand with the habit of command such hinds as they can never long withstand it. They grumbled something among themselves, and one of them at last made answer :

"Noble sir, it is our captain that we are bidden to arrest."

"True ; but your captain, like yourselves, is in this lady's pay ; and she, your true, your paramount commander, bids you arrest him." And now, whilst yet they hesitated, his quick wits flung them the bait that must prove most attractive. "He has shown himself to-day unfitted for the command entrusted him, and it may become a question, when he has been judged, of choosing one of you to fill the place he may leave empty."

Hinds were they in very truth ; the scum of the bravi that haunted the meanest borgo of Urbino. Their hesitation vanished, and such slight loyalty as they felt towards Ercole was overruled by the prospect of his position and his pay, should his disgrace become accomplished.

They called upon him to come forth from his refuge, where he still stood, dumb and stricken at this sudden turn events had taken. He sullenly refused to obey the call to yield, until Francesco—who now assumed command with a readiness that galled Gonzaga more and more—bade one of them go fetch an arquebuse and shoot the dog. At that he cried out for mercy, and came wading to the edge of the tank swearing that if the immersion had not drowned him it were a miracle, but he was poisoned.

Thus closed an incident that had worn a mighty ugly look, and it served to open Valentina's eyes to the true quality of the men Gonzaga had hired her. Maybe that it opened his own, for that amiable lute-thrummer was green of experience in these matters. She bade Gonzaga care for Francesco, and called one of the grinning pages from the gallery to be his esquire. A room was placed at his disposal for the little time that he might spend at Roccaleone whilst she debated what her course should be.

A bell tolled in the far southern wing of the castle beyond the second courtyard and summoned her to chapel, for there Fra Domenico said Mass each morning. And so she took her leave of Francesco, saying she would pray Heaven to direct her to a wise choice whether to fly from Roccaleone or whether to remain and ward off the onslaught of Gian Maria.

Francesco, attended by Gonzaga and the page, repaired to a handsome room under the Lion's Tower, which rose upon the south-eastern angle of the fortress. His windows overlooked the second, or inner, courtyard, across which Valentina and her ladies, were now speeding on their way to Mass.

Gonzaga made shift to stifle the resentment that he felt against this man, in whom he saw an interloper, and strove to treat him with the courtesy that was his due. He would even have gone the length of discussing with him the situation—prompted by a certain mistrust, and cunningly eager to probe the real motive that had brought this stranger to interest himself in the affairs of Valentina. But Francesco, wearily, yet with an unimpeachable politeness, staved him off, and requested that Lanciotto might be sent to attend him. Seeing the futility of his endeavours, Gonzaga withdrew in increased resentment, but with a heightened sweetness of smile and profoundness of courtesies.

He went below to issue orders for the raising of the bridge, and, finding the men singularly meek and tractable after the sharp lesson Francesco had read them, he vented upon them some of the vast ill-humour that possessed him. Next he passed on to his own apartments, and there he sat himself by a window overlooking the

castle gardens, with his unpleasant thoughts for only
company.

But presently his mood lightened and he took courage,
for he could be very brave when peril was remote. It
was best, he reflected, that Valentina should leave
Roccaleone. Such was the course he would advise and
urge. Naturally, he would go with her, and so he might
advance his suit as well elsewhere as in that castle. On
the other hand, if she remained, why, so would he, and,
after all, what if Gian Maria came ? As Francesco had
said, the siege could not be protracted, thanks to the
tangled affairs of Babbiano. Soon Gian Maria would be
forced to turn him homeward to defend his Duchy.   If,
then, for a little while they could hold him in check,
all would yet be well. Surely he had been over-quick to
despond.

He rose and stretched himself with indolent relish,
then pushing wide his casement he leaned out to
breathe the morning air. A soft laugh escaped him.
He had been a fool indeed to plague himself with fears
when he had first heard of Gian Maria's coming. Pro-
perly viewed, it became a service Gian Maria did him—
whether they remained or whether they went.   Love
has no stronger promoter than a danger shared, and a
week of such disturbances as Gian Maria was likely to
occasion them should do more to advance his suit than he
might hope to achieve in a whole month of peaceful
wooing. Then the memory of Francesco set a wrinkle
'twixt his brows, and he bethought him how taken Valentina had been with the fellow when first she had beheld
him at Acquasparta, and of how, as she rode that day,
she had seen naught but the dark eyes of this Knight
Francesco.

" Knight Francesco of what or where ? " he muttered
to himself. " Bah ! A nameless, homeless adventurer ;
a swashbuckling bully, reeking of blood and leather, and
fit to drive such a pack as Fortemani's. But with a lady
—what shall such an oaf attain, how shall he prevail ? "
He laughed the incipient jealousy to scorn, and his brow
grew clear, for now he was in an optimistic mood—perhaps a reaction from his recent tremors. " Yet, by the
Host ! " he pursued, bethinking him of the amazing

K

boldness Francesco had shown in the yard, " he has the strength of Hercules, and a way with him that makes him feared and obeyed. Pish ! " he laughed again, as, turning, he unhooked his lute from where it hung upon the wall. " The by-blow of some *condottiero* who blends with his father's bullying arrogance the peasant soul of his careless mother. And I fear that such a one as that shall touch the heart of my peerless Valentina ? Why, it is a thought that does her but poor honour."

And dismissing Francesco from his mind, he sought the strings with his fingers, and thrummed an accompaniment as he returned to the window, his voice, wondrous sweet and tender, breaking into a gentle love-song.

CHAPTER XV

Monna Valentina and her ladies dined at noon in a small chamber opening from the great hall, and thither were bidden Francesco and Gonzaga. The company was waited upon by the two pages, whilst Fra Domenico, with a snow-white apron girt about his portentous waist, brought up the steaming viands from the kitchen, where he had prepared them; for, like a true coventional, he was something of a master in the confection—and a very glutton in the consumption—of delectable comestibles. The kitchen was to him as the shrine of some minor cult, and if his breviary and beads commanded from him the half of the ecstatic fervour of his devotions to pot and pan, to cauldron and to spit, then was canonisation indeed assured him.

He set before them that day a dinner than which a better no prince commanded, unless it were the Pope. There were ortolans, shot in the valley, done with truffles that made the epicurean Gonzaga roll his eyes, translated through the medium of his palate into a very paradise of sensual delight. There was a hare, trapped on the hillside and stewed in Malmsey, of a flavour so delicate that Gonzaga was regretting him his heavy indulgence in the ortolans; there was trout, fresh caught in the stream below, and a wondrous pasty that turned liquid in the mouth. To wash down these good things there was stout red wine of Puglia and more delicate Malvasia, for in his provisioning of the fortress Gonzaga had contrived that, at least, they should not go thirsty.

" For a garrison awaiting siege you fare mighty well at Roccaleone," was Francesco's comment on that excellent repast.

It was the fool who answered him. He sat out of sight upon the floor, hunched against the chair of one of Valentina's ladies, who now and again would toss him down a morsel from her plate, much as she might have treated a favourite hound.

"You have the friar to thank for it," said he, in a muffled voice, for his mouth was crammed with pasty. "Let me be damned when I die if I make him not my confessor. The man who can so minister to bodies should deal amazingly well with souls. Fra Domenico, you shall confess me after sunset."

"You need me not," answered the monk, in disdainful wrath. "There is a beatitude for such as you—' blessed are the poor in spirit.' "

"And is there no curse for such as you, flashed back the fool. "Does it say nowhere—' Damned are the gross of flesh, the fat and rotund gluttons who fashion themselves a god of their own bellies ' ? "

With his sandalled foot the friar caught the fool a surreptitious kick.

"Be still, you adder, you bag of venom."

Fearing worse, the fool gathered himself up.

"Beware !" he cried shrilly. "Bethink you, friar, that anger is a cardinal sin. Beware, I say ! "

Fra Domenico checked his upraised hand and fell to muttering scraps of Latin, his lids veiling his suddenly downcast eye. Thus Peppe gained the door.

"Say, friar ; in my ear, now—Was that a hare you stewed, or an outworn sandal ? "

"Now, God forgive me," roared the monk, springing towards him.

"For your cooking ? Aye, pray—on your knees." He dodged a blow, ducked, and doubled back into the room. "A cook—you ? Pish ! you tun of convent lard ! Your ortolans were burnt, your trout swam in grease, your pasty——"

What the pasty may have been the company was not to learn, for Fra Domenico, crimson of face, had swooped down upon the fool, and would have caught him but that he dived under the table by Valentina's skirts and craved her protection from this gross maniac that held himself a cook.

"Now, hold your wrath, father," she said, laughing with the rest. "He does but plague you. Bear with him for the sake of that beatitude you cited, which has fired him to reprisals."

Mollified, but still grumbling threats of a beating to be bestowed on Peppe when the opportunity should better serve him, the friar turned to his domestic duties. They rose soon after, and at Gonzaga's suggestion Valentina paused in the great hall to issue orders that Fortemani be brought before her for judgment. In a score of ways, since their coming to Roccaleone, had Ercole been wanting in that respect to which Gonzaga held himself entitled, and this opportunity he seized with eagerness to vent his vindictive rancour.

Valentina begged of Francesco that he, too, would stay and help them with his wide experience, a phrase that sent an unpleasant pang through the heart of Romeo Gonzaga. It was perhaps as much to assert himself as to gratify his rancour against Fortemani that, having despatched a soldier to fetch the prisoner, he turned to suggest curtly that Ercole should be hanged at once.

"What boots a trial?" he demanded. "We were all witnesses of his insubordination, and for that there can be but one punishment. Let the animal hang!"

"But the trial is of your own suggestion," she protested.

"Nay, Madonna. I but suggested judgment. It is since you have begged Messer Francesco, here, to assist us that I opine you mean to give the knave a trial."

"Would you credit this dear Gonzaga with so much bloodthirstiness?" she asked Francesco. "Do you, sir, share his opinion that the captain should hang unheard? I fear me you do, for what I have seen of them your ways do not incline to gentleness."

Gonzaga smiled, gathering from that sentence how truly she apprised the coarse nature of this stranger. Francesco's answer surprised them.

"Nay, I hold Messer Gonzaga's an ill counsel. Show mercy to Fortemani now, where he expects none and you will have made a faithful servant of him. I know his kind."

"Ser Francesco speaks without the knowledge that we

have, Madonna," was Gonzaga's rude comment. "An
example that must be made if we would have respect and
orderliness from these men."

"Then make it an example of mercy," suggested
Francesco sweetly.

"Well, we'll see," was Valentina's answer. "I like
your counsel, Messer Francesco, and yet I see a certain
wisdom in Gonzaga's words. Though in such a case as
this I would sooner consort with folly than have a
man's death upon my conscience. But here he comes,
and, at least, we'll give him trial. Maybe he is penitent
by now."

Gonzaga sneered, and took his place on the right of
Valentina's chair, Francesco standing on her left ; and
in this fashion they disposed themselves to hold judgment
upon the captain of her forces.

He was brought in between two mailed men-at-arms,
his hands pinioned behind him, his tread heavy as that of
a man in fear, his eyes directed sullenly upon the waiting
trio, but sullenest of all upon Francesco, who had so
signally encompassed his discomfiture. Valentina spread
a hand to Gonzaga, and from Gonzaga waved it slightly
in the direction of the bully. Responsive to that gesture,
Gonzaga faced the pinioned captain truculently.

"You know your offence, knave," he bawled at him.
"Have you aught to urge that may deter us from
hanging you ? "

Fortemani raised his brows a moment in surprise at
this ferocity from one whom he had always deemed a very
woman. Then he uttered a laugh of such contempt that
the colour sprang to Gonzaga's cheek.

"Take him out——" he began furiously, when
Valentina interposed, setting a hand upon his arm.

"Nay, Gonzaga, your methods are all wrong. Tell
him—— Nay, I will question him myself. Messer
Fortemani, you have been guilty of an act of gross abuse.
You and your men were hired for me by Messer Gonzaga,
and to you was given the honourable office of captain
over them, that you might lead them in this service of
mine in the ways of duty, submission, and loyalty. In
stead of that, you were the instigator of that outrage this
morning when murder was almost done upon an

inoffensive man who was my guest.   What have you to say ? "

" That I was not the instigator," he answered sullenly.

" It is all one," she returned, " for at least it was done with your sanction, and you took a share in that cruel sport, instead of restraining it, as was clearly your duty. It is upon you, the captain, that the responsibility rests."

" Lady," he explained, " they are wild souls, but very true."

" True to their wildness, maybe," she answered him disdainfully.   Then she proceeded : " You will remember that twice before has Messer Gonzaga had occasion to admonish you.   These last two nights your men have behaved riotously within my walls.   There has been hard drinking, there has been dicing and such brawling once or trice as led me to think there would be throats cut among your ranks.   You were warned by Messer Gonzaga to hold your followers in better leash, and yet to-day, without so much as drunkenness to excuse them, we have this vile affair, with yourself for a ringleader in it."

There followed a pause, during which Ercole stood with bent head like one who thinks, and Francesco turned his wonder-laden glance upon this slight girl with the gentle brown eyes which had been so tender and pitiful.   Marvelling at the greatness of her spirit, he grew—all unconsciously—the more enslaved.

Gonzaga, all unconcerned in this, eyed Fortemani in expectation of his answer.

" Madonna," said the bully at last, " what can you look for from such a troop as this ?   Messer Gonzaga cannot have expected me to enlist acolytes for a business that he told me bordered upon outlawry.   Touching their drunkenness and the trifle of rioting, what soldiers have not these faults ?   When they have them not, neither have they merit.   The man that is tame in times of peace is a skulking woman in times of war.   For the rest, whence came the wine they drank ?   It was of Messer Gonzaga's providing."

" You lie, hound ! " blazed Gonzaga.   " I provided wine for Madonna's table, not for the men."

" Yet some found its way to them, which is well.   For water on the stomach makes a man poor-spirited.   Where

is the sin of a little indulgence, Madonna ? " he went on,
turning again to Valentina. " These men of mine will
prove their mettle when it comes to blows. They are
dogs perhaps—but mastiffs every one of them, and would
lose a hundred lives in your service if they had them."

" Aye, if they had them," put in Gonzaga sourly ;
but having no more than one apiece, they'll not care to
spare it."

" Nay, there you wrong them," cried Fortemani, with
heat. " Give them a leader strong enough to hold them,
to encourage and subject them, and they will go anywhere
at his bidding."

" And there," put in Gonzaga quickly, " you bring
back to the main issue. Such a leader you have shown
us that you are not. You have done worse. You have
been insubordinate when you should not only have been
orderly, but have enforced orderliness in others.
And for that, by my lights, you should be hanged.
Waste no more time on him, Madonna," he concluded,
turning to Valentina. " Let the example be made."

" But, Madonna——" began Fortemani, paling under
the tan of his rugged countenance.

Gonzaga silenced him.

" Your words are vain. You have been insubordinate,
and for insubordination there is but one penalty."

The bully hung his head, deeming himself lost, and
lacking the wit to retort as Francesco unexpectedly
retorted for him.

" Madonna, there your adviser is at fault. The
charge against the man is wrong. There has been no
insubordination."

" How ? " she questioned, turning to the Count.
" None, say you ? "

" A Solomon is arisen," sneered Gonzaga. Then
peevishly : " Waste not words with him, Madonna," he
pursued. " Our business is with Fortemani."

" But stay, my good Gonzaga. He may be right."

" Your heart is over tender," answered Romeo impatiently. But she had turned from him now, and was
begging Francesco to make his meaning clearer.

" Had he raised his hand against you, Madonna, or
even against Messer Gonzaga, or had he disobeyed an

order given him by either of you, then, and then only, could there be question of insubordination. But he has done none of these things. He is guilty of grossly misusing my servant, it is true, but there is no insubordination in that, since he was under no promise of loyalty to Lanciotto.''

They stared at him as though his words were words of recondite wisdom instead of the simple statement of a plain case, Gonzaga crestfallen, Fortemani with a light of hope and wonder shining in his eyes, and Madonna with a faint nodding of the head that argued agreement. They wrangled a while yet, Gonzaga bitter and vindictive and rashly scornful of both Francesco and Fortemani. But the Count so resolutely held the ground he had taken that in the end Valentina shrugged her shoulders, acknowledged herself convinced, and bade Francesco deliver judgment.

'' You are in earnest, Madonna ? '' quoth Francesco in surprise, whilst a black scowl disfigured the serenity of Gonzaga's brow.

'' I am indeed. Deal with him as you account best and most just, and it shall fare with him precisely as you ordain.''

Francesco turned to the men-at-arms. '' Unbind him, one of you,'' he said shortly.

'' I believe that you are mad,'' cried Gonzaga in a frenzy, but his mood sprang rather from the chagrin of seeing his interloper prevail where he had failed. '' Madonna, do not heed him.''

'' I pray you let be, my good Gonzaga,'' she answered soothingly, and Gonzaga, ready to faint from spite, obeyed her.

'' Leave him there, and go,'' was Paolo's next order to the men, and they departed, leaving the astonished Fortemani standing alone, unbound and sheepish.

'' Now mark me well, Messer Fortemani,'' Francesco admonished him. '' You did a cowardly thing, unworthy of the soldier that you would have men believe you. And for that, I think, the punishment you received at my hands has been sufficient, in that the indignity to which I submitted you has shaken your standing with your followers. Go back to them now and retrieve what you have lost, and see that in the future you are worthier. Let this be a lesson to you, Messer Fortemani. You have gone perilously near hanging, and you have had it proved to you that in moments of peril your men are ready to raise their hands against you. Why is that? Because you have not sought their respect. You have been too much of a fellow of theirs in their drinking and their brawling, instead of holding yourself aloof with dignity."

"Lord, I have learnt my lesson!" answered the cowed bully.

"Then act upon it. Resume your command, and discipline your men to a better order. Madonna, here, and Messer Gonzaga will forget this thing. Is it not so, Madonna? Is it not so, Messer Gonzaga?"

Swayed by his will and by an intuition that told her that to whatever end he might be working, he was working wisely, Valentina gave Fortemani the assurance Francesco begged, and Gonzaga was forced grudgingly to follow her example.

Fortemani bowed low, his face pale and his limbs trembling as not even fear had made them tremble. He advanced towards Valentina, and sinking on one knee he humbly kissed the hem of her gown.

"Your clemency, Madonna, shall give you no regret. I will serve you to the death, lady, and you, lord." At the last words he raised his eyes to Francesco's calm face. Then, without so much as a glance at the disappointed Gonzaga, he rose, and bowing again—a very courtier—he withdrew.

The closing of the door was to Gonzaga a signal to break out in a torrent of bitter reproofs against Francesco, reproofs that were stemmed midway by Valentina.

"You are beside yourself, Gonzaga," she exclaimed. "What has been done has been done with my sanction. I do not doubt the wisdom of it."

"Do you not? God send you never may! But that man will know no peace until he is avenged on us."

"Messer Gonzaga," returned Francesco, with an incomparable politeness, "I am an older man than are you, and maybe that I have seen more warring and more of such men. There is a certain valour lurks in that bully for all his blustering boastfulness and swagger, and there is, too, a certain sense of justice. Mercy he has had to-day, and time will show how right I am in having pardoned him in Madonna's name. I tell you, sir, that nowhere has Monna Valentina a more faithful servant than he is now likely to become."

" I believe you, Messer Francesco. Indeed, I am sure your act was wisdom itself."

Gonzaga gnawed his lip.

" I may be wrong," said he in grudging acquiescence " I hope, indeed, I may be."

CHAPTER XVI

GONZAGA UNMASKS

The four great outer walls of Roccaleone stood ranged into a mighty square, of which the castle proper occupied but half. The other half, running from north to south, was a stretch of garden broken into three terraces. The highest of these was no more than a narrow alley under the southern wall, roofed from end to end by a trellis of vines on beams blackened with age, supported by uprights of granite, square and roughly hewn.

Asteep flight of granite steps, weedy in the in terstices of the old stone, and terminating in a pair of couchant lions at the base, led down to the middle terrace, which was called the upper garden. This was slpit in twain by a very gallery of gigantic box-tress running down towards the lower terrace, and bearing eloquent witness to the age of that old garden. Into this gallery no sun ever penetrated by more than a furtive ray, and on the hottest day in summer a grateful cool dwelt in its green gloom. Rose gardens spread on either side of it, but neglect of late had left them rank with weeds.

The third and lowest of these terraces, which was longer and bróader than either of those above, was no more than a smooth stretch of lawn, bordered by acacias and plane-trees, from the extreme corner of which sprang a winding iron-railed staircase of stone leading to an eerie which corresponded diagonally with the Lion's Tower where the Count of Aquila was lodged.

On this green lawn, Valentina's ladies and a page beguiled the eventide of a game of bowls, their clumsiness at the unwonted pastime provoking the good-humoured banter of Peppe, who looked on, and their own still better-humoured laughter.

Fortemani, too, was there, brazening out the morning's affair, which it almost seemed he must have forgotten, so self-possessed and mightily at his ease was he. He was of the kind with whom shame strikes never very deeply, and he ruffled it gaily there, among the women, rolling his fierce eyes to ogle them seductively, tossing his gaudy new cloak with a high-born disdain—gloriously conscious that it would not rend in the tossing like the cloaks to which grim Circumstance had lately accustomed him—and strutting it like any cock upon a dunghill.

But the lesson he had learnt was not likely to share the same forgetfulness. Indeed, its fruits were to be observed already in the more orderly conduct of his men, four of whom, partisan on shoulder, were doing duty on the walls of the castle. They had greeted his return amongst them with sneers and derisive allusions to his immersion, but with a few choicely-aimed blows he had cuffed the noisiest into silence and a more subservient humour. He had spoken to them in a rasping, truculent tone, issuing orders that he meant should be obeyed, unless the disobeyer were eager for a reckoning with him.

Indeed, he was an altered man, and when that night his followers having drunk what he accounted enough for their good, and disregarding his orders that they should desist and get them to bed, he sent in quest of Monna Valentina. He found her in a conversation with Francesco and Gonzaga, seated in the loggia of the dining-room. They had been there since supper discussing the widsom of going and remaining, of fleeing or standing firm to receive Gian Maria. Their conference was interrupted now by Ercole with his complaint.

She despatched Gonzaga to quell the men, a course that Fortemani treated to a covert sneer. The fop went rejoicing at this proof that her estimate of his commanding qualities had nowise suffered by contrast with those of that swashbuckling Francesco. But his pride rode him to a bitter fall.

They made a mock of his remonstrances, and when he emulated Francesco's methods, addressing them with sharp ferocity, and dubbing them beasts and swine, they caught the false ring of his fierceness, which was as unlike the true as the ring of lead is unlike that of silver. They

jeered his insults, they mimicked his tenor voice, which
excitement had rendered shrill, and they bade him go
thrum a lute for his lady's delectation, and leave men's
work to men.

His anger rose, and they lost patience ; and from showing their teeth in laughter they began to show them in
snarls.   At this his ferocity deserted him.   Brushing past
Fortemani, who stood cold and contemptuous by the
doorway watching the failure he had expected, he returned with burning cheeks and bitter words to Madonna
Valentina.

She was dismayed at the tale he bore her, magnified
to cover his own shame.   Francesco sat quietly drum-
ming on the sill, his eyes upon the moonlit garden below,
and never by word or sign suggesting that he might succeed where Romeo had failed.   At last she turned to him.

" Could you——— ? " she began, and stopped, her eyes
wandering back to Gonzaga, loath to further wound a
pride that was very sore already.   On the instant
Francesco rose.

" I might try, Madonna," he said quietly, " although
Messer Gonzaga's failure gives me little hope.   And
yet it may be that he has taken the keen edge from their
assurance, and that, thus, an easier task awaits me.   I
will try, Madonna."   And with that he went.

" He will succeed, Gonzaga," she said, after he had
gone.   " He is a man of war, and knows the words to
which these fellows have no answer."

" I wish him well of his errand," sneered Gonzaga, his
pretty face white now with sullenness.   " And I'll wager
you he fails."

But Valentina disdained the offer, whose rashness was
more than proven when, at the end of some ten minutes,
Francesco re-entered, as imperturbable as when he
went.

" They are quiet now, Madonna," he announced.

She looked at him questioningly.   " How did you
accomplish it ? " she inquired.

" I had a little difficulty," he said, " yet not overmuch.
His eyes roved to Gonzaga, and he smiled.   " Messer
Gonzaga is too gentle with them.   Too true a courtier to
avail himself of the brutality that is necessary when we

deal with brutes. You should not disdain to use your hands upon them," he admonished the fop in all seriousness, and without a trace of irony. Nor did Gonzaga suspect any.

" I soil my hands on that vermin ? " he cried in a voice of horror. " I would die sooner."

" Or else soon after," squeaked Peppe, who had entered unobserved. "*Patronia mot*, you should have seen this paladin," he continued, coming forward. " Why, Orlando was never half so furious as he when he stood there telling them what manner of dirt they were, and bidding them to bed ere he drove them with a broomstick."

" And they went ? " she asked.

"Not at first," said the fool. " They had drunk enough to make them very brave, and one who was very drunk was so brave as to assault him. But Ser Francesco fells him with his hands, and calling Fortemani he bids him have the man dropped in a dungeon to grow sober. Then, without waiting so much as to see his orders carried out, he stalks away, assured that no more was needed. Nor was it. They rose up, muttering a curse or two, maybe—yet not so loud that it might reach the ears of Fortemani—and got themselves to bed."

She looked again at Francesco with admiring eyes and spoke of his audacity in commending terms. This he belittled ; but she persisted.

" You have seen much warring, sir," she half asked, half asserted.

" Why, yes, Madonna."

And here the writhing Gonzaga espied his opportunty.

" I do not call to mind your name, good sir," he purred.

Francesco half-turned towards him, and for all that his mind was working with a lightning quickness his face was indolently calm. To disclose his true identity he deemed unwise, for all connected with the Sforza brood must earn mistrust at the hands of Valentina. It was known that the Count of Aquila stood high in the favour of Gian Maria, and the news of his sudden fall and banishment could not have reached Guidobaldo's niece who had fled before the knowledge of it was in Urbino.

His name would awaken suspicion, and any story of
disgrace and banishment might be accounted the very
mask to fit a spy. There was this sleek, venomous
Gonzaga, whom she trusted and relied on, to whisper
insidiously into her ear.

"My name," he said serenely, "is, as I have told
you—Francesco."

"But you have another?" quoth Valentina, interest
prompting the question.

"Why, yes, but so closely allied to the first as to be
scarce worth reciting, I am Francesco Franceschi, a
wandering knight."

"And a true one, as I know." She smiled at him so
sweetly that Gonzaga was enraged.

"I have not heard the name before," he murmured,
adding : "Your father was——?"

"A gentleman of Tuscany."

"But not at Court?" suggested Romeo.

"Why, yes, at Court."

Then with a sly insolence that brought the blood to
Francesco's cheeks, though to the chaste mind of Valentina's it meant nothing. "Ah!" he rejoined. "But
then, your mother—— ?"

"Was more discriminating, sir, than yours," came the
sharp answer, and from the shadows the fool's smothered
burst of laughter added gall to it.

Gonzaga rose heavily, drawing a sharp breath, and the
two men stabbed each other with their eyes. Valentina,
uncomprehending, looked from one to the other.

"Sirs, sirs, what have you said?" she cried. "Why
all this war of looks?"

"He is over-quick to take offence, Madonna, for an
honest man," was Gonzaga's answer. "Like the snake
in the grass, he is very ready with his sting when we seek
to disclose him."

"For shame, Gonzaga," she cried, now rising too.
"What are you saying? Are you turned witless?
Come, sirs, since you are both my friends, be friends
each with the other."

"Most perfect syllogism?" murmured the fool,
unheeded.

"And you, Messer Francesco, forget his words. He

means them not. He is very hot of fancy, but sweet of heart, this good Gonzaga."

On the instant the cloud lifted from Francesco's brow.

"Why, since you ask me," he answered, inclining his head, "if he'll but say he meant no malice by his words, I will confess as much for mine."

Gonzaga, cooling, saw that haply he had gone too far, and was readier to make amends. Yet in his bosom he nursed an added store of poison, a breath of which escaped him as he was leaving Valentina, and after Francesco had already gone :

"Madonna," he muttered, "I mistrust that man."

"Mistrust him ? Why ? " she asked, frowning despite her faith in the magnificent Romeo.

"I know not why ; but it is here. I feel it." And with with his hand he touched the region of his heart. "Say that he is no spy, and call me a fool."

"Why, I'll do both," she laughed. Then more sternly added : " Get you to bed, Gonzaga. Your wits play you false. Peppino, call my ladies."

In the moment that they were left alone he stepped close up to her, spurred to madness by the jealous pangs he had that day endured. His face gleamed white in the candlelight, and in his eyes there was a lurking fierceness that gave her pause.

"Have your way, Madonna," he said, in a concentrated voice ; " but to-morrow, whether we go hence or whether we stay, he remains not with us."

She drew herself up to the full of her slender, graceful height, her eyes on a level with Gonzaga's own.

"That," she answered, "is as shall be decreed by me or him."

He breathed sharply, and his voice hardened beyond belief in one usually so gentle of tone and manner.

"Be warned, Madonna," he muttered, coming so close that with the slightest swaying she must touch him, " that if this nameless *sbirro* shall ever dare to stand twixt you and me, by God and His saints, I'll kill him ! Be warned, I say."

And the door reopening at that moment, he fell back, bowed, and, brushing past the entering ladies, gained the threshold. Here someone tugged at the prodigious foliated sleeves that spread beside him on the air like the wings of a bird. He turned and saw Peppino motioning him to lower his head.

" A word in your ear, Magnificent. There was a man once went out for wool that came back shorn."

Angrily cuffing the fool aside, he was gone.

Valentina sank down upon her window-seat in a turmoil of mingled anger and amazement that paled her cheek and set her bosom heaving. It was the first hint of his aims respecting her that Gonzaga had ever dared let fall, and the condition in which it left her boded ill for his ultimate success. Her anger he could have borne, had he beheld it, for he would have laid it to the score of the tone he had taken with her. But her incredulity that he could indeed have dared to mean that which her senses told her he had meant would have shown him how hopeless was his case and how affronted, how outraged in soul she had been left by this moment of self-revealing. He would have understood then that in her eyes he never had been, was never like to be, aught but a servant—and one, hereafter, that, deeming presumptuous, she would keep at greater distance.

But he, dreaming little of this as he paced his chamber, smiled at his thoughts, which flowed with ready optimism. He had been a fool to give way so soon, perhaps. The season was not yet; the fruit was not ripe enough for plucking; still, what should it signify that he had given the tree a slight premonitory shake? A little premature, perhaps, but it would predispose the fruit to fall. He bethought him of her never-varying kindness to him, her fond gentleness, and he lacked the wit to see that this was no more than the natural sweetness that flowed from her as freely as flows the perfume from the flower—because Nature has so fashioned it, and not because Messer Gonzaga likes the smell. Lacking that wit, he went in blissful confidence to bed, and smiled himself softly to his sleep.

Away in the room under the Lion's Tower the Count of Aquila, too, paced his chamber ere he sought his couch, and in his pacing caught sight of something that arrested his attention, and provoked a smile. In a corner, among his harness which Lanciotto had piled there, his shield threw back the light, displaying the Sforza lion quartered with the Aquila eagle.

"Did my sweet Gonzaga get a glimpse of that he would have no further need to pry into my parentage," he mused. And dragging the escutcheon from amongst that heap of armour, he softly opened his window and flung it far out, so that it dropped with a splash into the moat. That done, he went to bed, and he, too, fell asleep with a smile upon his lips and in his mind a floating vison of Valentina. She needed a strong and ready hand to guide her in this rebellion against the love-at-arms of Gian Maria, and that hand he swore should be his, unless she scorned the offer of it. And so, murmuring her name with a lingering fervour, of whose true significance he was all-nescient, he sank to sleep, nor waked again until a thundering at his door aroused him. And to his still dormant senses came the voice of Lanciotto, laden with the hurry and alarm.

"Awake, Lord! Up, afoot! We are beset."

CHAPTER XVII

THE ENEMY

THE Count leapt from his bed and hastened to throw wide the door to admit his servant, who with excited face and voice bore him the news that Gian Maria had reached Roccaleone in the night and was now encamped in the plain before the castle.

He was still at his tale when a page came with the message that Monna Valentina besought Messer Francesco's presence in the great hall. He dressed in all haste, and then, with Lanciotto at his heels, he descended to answer her summons.

As he crossed the second courtyard he beheld Valentina's ladies grouped upon the chapel steps in excited discussion of this happening with Fra Domenico, who, in full canonicals, was awaiting to say the morning's Mass. He gave them a courteous "Good morrow," and passed on to the banqueting-hall, leaving Lanciotto without.

Here he found Valentina in conference with Fortemani. She was pacing the great room as she talked; but, beyond that, there was no sign of excitement in her bearing, and if any fear of the issue touched her heart now that the moment for action was at hand, it was wondrously well suppressed. At sight of Francesco a look that was partly dismay and partly pleasure lighted her face. She greeted him with such a smile as she would bestow in that hour upon none but a trusted friend. Then, with a look of regret :

"I am beyond measure grieved, sir, that you should thus stand committed to my fortunes. They will have told you that already we are besieged, and so you will see

164

how your fate is now bound up with ours. For I fear me there is no road hence for you until Gian Maria raises this siege. The choice of going or remaining is no longer mine. We must remain and fight this battle out.

"At least, lady," he answered readily, gaily almost. "I cannot share your regrets for me. The act of yours may be a madness, Madonna. but it is the bravest, sweetest madness that ever was, and I shall be proud to play my part if you'll assign me one."

"But, sir, I have no claim upon you !"

"The claim that every beset lady has upon a true knight," he assured her. "I could ask no better employment for these arms of mine than in your defence against the Duke of Babbiano. I am at your service, and with a glad heart, Monna Valentina. I have seen something of war, and you may find me useful."

"Make him Provost of Roccaleone, Madonna" urged Fortemani, whose gratitude to the man who had saved his life was blent with an admiring appreciation of his powers, of which the bully had had such practical experience.

"You hear what Ercole says ?" she cried, turning to Francesco with a sudden eagerness that showed how welcome that suggestion was."

"It was too great an honour," he answered solemnly. "Yet, if you were to place in my hands that trust, I would defend it to my last breath."

And then, before he could answer him, Gonzaga entered by the side-door and frowned to see Francesco there before him. He was a trifle pale ; he carried his cloak on the right shoulder instead of the left, and in general his apparel was less meticulous than usual and showed signs of hasty donning. With a curt nod to the Count, and an utter ignoring of Fortemani—who was scowling upon him in memory of yesterday—he bowed low before Valentina.

"I am distraught, Madonna——" he began, when she cut him short.

"You have little cause to be. Have things fallen out other than we expected ?"

"Perhaps not. Yet I had hoped that Gian Maria would not allow his humour to carry him so far."

"You had hoped that—after the message Messer Francesco brought us?" And she looked him over with an eye of sudden understanding. Yet you expressed no such hope when you advised this flight to Roccaleone. You were all for fighting then. A martial ardour consumed you. Whence this change? Is it the imminence of danger that gives it a reality too grim for your appetite?

There was a scorn in her words that wounded him as she meant it should. His last night's rashness had shown her the need to leave him in no false opinion of the extent of her esteem, and, in addition, those last words of his had shown him revealed in a new light, and she liked him the less by it.

He inclined his head slightly, shame blazing red in his cheek, that he should be thus reproved before Fortemani and that upstart Francesco. That Francesco was an upstart was no longer a matter of surmise with him. His soul assured him of it.

"Madonna," he said, with some show of dignity, ignoring her gibes, "I came to bear you news that a herald from Gian Maria craves a hearing. Shall I hold parley with him for you."

"You are too good," she answered sweetly. "I will hear the man myself."

He bowed submissively, and then his eye moved to Francesco.

"We might arrange with him for the safe-conduct of this gentleman," he suggested.

"There is no hope they would accord it," she answered easily. "Nor could I hope so if they wanted, for Messer Francesco has consented to fill the office of Provost of Roccaleone. But we are keeping the messenger waiting. Sirs, will you attend me to the ramparts?"

They bowed and followed her, Gonzaga coming last, his tread heavy as a drunkard's, his face white to the lips in the bitter rage with which he saw himself superseded, and read his answer to the hot words that last night he had whispered in Valentina's ear.

As they crossed the courtyard Francesco discharged the first act of his new office in ordering a half-dozen men-at-arms to fall in behind them, to the end that they might

make some show upon the wall when they came to parley
with the herald.

They found a tall man on a tall grey horse whose pol-
ished helm shone like silver in the morning sun, and whose
haubergeon was almost hidden under a crimson tabard
ornamented with the Sforza lion. He bowed low as Valentina appeared, followed by her escort, aforemost in
which stood the Count of Aquila, his broad castor pulled
down upon his brow, so that it left his face in shadow.

"In the name of my master, the High and Mighty Lord
Gian Maria Sforza, Duke of Babbiano, I call upon you to
yield, lady, laying down your arms and throwing open
your gates."

There followed a pause, at the end of which she asked
him was that the sum of his message, or was there
something that he had forgotten. The herald, bowing
gracefully upon the arched neck of his caracoling palfrey,
answered her that what he had said was all he had been
bidden say.

She turned with a bewildered and rather helpless look
to those behind her. She wished that the matter might
be conducted with due dignity, and her convent rearing
left her in doubt of how this might best be achieved. She
addressed herself to Francesco.

"Will you give him his answer, my Lord Provost," she
said with a smile, and Francesco, stepping forward and
leaning on a merlon of that embattled wall, obeyed her.

"Sir Herald," he said, in a gruff voice that was unlike
his own, "will you tell me since when has the Duke of
Babbiano been at war with Urbino that he should thus
beset one of its fortresses and demand the surrender of
it?"

"His Highness," replied the herald, "is acting with
the full sanction of the Duke of Urbino in sending this
message to the Lady Valentina della Rovere."

At that Valentina elbowed the Count aside, and forget-
ting her purpose of conducting this affair with dignity,
she let her woman's tongue deliver the answer of her
heart.

"This message, sir, and the presence here of your
master, is but another of the impertinences that I have
suffered at his hands, and it is the crowning one. Take

you that message back to him, and tell him that when I am instructed by what right he dares to send you upon such an errand, I may render him an answer more germaine with his challenge.

" Would you prefer, Madonna, that his Highness shoud come himself to speak with you ? "

" There is nothing I should prefer less. Already has necessity compelled me to have more to say to Gian Maria than I could have wished." And with a proud gesture she signified that the audience was at an end, and turned to quit the wall.

She had a brief conference with Francesco, during which he consulted her as to certain measures of defence to be taken, and made suggestions, to all of which she agreed, her hopes rising fast to see that here, at least, she had a man with knowledge of the work to which he had set his hand. It lightened her heart and gave her a glad confidence to look on that straight, martial figure, the hand so familiarly resting on the hilt of the sword that seemed a part of him, and the eyes so calm ; whilst when he spoke of perils, they seemed to dwindle 'neath the disdain of them so manifest in his tone.

With Fortemani at his heels he went about the execution of the measures he had suggested, the bully following him now with the faithful wonder of a dog for its master, realising that here, indeed, was a soldier of fortune by comparison with whom the likes of himself were no better than camp-followers. Confidence, too, did Ercole gather from that magnetism of Francesco's unfaltering confidence ; for he seemed to treat the matter as a great jest, a comedy played for the Duke of Babbiano and at that same Duke's expense. And just as Francesco's brisk tone breathed confidence into Fortemani and Valentina, so, too, did it breathe it into Fortemani's wretched followers. They grew zestful in the reflection of his zest, and out of admiration for him they came to admire the business on which they were engaged and finally to take a pride in the part he assigned to each of them. Within an hour there was such diligent bustle in Roccaleone, such an air of grim gaiety and high spirits, that Valentina, observing it, wondered what manner of magician was this she had raised to the command of her fortress who in so little time could work so marvellous a change in the demeanour of her garrison.

Once only did Francesco's light-heartedness fail him, and this was when, upon visiting the armoury, he found but one single cask of gunpowder stored there. He turned to Fortemani to inquire where Gonzaga had bestowed it, and Fortemani being as ignorant as himself upon the subject he went forthwith in quest of Gonzaga. After ransacking the castle for him, he found him pacing the vine-alley in the garden in animated conversation with Valentina. At his approach the courtier's manner grew more subdued, and his brows sullen.

"Messer Gonzaga," Francesco hailed him. The courtier, surprised looked up. "Where have you hidden your store of powder?"

"Powder?" faltered Gonzaga, chilled by a sudden apprehension, "Is there none in the armoury?"

"Yes—one small cask, enough to load a cannon once or twice, leaving us nothing for our hand-guns. Is that your store?"

"If that is all there is in the armoury, that is all we have."

Francesco stood speechless, staring at him, a dull flush creeping into his cheeks. In that moment of wrath he forgot their positions, and gave never a thought to the smarting that must be with Gonzaga at the loss of rank he had suffered since Valentina had appointed a provost.

"And are these your methods of fortifying Roccaleone?" he asked in a voice that cut like a knife. "You have laid in a good store of wine, a flock of sheep, and endless delicacies, sir," he jeered. "Did you expect to pelt the enemy with these, or did you reckon upon no enemy at all?"

Now this question touched so closely upon the truth, that it fired in Gonzaga's bosom an anger that for the moment made a man of him. It was the last breath that blew into a blaze the smouldering wrath he carried in his soul.

His retort came fierce and hot. It was as unmeasured and contemptuous as Francesco's erst recriminations, and it terminated in a challenge to the Count to meet him on

horse or foot, with sword or lance, and that as soon as
might be.

But Valentina intervened and rebuked them both.
Yet to Francesco her rebuke was courteous, and ended
in a prayer that he should do the best with such resources
as Roccaleone offered ; to Gonzaga it was contemptuous in the last degree, for Francesco's question—which
Gonzaga had left unanswered—coming at a moment
when she was full of suspicions of Gonzaga and the ends
he had sought to serve in advising her upon a course
which he had since shown himself so utterly unfitted to
guide, had opened wide her eyes.   She remembered
how strangely moved he had been upon learning yesterday that Gian Maria was marching upon Roccaleone,
and how ardently he had advised flight from the fortress
—he that had so bravely talked of holding it against
the Duke.

They were still wrangling there in a most unseemly
fashion when a trumpet blast reached them from beyond
the walls.

" The herald again," she cried.   " Come, Messer
Francesco.   Let us hear what fresh message he brings."

She led Francesco away, leaving Gonzaga in the
shadow of the vines, reduced well-nigh to tears in the
extremity of his mortification.

The herald was returned with the announcement
that Valentina's answer left Gian Maria no alternative
but to await the arrival of Duke Guidobaldo, who was
then marching to join him.   The Duke of Urbino's
presence would be, he thought, ample justification in
her eyes for the challenge Gian Maria had sent, and
which he would send again when her uncle arrived to
confirm it.

Thereafter the remainder of the day was passed in
peace at Roccaleone, if we except the very hell of unrest
that surged in the heart of Romeo Gonzaga.   He sat
disregarded at supper that evening save by Valentina's
ladies and the fool, who occasionally rallied him upon his
glumness.   Valentina herself turned her whole attention
to the Count, and whilst Gonzaga—Gonzaga, the poet
of burning fancy, the gay songster, the acknowledged wit,
the mirror of courtliness—was silent and tongue-tied,

this ruffling, upstart swashbuckler entertained them with a sprightliness that won him every heart—always excepting that of Romeo Gonzaga.

Francesco made light of the siege in a manner that enlivened every soul present with relief. He grew merry at the expense of Gian Maria and made it very plain that he could have found naught more captivating to his war-like fancy than this business upon which an accident had embarked him. He was as full of confidence for the issue as he was full of eager anticipation of the fray itself.

It is wonderful that—never having known any but artificial men ; men of court and antechamber ; men of dainty ways and mincing, affected tricks of speech ; in short, such men as circumstance ordains shall surround the great—Monna Valentina's eyes should open very wide the better to behold this new pattern of a man ; who, whilst clearly a gentleman of high degree, carried with him an air of the camp rather than the *camerion*, was imbued by a spirit of chivalry and adventure, and ignored with a certain lofty dignity, as if beneath his observance, the poses that she was wont to see characterising the demeanour of the gentlemen of his Highness, her uncle.

He was young, moreover, yet no longer callow; comely, yet with a strong male comeliness ; he had a pleasantly modulated voice, yet one that they had heard swell into a compelling note of command ; he had the most joyous, careless laugh in all the world—such a laugh as endears a man to all that hear it—and he indulged it without stint.

Gonzaga sat glum and moody, his heart bursting with the resentment of the mean and the incompetent for the man of brilliant parts. But the morrow was to bring him worse.

The Duke of Urbino arrived next morning and rode up to the moat in person, attended only by a trumpeter who, for the third time, wound a note of challenge to the fortress.

As on the previous day, Valentina answered the summons, attended by Francesco, Fortemani and Gonzaga —the latter uninvited yet not denied, and following sullenly in her train, in a last, despairing attempt to assert himself one of her captains.

Francesco had put on his harness and came arrayed from head to foot in resplendent steel, to do worthy honour to the occasion. A bunch of plumes nodded in his helm, and for all that his beaver was open, yet the shadows of the head-piece afforded at the distance sufficient concealment to his features.

The sight of her uncle left Valentina unmoved. Well-beloved though he was of his people, between himself and his niece he had made no effort ever to establish relations of affection. Less than ever did he now seek to prevail by the voice of kinship. He came in the panoply of war, as a prince to a rebel subject, and in precisely such a tone did he greet her.

"Monna Valentina," he said—seeming entirely to over-look the circumstance that she was his kinswoman—"deeply though this rebellion grieves me, you are not to think that your sex shall gain you any privileges or any clemency. We will treat you precisely as we would any other rebel subject who acted as you have done."

"Highness," she replied, "I solicit no privilege beyond that to which my sex gives me the absolute right, and which has no concern with war and arms. I allude to the privilege of disposing of myself, my hand and heart as it shall please me. Until you come to recognise that I am a woman endowed with a woman's nature, and until, having realised it, you are prepared to submit to it and pass me your princely word to urge the Duke of Babbiano's suit no further with me, here will I stay in spite of you, your men-at-arms, and your paltry ally, Gian Maria, who imagines that love may be made successfully in armour, and that a way to a woman's heart is to be opened with cannon-shot."

"I think we shall bring you to a more subjective and dutiful frame of mind, Madonna," was the grim answer.

"Dutiful to whom?"

"To the State, a princess of which you have had the honour to be born."

"And what of my duty to myself, to my heart, and to my womanhood? Is no account to be taken of that?"

"These are matters, Madonna, that are not to be dis-cussed in shouts from the walls of a castle—nor, indeed, do I wish to discuss them anywhere. I am here to summon you to surrender. If you resist us, you do so at your peril."

"Then at my peril I will resist you—gladly. I defy you. Do your worst against me, disgrace your manhood and the very name of chivalry by whatsoever violence may occur to you, yet I promise you that Valentina della Rovere never shall become the wife of his Highness of Babbiano."

"You refuse to open your gates?" he returned in a voice that shook with anger.

"Utterly and finally."

"And you think to persist in this?"

"As long as I have life."

The Prince laughed sardonically.

"I wash my hands of the affair and of its consequences," he answered grimly. "I leave it in the care of your future husband, Gian Maria Sforza, and if, in his very natural eagerness for the nuptials, he uses your castle roughly, the blame of it must rest with you. But what he does he does with my full sanction, and I have come hither to advise you of it since you appeared in doubt. I beg that you will remain there for a few moments to hear what his Highness himself may have to say. I trust his eloquence may prove more persuasive."

He saluted ceremoniously, and, wheeling his horse about, he rode away. Valentina would have withdrawn, but Francesco urged her to remain and await the Duke of Babbiano's coming. And so they paced the battlements, Valentina in earnest talk with Francesco, Gonzaga following in moody silence with Fortemani, and devouring them with his eyes.

From their eminence they surveyed the bustling camp in the plain, where tents, green, brown and white, were being hastily erected by half-stripped soldiers. The little army altogether may have numbered a hundred men which, in his vainglory, Gian Maria accounted all that would be needed to reduce Roccaleone. But the most formidable portion of his forces rolled into the field even as they watched. It was heralded by a hoarse groaning of the wheels of bullock-carts to the number of ten, on each of which was borne a cannon. Other carts followed with ammunition and victuals for the men encamped.

They looked on with interest at the busy scene that was toward, and as they watched they saw Guidobaldo ride into the heart of the camp and dismount. Then from out of a tent more roomy and imposing than the rest advanced the short, stout figure of Gian Maria, not to be recognised at that distance save by the keen eyes of Francesco that were familiar with his shape.

A groom held a horse for him and assisted him to mount, and then, attended by the same trumpeter that had escorted Guidobaldo, he rode forward towards the castle. At the edge of the moat he halted, and at sight of Valentina and her company he doffed his feathered hat and bowed his straw-coloured head.

"Monna Valentina," he called, and when she stepped forth in answer he raised his little cruel eyes in a malicious glance and showed the round moon of his white face to be whiter even than its wont—a pallor atrabilious and almost green.

"I am grieved that his Highness, your uncle, should not have prevailed with you. Where he has failed, I may have little hope of succeeding—by the persuasion of words. Yet I would beg you to allow me to have speech of your captain, whoever he may be."

"My captains are here in attendance," she answered tranquilly.

"So! You have a plurality of them; to command—how many men?"

"Enough," roared Francesco, interposing, his voice sounding hollow from his helmet. "to blow you and your woman-besieging scullions to perdition."

The Duke stirred on his horse and peered up at the speaker. But there was too little of his face visible for recognition, whilst his voice was altered and his figure dissembled in its steel casing.

"Who are you, rogue?" he asked.

"Rogue in your teeth, be you twenty times a Duke," returned the other, at which Valentina laughed outright.

Never from the day when he had uttered his first wail had his Highness of Babbiano heard words of such import from the lips of living man. A purple flush mottled his cheeks at the indignity of it.

"Attend to me, knave!" he bellowed. "Whatever

betide the rest of this misguided garrison when ultimately it falls into my hands, for you I can promise a rope and a cross-beam."

" Bah ! " sneered the knight. " First catch your bird. Be none so sure that Roccaleone ever will fall into your hands. While I live you do not enter here, and my life, Highness, is to me a precious thing, which I will not part with lightly."

Valentina's eyes were mirthless now as she turned them upon that gleaming, martial figure standing so proudly at her side and seeming so well attuned to the proud defiance he hurled at the princely bully below.

" Hush, sir ! " she murmured. " Do not anger him further."

" Aye," groaned Gonzaga, " in God's name say no more, or you'll undo us hopelessly."

" Madonna," said the Duke, without further heeding Francesco. " I give you twenty-four hours in which to resolve upon your action. Yonder you see them bringing the cannon into camp. When you wake to-morrow you shall find those guns trained upon your walls. Meanwhile, enough said. May I speak a word with Messer Gonzaga ere I depart ? "

" So that you depart, you may say a word to whom you will," she answered contemptuously. And, turning aside she motioned Gonzaga to the crenel she abandoned.

" I'll swear that mincing jester is trembling already with the fear of what is to come," bawled the Duke, " and perhaps fear will show him the way to reason. Messer Gonzaga ! " he called, raising his voice. " As I believe the men of Roccaleone are in your service, I call upon you to bid them throw down that drawbridge, and in the name of Guidobaldo as well as my own I promise them free pardon and no hurt—saving only that rascal at your side. But if the knaves resist me, I promise you that when I shall have dashed Roccaleone stone from stone, not a man of you all will I spare."

Shaking like an aspen, Gonzaga stood there, his voice palsied and making no reply, whereupon Francesco leant forward again.

" We have heard your terms," he answered, " and we

are not like to heed them.   Waste not the day in vain threats."

"Sir, my terms were not for you.   I know not you ; I addressed you not, nor will I suffer myself to be addressed by you."

"Linger there another moment," answered the vibrating voice of the knight, "and you will find yourself addressed with a volley of arquebuse-shot.   Ola, there ! " he commanded, turning and addressing an imaginary body of men on the lower ramparts of the garden to his left.   "Arquebusiers to the postern !   Blow your matches !   Make ready !   Now, my Lord Duke, will you draw off, or must we blow you off ? "

The Duke's reply took the form of a bunch of blasphemous threats of how he would serve his interlocutor when he came to set hands on him.

"Present arms ! " roared the knight to his imaginary arquebusiers, whereupon, without another word, the Duke turned his horse and rode off in disgraceful haste, his trumpeter following hot upon his heels, pursued by a derisive burst of laughter from Francesco.

CHAPTER XVIII

TREACHERY

"Sir," gulped Gonzaga, as they were descending from the battlements, "you will end by having us all hanged. Was that a way to address a prince?"

Valentina frowned that he should dare rebuke her knight. But Francesco only laughed.

"By St. Paul! How would you have had me address him?" he inquired. "Would you have had me use cajolery with him—the lout? Would you have had me plead mercy from him and beg him in honeyed words to be patient with a wilful lady? Let be, Messer Gonzaga, we shall weather it yet, never doubt it."

"Messer Gonzaga's courage seems of a quality that wanes as the need for it increases," said Valentina.

"You are confounding courage Madonna, with foolhardy recklessness," the courtier returned. "You may learn it to your undoing."

That Gonzaga was not the only one entertaining this opinion they were soon to learn, for, as they reached the courtyard a burly, black-browed ruffian, Cappoccio by name, thrust himself in their path.

"A word with you, Messer Gonzaga, and you, Ser Ercole." His attitude was full of truculent insolence and all paused, Francesco and Valentina turning from him to the two men whom he addressed, and waiting to hear what he might have to say to them. "When I accepted service under you I was given to understand that I was entering a business that should entail little risk to my skin. I was told that probably there would be no fighting, and that if there were, it would be no more than a brush with the Duke's men. So, too, did you assure my comrades."

"Did you indeed?" quoth Valentina, intervening, and addressing herself to Fortemani, to whom Cappoccio's words had been directed.

"I did, Madonna," answered Ercole. "But I had Messer Gonzaga's word for it."

"Did you," she continued, turning to Gonzaga, "permit their engagement on that understanding?"

"On some such understanding, yes, Madonna," he was forced to confess.

She looked at him a moment in amazement. Then:

"Messer Gonzaga," she said at length, "I think that I begin to know you."

But Cappoccio, who was nowise interested in the extent of Valentina's knowledge of the man, broke in impetuously:

"Now we have heard what has passed between this new Provost here and his Highness of Babbiano. We have heard the terms that were offered, and his rejection of them, and I am come to tell you, Ser Ercole, and you, Messer Gonzaga, that I, for one, will not remain here to be hanged when Roccaleone shall fall into the hands of Gian Maria. And there are others of my comrades who are of the same mind."

Valentina looked at the rugged, determined features of the man, and fear for the first time stole into her heart and was reflected on her countenance. She was half-turning to Gonzaga to vent upon him some of the bitterness of her humour—for him she accounted to blame—when once again Francesco came to the rescue.

"Now, shame on you, Cappoccio, for a paltry hind! Are these words for the ears of a besieged and sorely harassed lady, craven?"

"I am no craven" the man answered hoarsely, his face flushing under the whip in Francesco's scorn. "Out in the open I will take my chances and fight in any cause that pays me. But this is not my trade—this waiting for the death of a trapped rat."

Francesco met his eyes steadily for a moment, then glanced at the other men, to the number of half-score or so—all, in fact, whom the duties he had apportioned them did not hold elsewhere. They hung in the rear of Cappoccio, all ears for what was being said, and their countenances plainly showing how their feelings were in sympathy with their spokesman.

"And you a soldier, Cappoccio ? " sneered Francesco. "Shall I tell you in what Fortemani was wrong when he enlisted you ? He was wrong in not hiring you for scullion duty in the castle kitchen."

"Sir Knight ! "

"Bah ! Do you raise your voice to me ? Do you think I am of your kind, animal, to be affrighted by sounds—however hideous ? "

"I am not affrighted by sounds."

"Are you not ? Why, then, all this ado about a bunch of empty threats cast at us by the Duke of Babbiano ? If you were indeed the soldier you would have us think you, would you come here and say, ' I will not die this way, or that ? Confess yourself a boaster when you tell us that you are ready to die in the open."

"Nay ! That am I not."

"Then, if you are ready to die out there, why not in here. Shall it signify aught to him that dies where he gets his dying done ? But reassure yourself, you woman, he added with a laugh, and in a voice loud enough to be heard by the others, " you are not going to die— neither here nor there."

"When Roccaleone capitulates——"

"It will not capitulate," thundered Francesco.

"Well, then—when it is taken."

"Nor will it be taken," the Provost insisted, with an assurance that carried conviction. "If Gian Maria had time unlimited at his command, he might starve us into submission. But he has not. An enemy is menacing his own frontiers, and in a few days—a week at most—he will be forced to get him hence to defend his crown."

"The greater reason for him to use stern measures and bombard us as he threatens," answered Cappoccio shrewdly, but rather in the tone of a man who expects to have his argument disproved. And Francesco, if he could not disprove it, would at least contradict it.

"Believe it not," he cried, with a scornful laugh. " I tell you that Gian Maria will never dare so much. And if he did, are these walls that will crumble at a few cannon-shots ? Assault he might attempt ; but I need not tell

a soldier that twenty men who are stout and resolute, as
I will believe you are for all your craven words, could hold
so strong a place as this against the assault of twenty
times the men the Duke has with him. And for the rest, if
you think I tell you more than I believe myself, I ask you
to remember how I am included in Gian Maria's threat.
I am but a soldier like you, and such risks as are yours are
mine as well. Do you see any sign of faltering in me ; any
sign of doubting the issue, or any fear of a rope that shall
touch me no more than it shall touch you ? There, Cappoccio ! A less merciful provost would have hanged you
for your words—for they reek of sedition. Yet I have
stood and argued with you, because I cannot spare a
brave man such as you will prove yourself. Let us hear
no more of your doubtings. They are unworthy. Be
brave and resolute, and you shall find yourself well rewarded when the baffled Duke shall be forced to raise
this siege."

He turned without waiting for the reply of Cappoccio—
who stood crestfallen, his cheeks reddened by shame
of his threat to get him hence—and conducted Valentina
calmly across the yard and up the steps of the hall.

It was his way never to show a doubt that his orders
would be obeyed, yet on this occasion scarce had the door
of the hall closed after them when he turned sharply to
the following Ercole.

" Get you an arquebuse," he said quickly, " and take
my man Lanciotto with you. Should those dogs still
prove mutinous, fire into any that attempt the gates—
fire to kill—and send me word. But above all, Ercole, do
not let them see you or suspect your presence ; that
were to undermine such effect as my words may have
produced."

From out of a woefully pale face Valentina raised
her brown eyes to his in a look that was as a stab to the
observing Gonzaga.

" I needed a man here," she said " and I think that
Heaven it must have been that sent you to my aid. But
do you think," she asked—and with her eyes she closely
scanned his face for any sign of doubt—" that they are
pacified ? "

" I am assured of it, Madonna. Come, there are

signs of tears in your eyes, and—by my soul !—there is naught to weep at.''

" I am but a woman, after all,'' she smiled up at him, " and so, subject to a woman's weakness. It seemed as if the end were indeed come just now. It had come, but for you. If they should mutiny——''

"They shall not, while I am here,'' he answered, with a cheering confidence. And she, full of faith in this true knight of hers, went to seek her ladies and to soothe in her turn any alarm to which they might have fallen a prey.

Francesco went to disarm, and Gonzaga to take the air upon the ramparts, his heart a very bag of gall. His hatred for the interloper was as nothing now to his rage against Valentina, a rage that had its birth in a wondering uncomprehension of how she should prefer that coarse, swashbuckling bully to himself, the peerless Gonzaga. And as he walked there, under the noontide sky, the memory of Francesco's assurance that the men would not mutiny returned to him, and he caught himself most ardently desiring that they might—if only to bear it home to Valentina how misplaced was her trust, how foolish her belief in that loud boaster. He thought next—and with increasing bitterness—of his own brave schemes, of his love for Valentina and of how assured he had been that his affections were returned, before this ruffler came amongst them. He laughed in bitter scorn as the thought returned to her preferring Francesco to himself.

Well, it might be so now—now that the times were warlike, and this Francesco was such a man as shone at his best in them. But what manner of companion would this *sbirro* make in times of peace ? Had he the wit, the grace, the beauty even that was Gonzaga's ? Circumstance, it seemed to him, was to blame, and he roundly cursed that same Circumstance. In other surroundings, he was assured that she would not have cast an eye upon Francesco whilst he, himself, was by ; and if he recalled their first meeting at Acquasparta, it was again to curse Circumstance for having placed the knight in such case as to appeal to the tenderness that is a part of woman's nature.

He reflected—assured that he was right—that if Francesco had not come to Roccaleone, he might by now have been wed to Valentina ; and once wed, he could throw down the bridge and march out of Roccaleone, assured that Gian Maria would not care to espouse his widow, and no less assured that Guidobaldo— who was at heart a kind and clement prince—would be content to let be what was accomplished, since there would be naught gained beyond his niece's widowhood in hanging Gonzaga. It was the specious argument that had lured him upon this rash enterprise, the hopes that he was confident would have fructified but for the interloping of Francesco.

He stood looking down at the tented plain, with black rage and black despair blotting the beauty from the sunlight of that May morning, and then it came to him that since there was naught to be hoped from his old plans, might it not be wise to turn his attention to new ones that would at least save him from hanging For he was assured that whatever might betide the others, his own fate was sealed whether Roccaleone fell or not. It would be remembered against him that the affair was of his instigating, and from neither Gian Maria nor Guidobaldo might he look for mercy.

And now the thought of extricating himself from his desperate peril turned him cold by its suddenness. He stood very still a moment ; then looked about him as though he feared that some watching spy might read on him the ugly intention that of a sudden had leapt to life in his heart. Swiftly it spread and took more definite shape, the reflection of it showing now upon his smooth, handsome face and disfiguring it beyond belief. He drew away from the wall and took a turn or two upon the ramparts, one hand behind him, the other raised to support his drooping chin. Thus he brooded for a little while. Then with another of his furtive glances, he turned to the north-western tower and entered the armoury. There he rummaged until he had found the pen, ink, and paper that he sought, and with the door wide open—the better that he might hear the sound of approaching steps—he set himself feverishly to write. It was soon done, and he stood up, waving the sheet to dry the ink. Then he looked it over again, and this is what he had written :

I have it in my power to stir the garrison to mutiny and to throw open the gates of Roccaleone. Thus shall the castle fall immediately into your hands, and you shall have a proof of how little I am in sympathy with this rebellion of Monna Valentina's. What terms do you offer me if I accomplish it ? Answer me now, and by the same means as I am employing, but dispatch not your answer if I show myself upon the ramparts.

Romeo Gonzaga.

He folded the paper, and on the back he wrote the superscription—*To the High and Mighty Duke of Babbiano.* Then opening a large chest that stood against the wall, he rummaged a moment, and at last withdrew an arbalest quarrel. About the body of this he tied his note. Next, from the wall he took down a cross-bow, and from a corner a moulinet for winding it. With his foot in the stirrup he made the cord taut and set the shaft in position.

And now he closed the door, and, going to the window, which was little more than an arrow-slit, he shouldered his arbalest. He took careful aim in the direction of the ducal tent and loosed the quarrel. He watched its flight, and it almost thrilled him with pride in his archery to see it strike the tent at which he had aimed and set the canvas shuddering.

In a moment there was a commotion. Men ran to the spot, others emerged from the tent, and amongst the latter Gonzaga recognised the figures of Gian Maria and Guidobaldo.

The bolt was delivered to the Duke of Babbiano, who, with an upward glance at the ramparts, vanished into the tent once more.

Gonzaga moved from his eerie, and set wide the door of the tower so that his eyes could range the whole of the sun-bathed ramparts. Returning to his window, he waited impatiently for the answer. Nor was his impatience to endure long. At the end of some ten minutes Gian Maria reappeared, and, summoning an archer to his side, he

delivered him something and made a motion of his hand
towards Roccaleone.   Gonzaga moved to the door and
stood listening breathlessly.   At the least sign of an
approach he would have shown himself, and thus, by
the provision made in his letter, have cautioned the archer
against shooting his bolt.   But all was quiet, and so
Gonzaga remained where he was until something flashed
like a bird across his vision, struck sharply against the
posterior wall, and fell with a tinkle on the broad stones
of the rampart.   A moment later the answer from Gian
Maria was in his hands.

He swiftly unwound it from the shaft that had brought
it, and dropped the bolt into a corner.   Then unfolding
the letter, he read it, leaning against one of the merlons of
the wall :

*If you can devise a means to deliver Roccaleone at once
into my hands you shall earn my gratitude, full pardon for
your share in Monna Valentina's rebellion, and the sum of
a thouasnd gold florins.*

                                        Gian Maria.

As he read, a light of joy leapt to his eyes.   Gian Maria's
terms were very generous.   He would accept them, and
Valentina should realise when too late upon what manner
of broken reed she leaned in relying upon Messer Francesco.   Would he save her now, as he so loudly boasted ?
Would there indeed be no mutiny, as he so confidently
prophesied ?   Gonzaga chuckled evilly to himself.   She
should learn her lesson, and when she was Gian Maria's
wife she might perhaps repent her of her treatment of
Romeo Gonzaga.

He laughed softly to himself.   Then suddenly he turned
cold, and he felt his skin roughening.   A stealthy step
sounded behind him.

He crumpled the Duke's letter in his hand, and in the
alarm of the moment he dropped it over the wall.
Seeking vainly to compose the features that a chilling
fear had now disturbed, he turned to see who came.

Behind him stood Peppe, his solemn eyes bent with
uncanny intentness upon Gonzaga's face.

" You are seeking me ? " quoth Romeo, and the quiver in his voice sorted ill with his arrogance.

The fool made a grotesque bow.

" Monna Valentina desires that you attend her in the garden, Illustrious."

CHAPTER XIX

PLOT AND COUNTERPLOT

PEPPE'S quick eyes had seen Gonzaga crumple and drop the paper, no less than he had observed the courtier's startled face, and his suspicions had been aroused. He was by nature prying, and experience had taught him that the things men seek to conceal are usually the very things it imports most to have knowledge of. So when Gonzaga had gone in obedience to Valentina's summons the jester peered carefully over the battlements.

At first he saw nothing, and he was concluding with disappointment that the thing Gonzaga had cast from him was lost in the torrential waters of the moat. But presently, lodged on a jutting stone, above the foaming stream into which it would seem that a miracle had prevented it from falling, he espied a ball of crumpled paper. He observed with satisfaction that it lay some ten feet immediately below the postern gate by the drawbridge.

Secretly, for it was not Peppe's way to take men into his confidence where it might be avoided, he got himself a coil of rope. Having descended and quietly opened the postern, he made one end fast and lowered the other to the water with extreme care, lest he should dislodge, and so lose, that paper.

Assuring himself again that he was unobserved, he went down, hand over hand, like a monkey, his feet against the rough-hewn granite of the wall. Then, with a little swinging of the rope, he brought himself nearer that crumpled ball, his legs now dangling in the angry water, and by a mighty stretch that all but precipitated him into the torrent he seized the paper and transferred it to his teeth. Then, hand over hand again, and with a frantic haste, for he feared observation, not only from the castle sentries but also from the watchers in the besieger's camp, he climbed back to the postern, exulting in that he had gone unobserved, and contemptuous for the vigilance of those that should have observed him.

Softly he closed the wicket, locked it and shot home the bolts at top and base, and went to replace the key on its nail in the guardroom, which he found untenanted. Next, with that mysterious letter in his hand, he scampered off across the courtyard and through the porch leading to the domestic quarters, nor paused until he had gained the kitchen, where Fra Domenico was roasting the quarter of a lamb that he had that morning butchered. For now that the siege was established there was no more fish from the brook, nor hares and ortolans from the countryside.

The friar cursed the fool roundly, as was his wont upon every occasion, for he was none so holy that he disdained the milder forms of objurgatory oaths. But Peppe for once had no vicious answer ready, a matter that led the Dominican to ask him was he ill.

Never heeding him, the fool unfolded and smoothed the crumpled paper in a corner by the fire. He read it and whistled, then stuffed it into the bosom of his absurd tunic.

" What ails you ? " quoth the friar. " What have you there ? "

" A recipe for a dish of friar's brains. A most rare delicacy, and rendered costly by virtue of the scarcity of the ingredients." And with that answer Peppe was gone, leaving the monk with an ugly look in his eyes and an unuttered imprecation on his tongue.

Straight to the Count of Aquila went the fool with his letter. Francesco read it and questioned him closely as to what he knew of the manner in which it had come into Gonzaga's possession. For the rest, those lines, far from causing him the uneasiness Peppe expected, seemed a source of satisfaction and assurance to him.

" He offers a thousand gold florins," he muttered, " in addition to Gonzaga's liberty and advancement.

Why, then, I have said no more than was true when
I assured the men that Gian Maria was but idly
threatening us with bombardment. Keep this matter
secret, Peppe."

"But you will watch Messer Gonzaga ? " quoth the
fool.

"Watch him ? Why, where is the need ? You do
not imagine him so vile that this offer could tempt
him ? "

Peppe looked up, his great whimsical face screwed
into an expression of cunning doubt.

"You do not think, lord, that he invited it ? "

"Now, shame on you for that thought. Messer
Gonzaga may be an idle lute-thrummer, a poor-spirited
coward ; but a traitor——— ! And to betray Monna
Valentina ! No, no."

But the fool was far from reassured. He had had the
longer acquaintance of Messer Gonzaga, and his shrewd
eyes had long since taken the man's exact measure.
Let Francesco scorn the notion of betrayal at Romeo's
hands ; Peppe would dog him like a shadow. This
he did for the remainder of that day, clinging to Gonzaga
as if he loved him dearly, and furtively observing the
man's demeanour. Yet he saw nothing to confirm his
suspicions beyond a certain preoccupied moodiness on
the courtier's part.

That night, as they supped, Gonzaga pleaded toothache, and with Valentina's leave he quitted the table
at the very outset of the meal. Peppe rose to follow
him, but as he reached the door his natural enemy, the
friar—ever anxious to thwart him where he could—
caught him by the nape of the neck and flung him
unceremoniously back into the room.

"Have you a toothache too, good-for-naught ? "
quoth the *frate*. "Stay you here and help me to wait
upon the company."

"Let me go, good Fra Domenico," the fool whispered
in a voice so earnest that the monk left his way clear.
But Valentina's voice now bade him stay with them,
and so his opportunity was lost.

He moved about the room a very dispirited, moody
fool, with no quip for anyone, for his thoughts were all

on Gonzaga and the treason that he was sure he was
hatching. Yet, faithful to Francesco, who sat all
unconcerned, and not wishing to alarm Valentina, he
choked back the warning that rose to his lips, seeking
to convince himself that his fears sprang perhaps from
an excess of suspicion. Had he known how well-
founded indeed they were he might have practised less
self-restraint.

For whilst he moved sullenly about the room, assisting
Fra Domenico with the dishes and platters, Gonzaga
paced the ramparts beside Cappoccio, who was on
sentry duty on the north wall.

His business called for no great diplomacy, nor did
Gonzaga employ much. He bluntly told Cappoccio
that he and his comrades had allowed Messer Francesco's
glib tongue to befool them that morning, and that the
assurances Francesco had given them were not worthy
of an intelligent man's consideration.

" I tell you, Cappoccio," he ended, " that to remain
here and protect this hopeless resistance will cost you
your life at the unsavoury hands of the hangman. You
see I am frank with you."

Now for all that what Gonzaga told him might sort
excellently well with the ideas he had himself entertained,
Cappoccio was of a suspicious nature, and his suspicions
whispered to him now that Gonzaga was actuated by
some purpose he could not gauge.

He stood still, and, leaning with both hands upon his
partisan, he sought to make out the courtier's features
in the dim light of the rising moon.

" Do you mean," he asked, and in his voice sounded
the surprise with which Gonzaga's odd speech had
filled him, " that we are foolish to have listened to
Francesco, and that we should be better advised to
march out of Roccaleone ? "

" Yes ; that is what I mean."

" But why," he insisted, his surprise increasing, " do
you urge such a course upon us ? "

" Because, Cappoccio," was the plausible reply,
" like yourselves, I was lured into this business by
insidious misrepresentations. The assurances that I
gave Fortemani, and with which he enrolled you into

his service, were those that had been given to me.
I did not bargain with such a death as awaits us here,
and I frankly tell you that I have no stomach for
it."

"I begin to understand," murmured Cappoccio,
sagely wagging his head, and there was a shrewd insolence
in his tone and manner. "When we leave Roccaleone
you come with us?"

Gonzaga nodded

"But why do you not say these things to Fortemani?" questioned Cappoccio, still doubting.

"Fortemani!" echoed Gonzaga. "By the Host,
no! The man is bewitched by that plausible rogue,
Francesco. Far from resenting the fellow's treatment
of him, he follows and obeys his every word, like the
mean-spirited dog that he is."

Again Cappoccio sought to scrutinise Gonzaga's face.
But the light was indifferent.

"Are you dealing with me fairly?" he asked. "Or
does some deeper purpose lie under your wish that he
should rebel against the lady?"

"My friend," answered Gonzaga, "do you but wait
until Gian Maria's herald comes for his answer in the
morning. Then you will learn again the terms on which
your lives are offered you. Do nothing until then.
But when you hear yourselves threatened with the rope
and the wheel, bethink you of what course you will be
best advised in pursuing. You ask me what purpose
inspires me. I have already told you—for I am as
open as the daylight with you—that I am inspired by
the purpose of saving my own neck. Is not that purpose
enough?"

A laugh of such understanding as would have set
a better man on fire with indignation was the answer
he received.

"Why, yes; it is more than enough. To-morrow,
then, my comrades and I march out of Roccaleone.
Count upon that."

"But do not accept my word. Wait until the herald
comes again. Do nothing until you have heard the
terms he brings."

"Why, no, assuredly not."

" And do not let it transpire among your fellows that
it is I who have suggested this."

" Why, no.   I'll keep your secret," laughed the bravo
offensively, resuming his sentinel's pacing.

Gonzaga sought his bed.   A fierce joy consumed him
at having so consummately planned Valentina's ruin,
yet he did not wish to face her again that night.

But when on the morrow the herald wound his horn
again beneath the castle walls, Gonzaga was prominent
in the little group that attended Monna Valentina.
The Count of Aquila was superintending the work to
which he had set a half-score of men.   With a great
show, and as much noise as possible—by which Francesco
intended that the herald should be impressed—they
were rolling forward four small culverins and some three
cannons of larger calibre, and planting them so that
they made a menacing show in the crenels of the parapet.

Whilst watching and directing the men, he kept his
ears open for the message, and he heard the herald
again recite the terms on which the garrison might
surrender, and again the threat to hang every man
from the castle walls if they compelled him to reduce
them by force of arms.   He brought his message to an
end by announcing that in his extreme clemency Gian
Maria accorded them another half-hour's grace in which
to resolve themselves upon their course.   Should the
end of that time still find them obstinate, the bombardment would commence.   Such was the message that in
another of his arrow-borne letters Gonzaga had suggested
Gian Maria should send.

It was Francesco who stepped forward to reply.   He
had been stooping over one of the guns, as if to assure
himself of the accuracy of its aim, and as he rose he pronounced himself satisfied in a voice loud enough for the
herald's hearing.   Then he advanced to Valentina's side,
and whilst he stood there delivering his answer he never
noticed the silent departure of the men from the wall.

" You will tell his Highness of Babbiano," he replied,
" that he reminds us of the boy in the fable who cried
' Wolf !' too often.   Tell him, sir that his threats
leave this garrison as unmoved as do his promises.
If so be that he intends in truth to bombard us, let
him begin forthwith.   We are ready for him, as you

perceive. Maybe he did not suppose us equipped with cannon; but there they stand. Those guns are trained upon his camp, and the first shot h efires upon us shall be a signal for such a reply as he little dreams of. Tell him, too, that we expect no quarter, and will yield none. We are unwilling for bloodshed, but if he drives us to it and executes his purpose of employing cannon, then the consequences be upon his own head. Bear him that answer, and tell him to send you no more with empty threats."

The herald bowed upon the withers of his horse. The arrogance, the cold imperiousness of the message struck him dumb with amazement. Amazement was his, too, that Roccaleone should be armed with cannon, as with his own eyes he saw. That those guns were empty he could not guess, nor could Gian Maria when he heard a message that filled him with rage, and would have filled him with dismay, but that he counted upon the mutiny which Gonzaga had pledged himself to stir up.

As the herald was riding away a gruff laugh broke from Fortemani, who stood behind the Count.

Valentina turned to Francesco with eyes that beamed admiration and a singular tenderness.

"Oh, what had I done without you, Messer Francesco?" she cried, for surely the twentieth time since his coming. "I tremble to think how things had gone without your wit and valour to assist me." She never noticed the malicious smile that trembled on Gonzaga's pretty face. "Where did you find the powder?" she asked innocently, for her mind had not yet caught that humour of the situation that had drawn a laugh from Fortemani.

"I found none," answered Francesco, smiling from the shadow of his helm. "My threats"—and he waved his hand in the direction of that formidable array of guns—"are as empty as Gian Maria's. Yet I think they will impress him more than his do us. I will answer for it, Madonna, that they deter him from bombarding us if so be that he ever intended to. So let us go and break our fast with a glad courage."

"Those guns are empty?" she gasped. "And you could talk so boldly and threaten so defiantly!"

Mirth crept into her face and thrust back the alarm, a little of which had peeped from her eyes even as she was extolling Francesco.

"There!" he cried joyously. "You are smiling now, Madonna. Nor have you cause for aught else. Shall we descend? This early morning work has given me the hunger of a wolf."

She turned to go with him, and in that moment Peppe, his owlish face spread over with alarm, dashed up the steps from the courtyard.

"Madonna!" he gasped breathless. "Messer Francesco! The men—Cappoccio—— He is haranguing them. He—is inciting them to treachery."

So, in gasps, he got out his tale, which swept the mirth again from Valentina's eyes and painted very white her cheek. Strong and brave though she was, she felt her senses swimming at that sudden revulsion from confidence to fear. Was all indeed ended at the very moment when hope had reached its high meridian?

"You are faint, Madonna; lean on me."

It was Gonzaga who spoke. But beyond the fact that the words had been uttered, she realised nothing. She saw an arm advanced, and she took it. Then she dragged Gonzaga with her to the side overlooking the courtyard that with her own eyes she might have evidence of what was toward.

She heard an oath—a vigorous, wicked oath—from Francesco, followed by a command, sharp and rasping.

"To the armoury yonder, Peppe! Fetch me a two-handed sword—the stoutest you can find. Ercole, come with me. Gonzaga—— Nay, you had best stay here. See to Monna Valentina."

He stepped to her side now, and rapidly surveying the surging scene below, where Cappoccio was still addressing the men. At sight of Francesco they raised a fierce yell, as might a pack of dogs that have sighted their quarry.

"To the gates!" was the shout. "Down the drawbridge! We accept the terms of Gian Maria. We will not die like rats."

"By God, but you shall, if I so will it!" snarled Francesco through his set teeth. Then turning his

N

head in a fever of impatience : " Peppe," he shouted,
" will you never bring that sword ? "

The fool came up at that moment, staggering under
the weight of a great double-edged two-hander, equipped
with lugs, and measuring a good six feet from point to
pummel. Francesco caught it from him, and bending,
he muttered a swift order in Peppino's ear.

" . . . In the box that stands upon the table in my
chamber," Gonzaga overheard him say. " Now go,
and bring it to me in the yard. Speed you, Peppino ! "

A look of understanding flashed up from the hunchback's eyes, and as he departed at a run Francesco
hoisted the mighty sword to his shoulder as though its
weight were that of a feather. ·In that instant Valentina's white hand was laid upon the brassart that steeled
his fore-arm.

" What will you do ? " she questioned in a whisper,
her eyes dilating with alarm.

" Stem the treachery of that rabble," he answered
shortly. " Stay you here, Madonna. Fortemani and
I will pacify them—or make an end of them." And
so grimly did he say it that Gonzaga believed it to lie
within his power.

" But you are mad ! " she cried, and the fear in her
eyes increased. " What can you do against twenty ? "

" What God pleases," he answered, and for a second
put the ferocity from his heart that he might smile
reassurance.

" But you will be killed," she cried. " Oh ! don't go,
don't go ! Let them have their way, Messer Francesco.
Let Gian Maria invest the castle. I care not, so that
you do not go."

Her voice, and the tale it told of sweet anxiety for his
fate overruling everything else in that moment—even
her horror of Gian Maria—quickened his blood to the
pace of ecstasy. He was taken by a wild longing to
catch her in his arms—this lady hitherto so brave and
daunted now by the fear of his peril only. Every fibre
of his being urged him to gather her to his breast whilst
he poured courage and comfort into her ear. He
fainted almost with desire to kiss those tender eyes,
upturned to his in her piteous pleading that he should

not endanger his own life.   But suppressing all, he only smiled, though very tenderly.

" Be brave, Madonna, and trust in me a little.   Have I failed you yet ?   Need you, then, fear that I shall fail you now ? "

At that she seemed to gather courage.   The words re-awakened her confidence in his splendid strength.

" We shall laugh over this when we break our fast," he cried.   " Come, Ercole ! "   And without waiting for more he leapt down the steps with an agility surprising in one so heavily armed as he.

They were no more than in time.   As they gained the courtyard the men came sweeping along towards the gates, their voices raucous and threatening.   They were full of assurance.   All hell, they thought, could not have hindered them, and yet at sight of that tall figure, bright as an angel, in his panoply of glittering steel, with that great sword poised on his left shoulder, some of the impetuousness seemed to fall from them.

Still they advanced, Cappoccio's voice shouting encouragement.   Almost were they within range of that lengthy sword, when of a sudden it flashed from his shoulder and swept a half-circle of dazzling light before their eyes.   Round his head it went, and back again before them, handled as though it had been a whip, and bringing them, silent, to a standstill.   He bore it back to his shoulder, and alert for the first movement, his blood on fire, and ready to slay a man or two should the example become necessary, he addressed them.

" You see what awaits you if you persist in this," he said in a dangerously quiet voice.   " Have you no shame, you herd of cowardly animals !   You are loud-voiced enough where treason to the hand that pays you is in question ; but there, it seems, your valour ends."

He spoke to them now in burning words.   He recapitulated the arguments which yesterday he had made use of to quell the mutinous spirit of Cappoccio. He assured them that Gian Maria threatened more than he could accomplish ; and so, perhaps, more than he could fulfil if they were so foolish as to place

themselves in his power. Then safety, he pointed out to
them, lay here, behind these walls. The siege could not
long endure. They had a stout ally in Cæsar Borgia,
and he was marching upon Babbiano by then, so that
Gian Maria must get him home perforce ere long.
Their pay was good, he reminded them, and if the
siege were soon raised they should be well rewarded.

"Gian Maria threatens to hang you when he captures
Roccaleone. But even should he capture it, do you
think he would be allowed to carry out so inhuman a
threat? You are mercenaries, after all, in the pay
of Monna Valentina, on whom and her captains the
blame must fall. This is Urbino, not Babbiano, and
Gian Maria is not master here. Do you think the noble
and magnanimous Guidobaldo would let you hang?
Have you so poor an opinion of your Duke? Fools!
You are as safe from violence as are those ladies in the
gallery up there. For Guidobaldo would no more think
of harming you than of permitting harm to come to
them. If any hanging there is it will be for me, and
perhaps for Messer Gonzaga who hired you. Yet, do
I talk of throwing down my arms? What think you
holds me here? Interest—just as interest holds you—
and if I think the risk worth taking, why should not
you? Are you so tame and so poor-spirited that a
threat is to vanquish you? Will you become a byword
in Italy, and when men speak of cowardice will you have
them say: 'Craven as Monna Valentina's garrison'?"

In this strain he talked to them, now smiting hard
with his scorn, now cajoling them with his assurances,
and breeding confidence anew in their shaken spirits.
It was a thing that went afterwards to the making of an
epic that was sung from Calabria to Piedmont, how
this brave knight, by his words, by the power of his
will and the might of his presence, curbed and subdued
that turbulent score of rebellious hinds.

And from the wall above Valentina watched him, her
eyes sparkling with tears that had not their source in
sorrow nor yet in fear, for she knew that he must
prevail. How could it be else with one so dauntless?

Thus thought she now. But in the moment of his
going, fear had chilled her to the heart, and when she

first saw him take his stand before them she had turned
half-distraught, and begged Gonzaga not to linger at
her side but to go lend what aid he could to that brave
knight who stood so sorely in need of it. And Gonzaga
had smiled a smile as pale as January sunshine, and his
soft blue eyes had hardened in their glance. Not
weakness now was it that held him there, well out of
the dangerous turmoil. For he felt that had he possessed the strength of Hercules and the courage of
Achilles he would not in that instant have moved a step
to Francesco's aid. And as much he told her.

" Why should I, Madonna ? " he had returned coldly.
" Why should I raise a hand to help the man whom you
prefer to me ? Why should I draw sword in the cause
of this fortress ? "

She looked at him with troubled eyes. " What are
you saying, my good Gonzaga ? "

" Aye—your good Gonzaga ! " he mocked her bitterly.
" Your lap-dog, your lute-thrummer ; but not man
enough to be your captain ; not man enough to earn
a thought that is kinder than any earned by Peppe or
your hounds. I may endanger my neck to save you,
to bring you hither to a place of safety from Gian Maria's
persecution, and be cast aside for one who, it happens,
has a little more knowledge of this coarse trade of arms.
Cast me aside if you will," he pursued, with increasing
bitterness, " but having done so, do not ask me to serve
you again. Let Messer Francesco fight it out——"

" Hush, Gonzaga ! " she interrupted. " Let me hear
what he is saying."

And her tone told the courtier that his words had been
lost upon the morning air. Engrossed in the scene below,
she had not so much as listened to his bitter tirade.
For now Francesco was behaving oddly. The fool was
returned from the errand on which he had been despatched, and Francesco called him to his side. Lowering
his sword he received a paper from Peppe's hand.

Burning with indignation at having gone unheeded,
Gonzaga stood gnawing his lip, whilst Valentina craned
forward to catch Francesco's words.

" I have here a proof," he cried, " of what I tell you—
proof of how little Gian Maria is prepared to carry out

his threats of cannon. It is that fellow Cappoccio has seduced you with his talk. And you, like the sheep you are, let yourselves be driven by his foul tongue. Now listen to the bribe that Gian Maria offers to one within these walls if he can contrive a means to deliver Roccaleone into his hands." And to Gonzaga's paralysing consternation, he heard Francesco read the letter with which Gian Maria had answered his proposed betrayal of the fortress. He went white with fear and he leant against the low wall to steady the tell-tale trembling that had seized him. Then Francesco's voice, scornful and confident, floated up to his ears. " I ask you, my friends, would his Highness of Babbiano be disposed to the payment of a thousand gold florins if by bombardment he thought to break a way into Roccaleone ? This letter was written yesterday. Since then we have made a brave display of cannon ourselves ; and if yesterday he dared not fire, think you he will to-day ? But here, assure yourselves, if there is one amongst you that can read."

He held out the letter to them. Cappoccio took it, and calling one Aventano, he held it out in his turn. This Aventano, a youth who had been partly educated for the Church but had fallen from that lofty purpose, now stood forward and took the letter. He scrutinised it, read it aloud, and pronounced it genuine.

"Whom is it addressed to ? " demanded Cappoccio.

"Nay, nay ! " cried Francesco. " What need for that ? "

"Let be," Cappoccio answered, almost fiercely. " If you would have us remain in Roccaleone, let be. Aventano, tell me."

" To Messer Romeo Gonzaga," answered the youth in a voice of wonder.

So evil a light leapt to Cappoccio's eye that Francesco carried his free hand to the sword which he had lowered. But Cappoccio only looked up at Gonzaga and grinned malevolently. It had penetrated his dull wits that he had been the tool of a Judas who sought to sell the castle for a thousand florins. Further than that Cappoccio did not see ; nor was he very resentful, and his grin was rather of mockery than of anger. He was troubled by no lofty notions of honour that should cause him to see in this deed of Gonzaga's anything more than such a trickster's act as it is always agreeable to foil. And then, to the others, who knew naught of what was passing in Cappoccio's mind, he did a mighty strange thing. From being the one to instigate them to treachery and mutiny he was the one now to raise his voice in a stout argument of loyalty. He agreed with all that Messer Francesco had said, and he, for one, ranged himself on Messer Francesco's side to defend the gates from any traitors who sought to open them to Gian Maria Sforza.

His defection from the cause of mutiny was the signal for the utter abandoning of that cause itself, and another stout ally came opportunely to weigh in Francesco's favour was the fact that the half-hour of grace was now elapsed and Gian Maria's guns continued silent. He drew their attention to the fact with a laugh, and bade them go in peace, adding the fresh assurance that those guns would not speak that day, nor the next, nor indeed ever.

Utterly conquered by Francesco and—perhaps even more—by his unexpected ally, Cappoccio, they slunk shamefacedly away to the food and drink that he bade them seek at Fra Domenico's hands.

CHAPTER XX

THE LOVERS

"How came that letter to your hands?" Valentina asked Gonzaga, when presently they stood together in the courtyard, whither the courtier had followed her when she descended.

"Wrapped round an arbalest-bolt that fell on the ramparts yesterday whilst I was walking there alone," returned Gonzaga coldly.

He had by now regained his composure. He saw that he stood in deadly peril, and the very fear that possessed him seemed, by an odd paradox, to lend him the strength to play his part.

Valentina eyed him with something of mistrust in her glance. But on Francesco's clear countenance no shadow of suspicion showed. His eyes almost smiled as he asked Gonzaga:

"Why did you not bear it to Monna Valentina?"

A flush reddened the courtier's cheeks. He shrugged his shoulders impatiently, and in a voice that choked with anger he delivered his reply.

"To you, sir, who seem bred in camps and reared in guardrooms, the fulness of this insult offered me by Gian Maria may not be apparent. It may not be yours to perceive that the very contact of that letter soiled my hands, that it shamed me unutterably to think that that loutish Duke should have deemed me a target for such a shaft. It were idle, therefore, to seek to make you understand how little I could bear to submit to the further shame of allowing another to see the affront that I was powerless to avenge. I did, sir, with that letter the only thing conceivable. I crumpled it in my hand and cast it from me, just as I sought to cast its

200

contents from my mind. But your watchful spies, Ser Francesco, bore it to you, and if my shame has been paraded before the eyes of that rabble soldiery, at least it has served the purpose of saving Monna Valentina. To do that I would, if the need arose, immolate more than the pride that caused me to be silent on the matter of this communication."

He spoke with such heat of sincerity that he convinced both Francesco and Valentina, and the lady's eyes took on a softer expression as she surveyed Gonzaga—this poor Gonzaga whom, her heart told her, she had sorely wronged in thought. Francesco, ever generous, took his passionate utterances in excellent part.

"Messer Gonzaga, I understand your scruples. You do me wrong to think that I should fail in that."

He checked the suggestion he was on the point of renewing that, nevertheless, Gonzaga would have been better advised to have laid that letter at once before Monna Valentina. Instead, he dismissed the subject with a laugh, and proposed that they should break their fast so soon as he had put off his harness.

He went to do so, whilst Valentina bent her steps towards the dining-room, attended by Gonzaga, to whom she now sought to make amends for her suspicions by an almost excessive friendliness of bearing.

But there was one whom Gonzaga's high-sounding words in connection with that letter had left cold. This was Peppe, that most wise of fools. He hastened after Francesco, and while the knight was disarming he came to voice his suspicions. But Francesco drove him out with impatience, and Peppe went sorrowing and swearing that the wisdom of the fool was truly better than the folly of the wise.

Throughout that day Gonzaga hardly stirred from Valentina's side. He talked with her in the morning at great length and upon subjects poetical or erudite, by which he meant to display his vast mental superiority over the swashbuckling Francesco. In the evening, when the heat of the day was spent, and whilst that same Messer Francesco was at some defensive measures on the walls, Gonzaga played at bowls with Valentina

and her ladies—the latter having now recovered from
the panic to which earlier they had been a prey.

That morning Gonzaga had stood at bay, seeing his
plans crumble. That evening, after the day spent in
Valentina's company—and she so sweet and kind to
him—he began to take heart of grace once more, and his
volatile mind whispered to his soul the hope that,
after all, things might well be as he had first intended
if he but played his cards adroitly and did not mar his
chances by the precipitancy that had once gone near
to losing him. His purpose gathered strength from
a message that came that evening from Gian Maria,
who was by then assured that Gonzaga's plan had failed.
He sent word that, being unwilling to provoke the
bloodshed threatened by the reckless madman who
called himself Monna Valentina's Provost, he would
delay the bombardment, hoping that in the meantime
hunger would beget in that rebellious garrison a more
submissive mood.

Francesco read the message to Madonna's soldiers,
and they received it joyously. Their confidence in
him increased a hundredfold by this proof of the accuracy
of his foresight. They were a gay company at supper
in consequence, and gayest of all was Messer Gonzaga,
most bravely dressed in a purple suit of taby silk to
honour so portentous an occasion.

Francesco was the first to quit the table, craving
Monna Valentina's leave to be about some duty that
took him to the walls. She let him go, and afterwards
sat pensive, nor heeded now Romeo's light chatter, nor
yet the sonnet of Petrarca that presently he sang the
company. Her thoughts were all with him that had
left the board. Scarcely a word had she exchanged with
Francesco since that delirious moment when they had
looked into each other's eyes upon the ramparts and
seen the secret that each was keeping from the other.
Why had he not come to her ? she asked herself. And
then she bethought her of how Gonzaga had all day
long been glued to her side, and she realised, too, that it
was she had shunned Francesco's company, grown of a
sudden strangely shy.

But greater than her shyness was now her desire to

be near him and to hear his voice ; to have him look again upon her as he had looked that morning, when in terror for him she had sought to dissuade him from opposing the craven impulse of men-at-arms. A woman of mature age, or one riper in experience, would have waited for him to seek her out. But Valentina, in her sweet naturalness, thought never of subterfuge or of dalliant wiles. She rose quietly from the table ere Gonzaga's song was done, and as quietly she slipped from the room.

It was a fine night, the air heavy with the vernal scent of fertile lands, and the deep cobalt of the heavens a glittering, star-flecked dome, in a lighter space of which floated the half-dusk of the growing moon. Such a moon, she bethought her, as she had looked at with thoughts of him, the night after their brief meeting at Acquasparta. She had gained that north rampart on which he had announced that duty took him, and yonder she saw a man—the only tenant of the wall— leaning upon the embattled parapet, looking down at the lights of Gian Maria's camp. He was bareheaded, and by the gold coif that gleamed in his hair she knew him. Softly she stole up behind him.

" Do we dream here, Messer Francesco ? " she asked him, as she reached his side, and there was laughter running through her words.

He started round at the sound of her voice, then he laughed too, softly and gladly.

" It is a night for dreams, and I was dreaming indeed. But you have scattered them."

" You grieve me," she rallied him. " For assuredly they were pleasant, since, to come here and indulge them, you left—us."

" Aye—they were pleasant," he answered. " And yet, they were fraught with a certain sadness, but idle as is the stuff of dreams. They were yours to dispel, for they were of you."

" Of me ? " she questioned, her heart-beats quickening and bringing to her cheeks a flush that she thanked the night for concealing.

" Yes, Madonna—of you and our first meeting in the woods at Acquasparta. Do you recall it ? "

" I do, I do," she murmured fondly.

" And do you recall how I then swore myself your knight and ever your champion ? Little did we dream how the honour that I sighed for was to be mine."

She made him no answer, her mind harking back to that first meeting on which so often and so fondly she had pondered.

" I was thinking, too," he said presently, " of that man Gian Maria in the plain yonder, and of this shameful siege."

" You—you have no misgivings ? " she faltered, for his words had disappointed her a little.

" Misgivings ? "

" For being here with me. For being implicated in what they call my rebellion ? "

He laughed softly, his eyes upon the silver gleam of waters below.

" My misgivings are all for the time when this siege shall be ended ; when you and I shall have gone each our separate way," he answered boldly. He turned to face her now, and his voice rang a little tense. " But for being here to guide this fine resistance and lend you the little aid I can—— No, no, I have no misgivings for that. It is the dearest frolic ever my soldiering led me into. I came to Roccaleone with a message of warning ; but underneath, deep down in my heart, I bore the hope that mine should be more than a messenger's part ; that mine it might be to remain by you and do such work as I am doing."

" Without you they would have forced me by now to surrender."

" Perhaps they would. But while I *am* here I do not think they will. I burn for news of Babbiano. If I could but tell what is happening there I might cheer you with the assurance that this siege can last but a few days longer. Gian Maria must get him home or submit to the loss of his throne. And if he loses that your uncle would no longer support so strenuously his suit with you. To you, Madonna, this must be a cheering thought. To me—alas ! Why should I hope for it ? "

He was looking away now into the night, but his voice

quivered with emotion that was in him. She was silent, and, emboldened perhaps by that silence of hers, encouraged by the memory of what he had seen that morning reflected in her eyes :

" Madonna," he cried, " I would it might be mine to cut a road for you through that besieging camp and bear you away to some blessed place where there are neither courts nor princes. But since this may not be, Madonna *mia*, I would that this siege might last for ever."

And then—was it the night breeze faintly stirring through his hair that mocked him with the whisper, " So indeed I would ? " He turned to her ; his hand, brown and nervous, fell upon hers, ivory-white, where it rested on the stone.

" Valentina ! " he cried, his voice no louder than a whisper, his eyes ardently seeking her averted ones. And then, as suddenly as it had leapt up, was the fire in his glance extinguished. He withdrew his hand from hers, he sighed and shifted his gaze to the camp once more.
" Forgive, forget, Madonna," he murmured bitterly, " that which in my madness I have presumed."

Silent she stood for a long moment ; then she edged nearer to him, and her voice murmured back : " What if I account it no presumption ? "

With a gasp he swung round to face her, and they stood very close, glance holding glance, and hers the less timid of the two. They thus remained for a little space. Then shaking his head and speaking with an infinite sadness :

" It were better that you did, Madonna," he made answer.

" Better ? But why ? "

" Because I am no duke, Madonna."

" And what of that ? " she cried, to add with scorn : " Out yonder sits a duke. Oh, sir, how shall I account presumptuous in you the very words that I would hear ? What does your rank signify to me ? I know you for the truest knight, the noblest gentleman, and the most valiant friend that ever came to the aid of distressed maiden. Do you forget the very principles that have led me to make this resistance ?—that I am a woman, and ask of life no more than is a woman's due—and no less."

There she stopped ; again the blood suffused her cheeks as she bethought her of how fast she talked and of how bold her words might sound. She turned slightly from him and leant now upon the parapet, gazing out into the night. And as she stood thus a very ardent voice it was that whispered in her ear :

" Valentina, by my soul, I love you ! " And there that whisper, which filled her with an ecstasy that was almost painful in its poignancy, ended sharply as if throttled. Again his hand sought hers, which was yielded to him as she would have yielded her whole life to his sweet bidding, and now his voice came less passionately.

" Why delude ourselves with cruel hopes, my Valentina ? " he was saying. " There is the future. There is the time when this siege shall be done with and when, Gian Maria having got him home, you will be free to depart. Whither will you go ? "

She looked at him as if she did not understand the question, and her eyes were troubled, although in such light as there was he could scarce see this.

" I will go whither you bid me. Where else have I to go ? " she added, with a note of bitterness.

He started. Her answer was so far from what he had expected.

" But your uncle——? "

" What duty do I owe to him ? Oh, I have thought of it, and until—until this morning, it seemed that a convent must be my ultimate refuge. I have spent most of my young life at Santa Sofia, and the little that I have seen of the world at my uncle's court scarce invites me to see more of it. The Mother Abbess loves me a little. She would take me back, unless——"

She broke off and looked at him, and before that look of absolute and sweet surrender his senses swam. That she was niece to the Duke of Urbino he remembered no more than that he was Count of Aquila, well-born, but of none too rich estate, and certainly no more a match for her in Guidobaldo's eyes than if he had been the simple knight-errant that he seemed.

He moved closer to her, his hands—as if obeying a bidding greater than his will, the bidding of that glance of hers, perhaps—took her by the shoulders whilst his whole soul looked at her from his eyes. Then, with a stifled cry, he caught her to him. For a moment she lay, palpitant, within his arms, her tall, bronze head on a level with his chin, her heart beating against his heart. Stooping suddenly, he kissed her on the lips. She suffered it with an unresistance that invited. But when it was done, she gently put him from her ; and he, obedient to her slightest wish, curbed the wild ardour of his mood and set her free.

"*Anima, mia* ! " he cried rapturously. " You are mine now, betide what may. Not Gian Maria nor all the dukes in Christendom shall take you from me."

She set her hand upon his lips to silence him, and he kissed the palm, so that laughing she drew back again. And now from laughter she passed to a great solemnity and with arm outstretched towards the ducal camp : " Win me a way through those lines," said she, " and bear me away from Urbino—far away where Guidobaldo's power and the vengeance of Gian Maria may not follow us—and you shall have won me for your own. But until then, let there be a truce to—to this, between us. Here is a man's work to be done, and if I am weak, as to-night, I may weaken you, and then we should both be undone. It is upon your strength I count, Franceschino *mio*, my true knight."

He would have answered her. He had much to tell her—who and what he was. But she pointed to the head of the steps, where a man's figure loomed.

" Yonder comes the sentinel," she said. " Leave me now, dear Francesco. Go. It is growing late."

He bowed low before her, obedient ever, like the true knight he was, and took his leave of her, his soul on fire.

Valentina watched his retreating figure until it had vanished round the angle of the wall. Then with a profound sigh that was as a prayer of thanksgiving for this great good that had come into her life she leaned upon the parapet and looked out into the darkness, her cheeks flushed, her heart still beating high. She laughed softly to herself out of the pure happiness of her mood. The camp of Gian Maria became a subject for her scorn. What should his might avail whilst she had such a champion to defend her now and hereafter?

There was an irony in that siege on which her fancy fastened. By coming thus in arms against her Gian Maria sought to win her for his wife; yet all that he had accomplished was to place her in the arms of the one man whom she had learnt to love by virtue of this very siege. The mellow warmth of that night, the ambient perfume of the fields were well-sorted to her mood, and the faint breeze that breathed caressingly upon her cheek seemed to re-echo the melodies her heart was giving forth. In that hour those old grey walls of Roccaleone seemed to enclose for her a very paradise, and the snatch of an old love-song stole softly from her parted lips. But like a paradise—alas!—it had its snake that crept up unheard behind her and was presently hissing in her ear. And its voice was the voice of Romeo Gonzaga.

"It comforts me, Madonna, that there is one, at least, in Roccaleone has the heart to sing."

Startled out of her happy pensiveness by that smooth and now unutterably sinister voice, she turned to face its owner.

She saw the white gleam of his face and something of the anger that smouldered in his eye, and, despite herself, a thrill of alarm ran through her like a shudder. She looked beyond him to a spot where lately she had seen the sentry. There was no one there nor anywhere upon that wall. They were alone, and Messer Gonzaga looked singularly evil.

For a moment there was a tense silence, broken only by the tumbling waters of the torrent-moat and the hoarse challenge of a sentry's "*Chi, va la?*" on Gian Maria's camp. Then she turned nervously, wondering how much he might have heard of what had passed between herself and Francesco, how much have seen.

"And yet, Gonzaga," she answered him, "I left you singing below when I came away."

"To wanton it here in the moonlight with that damned swashbuckler, that brigand, that kennel-bred beast of a *sbirro*!"

" Gonzaga ! You would dare ! "

" Dare ? " he mocked her, beside himself with passion. " Is it you who speak of daring—you, the niece of Guidobaldo da Montefeltro, a lady of the noble and illustrious house of Rovere, who cast yourself into the arms of a low-born vassal such as that, a *masnadiero*, a bandit, a bravo ? And can you yet speak of daring and take that tone with me, when shame should strike you either dead or dumb ? "

" Gonzaga," she answered him, her face as white as his own, but her voice steady and hard with anger, " leave me now—upon the instant, or I will have you flogged—flogged to the bone."

A moment he stared at her like a man dazed. Then he tossed his arms to Heaven, and letting them fall heavily to his sides he shrugged his shoulders and laughed evilly. But of going he made no shift.

" Call your men," he answered her, in a choking voice. " Do your will on me. Flog me to the bone or to the death—let that be the reward of all that I have done, all that I have risked, all that I have sacrificed to serve you. It were of a piece with your other actions."

Her eyes sought his in the gloom, her bosom heaving wildly in her endeavours to master herself before she spoke.

" Messer Gonzaga," said she at last. " I'll not deny that you served me faithfully in the matter of my escape from Urbino——"

" Why speak of it ? " he sneered. " It was a service of which you but avail yourself until another offered on whom you might bestow your favour and the supreme command of your fortress. Why speak of it ? "

" To show you that the service you allude to is now paid," she riposted sternly. " By reproaching me you have taken payment, and by insulting me you have stamped out my gratitude."

" A most convenient logic yours," he mocked. " I am cast aside like an out-worn garment, and the garment is accounted paid for because through much hard usage it has come to look a little threadbare."

And now it entered her mind that perhaps there was

O

some justice in what he said.   Perhaps she had used him a little hardly.

"Do you think, Gonzaga," she said, and her tone was now a shade more gentle, "that because you have served me you may affront me, and that knight who has served me also, and——"

"In what can such service as his compare with mine ? What has he done that I have not done more ? "

"Why, when the men rebelled here——"

"Bah !   Cite me not that.   Body of God !   it is his trade to lead such swine.   He is one of themselves. But for the rest, what has such a man as this to lose by his share in your rebellion compared with such a loss as mine must be ? "

"Why, if things go ill, I take it he may lose his life," she answered in a low voice.   "Can you lose more ? "

He made a gesture of impatience.

"If things go ill—yes.   It may cost him dearly. But if they go well, and this siege is raised, he has nothing more to fear.   Mine is a parlous case.   However ends this siege, for me there will be no escape from the vengeance of Gian Maria and Guidobaldo.   They know my share in it.   They know that your action was helped by me and that without me you could never have equipped yourself for such resistance.   Whatever may betide you and this Ser Francesco, for me there will be no escape."

She drew a deep breath then set him the obvious question :

"Did you not consider it—did you not weigh those chances—before you embarked upon this business, before you, yourself, urged me to this step ? "

"Aye, did I," he answered sullenly.

"Then, why these complaints now ? "

He was singularly, madly frank with her in his reply. He told her that he had done it because he loved her, because she had given him signs that his love was not in vain.

"I gave you signs ? " she interrupted him.   "Mother in Heaven !   Recite these signs that I may know them."

"Were you not ever kind to me ? " he demanded.

" Did you not ever manifest a liking for my company ?
Were you not ever pleased that I should sing to you the
songs that in your honour I had made ? Was it not to
me you turned in the hour of your need ? "

" See now how poor a thing you are, Gonzaga ! " she
answered witheringly. " A woman may not smile on
you, may not give you a kind word, may not suffer you
to sing to her, but you must conclude she is enamoured
of you. And if I turned to you in my hour of need, as
you remind me, need that be a sign of my infatuation ?
Does every cavalier so think when a helpless woman
turns to him in her distress ? But even so," she continued, " how should all that diminish the peril you
now talk of ? Even were your suit with me to prosper,
would that make you any the less Romeo Gonzaga, the
butt of the anger of my uncle and Gian Maria ? Rather
do I think that it should make you more."

But he disillusioned her. He did not scruple, in his
angry mood, to lay before her his reasonings that as her
husband he would be screened.

She laughed aloud at that.

" And so it is by such sophistries as these that your
presumption came to life ? "

That stung him. Quivering with the passion that
obsessed him, he stepped close up to her.

" Tell me, Madonna—why shall we account presumption in Romeo Gonzaga a suit that in a nameless adventurer we encourage ? " he asked, his voice thick and
tremulous.

" Have a care," she bade him.

" A care of what ? " he flashed back. " Answer me,
Monna Valentina. Am I so base a man that by the
very thought of love for you I must presume, whilst
you can give yourself into the arms of this swashbuckling
bravo, and take his kisses ? Your reasoning sorts ill
with your deeds."

" Craven ! " she answered him. " Dog that you
are ! " And before the blaze of passion in her eyes he
recoiled, his courage faltering. She cropped her anger
in mid-career and in a dangerously calm voice she bade
him see to it that by morning he was no longer in
Roccaleone. " Profit by the night," she counselled

him, " and escape the vigilance of Gian Maria as best you can. Here you shall not stay."

At that a great fear took possession of him, putting to flight the last remnant of his anger. Nor fear alone was it, to do him justice. It was also the realisation that if he would take payment from her for this treatment of him, if he would slake his vengeance, he must stay. One plan had failed him. But his mind was fertile, and he might devise another that might succeed and place Gian Maria in Roccaleone. Thus should he be amply venged. She was turning away, having pronounced his banishment, but he sprang after her, and upon his knees he now besought her piteously to hear him yet awhile.

And she, regretting her already of her harshness, and thinking that perhaps in his jealousy he had been scarce responsible for what he had said, stood still to hear him.

" Not that, not that, Madonna," he wailed, his tone suggesting the imminence of tears. " Do not send me away. If die I must, let me die here at Roccaleone, helping the defence to my last breath. But do not cast me out to fall into the hands of Gian Maria. He will hang me for my share in this business. Do not requite me thus, Madonna. You owe me a little, surely ; and if I was mad when I talked to you just now, it was love of you that drove me—love of you and suspicion of that man of whom none of us know anything. Madonna, be pitiful a little. Suffer me to remain."

She looked down at him, her mind swayed between pity and contempt. Then pity won the day in the wayward but ever gentle heart of Valentina. She bade him rise.

" And go, Gonzaga. Get you to bed, and sleep you into a saner frame of mind. We will forget all this that you have said, so that you never speak of it again— nor of this love you say you bear me."

The hypocrite caught the hem of her cloak and bore it to his lips.

" May God keep your heart ever as pure and noble and forgiving," he murmured brokenly. " I know how little I am deserving of your clemency. But I shall repay you, Madonna," he protested—and truly meant it, though not in the sense it seemed.

CHAPTER XXI

THE PENITENT

A WEEK passed peacefully at Roccaleone; so peacefully that it was difficult to conceive that out there in the plain sat Gian Maria with his five-score men besieging them.

This inaction fretted the Count of Aquila, as did the lack of news from Fanfulla; and he wondered vaguely what might be taking place at Babbiano that Gian Maria should be content to sit idly before them, as though he had months at his disposal in which to starve them into yielding. The mystery would have been dispelled had he known that he had Gonzaga to thank for this singular patience of Gian Maria's. For the courtier had found occasion to send another letter-carrying shaft into the Duke's camp, informing them of how and why the last plot had failed, and urging Gian Maria to wait and trust in him to devise a better scheme for delivering the castle into his power. He had promised boldly and confidently enough, and Gian Maria, facts showed, had trusted to that promise of his, and awaited its fulfilment. But tax his mind though he did incessantly, no inspiration came to him, no scheme suggested itself by which he might accomplish his treacherous purpose.

He employed the time cunningly to win back Valentina's favour and confidence. On the morning after his stormy interview with Guidobaldo's niece he had confessed himself to Fra Domenico, and approached the Sacrament. Every morning thereafter he appeared at Mass, and by the piety and fervour of his devotions became an example to all the others. Now this was not lost on Valentina, who was convent-bred, and in a measure devout. She read in this singular alteration of his ways the undoubtable indication of an altered character. That he had

approached the Sacrament on the morning after his wild
words to her she took to mean that he repented him the
viciousness of the animosity he had entertained ; that
he continued so extremely devout thereafter she construed into meaning that his repentance was sincere and
persistent.

And so she came to ask herself whether indeed he had
not been as much sinned against as sinning, and she
ended by assuring herself that in a measure the fault was
hers. Seeing him so penitent, and concluding from it
that he was not likely to transgress again, she readmitted
him to her favour, and, little by little, the old friendly
state was re-established and was the sounder, perhaps,
by virtue of her confidence that after what had passed he
would not again misunderstand her.

He did not, nor did he again allow his optimism and
every-read vanity to cozen him with false hopes.   He
read her with exact precision, and whilst the reading but
served to embitter him the more and render him more
steadfast in his vengeful purpose, it, nevertheless,
made him smile the more sweetly and fawn the more
obsequiously.

And not content with this, he did not limit his syco-
phancy to Valentina, but sought also by a smiling per-
sistence to ingratiate himself with Francesco.   No voice
in Roccaleone—not even that of the bully Ercole—was
raised more often or more enthusiastically to praise and
glorify their Provost.   Valentina, observing this and
accepting it as another sign of his contrition for the past
and purpose of amendment for the future, grew yet more
cordial towards him.   He was not lacking in astuteness,
this pretty Ser Romeo, nor in knowledge of a woman's
heart and the apprehension of the fact that there is no
flattery she prefers to that which has for object the man
she loves.

Thus did Gonzaga conquer the confidence and esteem
of all during that peaceful week.   He seemed a changed
man, and all save Peppe saw in this change a matter
for increased trust and friendship towards him.   But the
astute fool looked on and pondered.   Such transforma-
tions as these were not effected in a night.   He was no
believer in any human chrysalis that shall make of the

grub of yesterday the butterfly of to-day. And so, in this fawning, smiling, subservient Gonzaga, he saw nothing but an object of mistrust, a fellow to be watched with the utmost vigilance. To this vigilance the hunchback applied himself with a zeal born of his cordial detestation of the courtier. But Gonzaga, aware of the fool's mistrust and watchfulness, contrived for once to elude him and to get a letter to Gian Maria setting forth the ingenious plan he had hatched.

The notion had come to him that Sunday at Mass. On all sanctified days it was Monna Valentina's way to insist that the entire garrison, with the exception of one single sentinel—and this only at Francesco's very earnest urging—should attend the morning service. Like an inspiration it came to him that such a half-hour as that would be a most opportune season in which to throw open the gates of Roccaleone to the besiegers. The following Wednesday was the feast of Corpus Christi. Then would be his opportunity.

Kneeling there, with head bent in ecstatic devotion, he matured his treacherous plan. The single sentry he could suborn, or else—if bribery failed—poniard. He realised that single-handed he might not lower the cumbrous drawbridge, nor would it be wise, even if possible, for the noise of it might give the alarm. But there was the postern. Gian Maria must construct him a light portable bridge and have it in readiness to span the moat and silently pour his soldiers into the castle through that little gate.

And so, the plot matured and every detail clear, he got him to his chamber and penned the letter that was to rejoice the heart of Gian Maria. He chose a favourable moment to despatch it, as he had despatched the former ones, tied about the quarrel of an arbalest, and he saw Gian Maria's signal—which the letter had provided—that the plan would be adopted. Humming a gay measure, jubilant at the prospect of seeing himself so amply avenged, Gonzaga passed down and out into the castle gardens to join the ladies in their merry-making over a game of hoodman blind.

Now, however much the Duke of Babbiano may have congratulated himself upon the ally he possessed in

Gonzaga and the cunning scheme the latter had devised
for placing him in possession of Roccaleone, there came
news to him on the morrow that caused him to rejoice a
hundredfold more fervently. His subjects of Babbiano
were in a condition approaching open rebellion resulting
from the disquieting rumours that Cæsar Borgia was
arming at Rome for a descent upon the Duchy, and the
continued absence of Gian Maria in such a season upon
a wooing that they deemed ill-timed. A strong party had
been formed, and the leaders had nailed upon the Palace
gates a proclamation that, unless Gian Maria returned
within three days to organise the defence of Babbiano,
they would depose him and repair to Aquila to invite his
cousin, Francesco del Falco—whose patriotism and military skill were known to all—to assume the crown of
Babbiano and protect them.

At the news, and upon reading the proclamation, which
Alvari had brought with him, Gian Maria flew into one of
those fits of rage that made his name a byword in Babbiano. Presently, however, he cooled. There was
Gonzaga yonder, who had promised to admit him to
Roccaleone on Wednesday. That left him time to first
possess himself of his reluctant bride and then ride hard
to Babbiano, to arrive there before the expiry of the three
days' grace his subjects gave him.

He conferred with Guidobaldo, and urged that a priest
should be in waiting to wed them as soon as he should
have brought her out of the fortress. Upon that detail
they were within an ace of quarrelling. Guidobaldo
would not at first agree to such hasty nuptials ; they
were unfitting the dignity and the station of his niece,
and if Gian Maria would wed her he must come to Urbino
and let the ceremony be performed by a cardinal. Well
was it, then, for Gian Maria that he mastered his wonted
hastiness and curbed the hot, defiant retort that rose to
his lips. Had he done so, an enduring rupture between
them would probably have ensued ; for Guidobaldo was
not one to permit himself to be hectored, and, after all,
he amply realised that Gian Maria had more need of him
than he of Gian Maria. And this in that moment the
Duke of Babbiano realised too, and realising it he set
himself to plead where otherwise he might have demanded,

to beg as a favour that which otherwise he might have commanded with a threat. And so he won Guidobaldo—although reluctant—to his wishes in the matter, and in his good-nature the Duke of Urbino consented to pocket the dignity that prompted him to see the ceremony performed with princely pomp.

This being settled, Gian Maria blessed Gonzaga who rendered it all possible and came most opportunely to his aid where without him he should have been forced to resort to cannon and bloodshed.

With Gonzaga the only shadow of doubt that remained to mar the perfect certainty of his success lay in his appreciation of Francesco's daring character and resourceful mind, and now, as if the gods were eager to favour him to the very last degree—a strange weapon to combat this was unexpectedly thrust into his hand.

It happened that Alvari was not the only messenger who travelled that day to Roccaleone. There followed him, by some hours, the Count of Aquila's servant, Zaccaria, who rode hard and reached the approaches of the castle by sunset. His destination being the fortress itself, he was forced to wait in the woods until night had fallen, and even then his mission was fraught with peril.

It befell that somewhere near the second hour of night, the moon being overcast at the time—for there were threats of a storm in the sky—the sentinel on the eastern wall heard a sound of splashing in the moat below, accompanied by the stertorous breathing of a swimmer whose mouth was not well above water. He challenged the sound, but receiving no reply he turned to go and give the alarm, and ran into the arms of Gonzaga, who had come up to take the air.

" Illustrious," he exclaimed, " there is someone swimming the moat."

" Eh ? " cried Gonzaga, a hundred suspicions of Gian Maria running through his mind. " Treachery ? "

" It is what I thought."

Gonzaga took the man by the sleeve of his doublet and drew him back to the parapet. They peered over, and from out of the blackness they were hailed by a faint " Olá ! "

" Who goes there ? " demanded Romeo.

"A friend," came the answer softly. "A messenger from Babbiano with letters for the Lord Count of Aquila. Throw me a rope, friends, before I drown in this trough."

"You rave, fool!" answered him Gonzaga. "We have no counts at Roccaleone."

"Surely, sir sentinel," replied the voice, "my master, Messer Francesco del Falco, is here. Throw me a rope, I say."

"Messer Fran——" began Gonzaga. Then he made a noise like a man choking. It was as if a sudden light of revelation had flooded his brain. "Get a rope," he harshly bade the sentry. "In the armoury yard, Despatch, fool!" he added sharply, now fearing interruption.

In a moment the man was back, and the rope was lowered to the visitor below. A few seconds later Zaccaria stood on the ramparts of Roccaleone, the water dripping from his sodden garments and gathering in a pool about his feet.

"This way," said Gonzaga, leading the man towards the armoury tower, where a lanthorn was burning. By the light of it he surveyed the newcomer, and bade the sentry close the door and remain within call, without.

Zaccaria looked startled at the order. This was scarcely the reception he had expected after so imperilling his life to reach the castle with his letter.

"Where is my lord?" he inquired through teeth that chattered from the cold of his immersion, wondering vaguely who this very magnificent gentleman might be.

"Is Messer Francesco del Falco your lord?" asked Romeo.

"He is, sir. I have had the honour to serve him these ten years. I bring him letters from Messser Fanfulla degli Arcipreti. They are very urgent. Will you lead me to him?"

"You are very wet," murmured Gonzaga solicitously. "You will take your death from cold, and the death of a man so brave as to have found a way through Gian Maria's lines were truly deplorable." He stepped to the door. "Olà!" he called to the sentry "Take this brave fellow up there and find him a change of raiment." He pointed to the upper chamber of the tower, where, indeed, such things were stored.

"But the letter, sir!" cried Zaccaria impatiently. "It is very urgent, and hours have I wasted already in waiting for the night."

"Surely you can wait until you have changed your garments? Your life, I take it, is of more account than the loss of a few moments."

"But my orders from Messer degli Arcipreti were that I must lose not an instant."

"Oh, *si, si!*" cried Gonzaga, with a show of good-tempered impatience. "Give me the letter, then, and I will take it to the Count while you are stripping those wet clothes."

Zaccaria eyed him a moment in doubt. But he looked so harmless in his finery, and the expression of his comely face was so winning and honest, that the man's hesitancy faded as soon as it sprang up. Removing his cap, he drew from within the crown the letter which he had placed there to keep dry. This package he now handed to Gonzaga, who, with a final word of instruction to the sentry touching the finding of raiment for the messenger, stepped out to go his errand. But outside the door he paused, and called the sentry to him again.

"Here is a ducat for you," he whispered. "Do my bidding and you shall have more. Detain him in the tower till I return, and on no account let him be seen or heard by anyone."

"Yes, Excellency," the man replied. "But what if the captain comes and finds me absent from my post?"

"I will provide for that. I will tell Messer Fortemani that I have employed you on a special matter and ask him to replace you. You are dispensed sentry duty for to-night."

The man bowed and quietly withdrew to attend to his prisoner, for in that light he now regarded Zaccaria.

Gonzaga sought Fortemani in the guardroom below, and did as he had promised the sentry.

"But," snapped Ercole, reddening, "by whose authority have you done this? By what right do you send sentinels on missions of your own? *Christo Canto!* Is the castle to be invaded while you send my watchmen to fetch your comfit-box or a book of verses?"

"You will remember——" began Romeo, with an air of overwhelming dignity.

"Devil take you and him that sent you!" broke in the bully. "The Messer Provost shall hear of this."

"On no account," cried Gonzaga, now passing from anger to alarm, and snatching the skirts of Fortemani's cloak as the captain was in the act of going out to execute his threat. "Ser Ercole, be reasonable, I beg of you. Are we to alarm the castle and disturb Monna Valentina over a trumpery affair such as this? Man, they will laugh at you."

"Eh?" There was nothing Ercole relished less than to be laughed at. He pondered a moment, and it occurred to him that perhaps he was making much of nothing. Then: "You, Aventano," he called, "take your partisan and patrol the eastern rampart. There, Messer Gonzaga, I have obeyed your wishes; but Messer Francesco shall hear of it when he comes his rounds."

Gonzaga left him. Francesco would not make his rounds for another hour, and by then it would not matter that Fortemani told him. In one way or another he would be able to account for his action.

He crossed the courtyard and then mounted the steps leading to his own chamber. Once there, he closed and barred the door. He kindled a light, and, flinging the letter on the table, he sat and contemplated its exterior and the great red seal that gleamed in the yellow light of his taper.

So! This knight-errant, this man whom he had accounted a low-born hind, was none other than the famous Count of Aquila, the well-beloved of the people of Babbiano, the beau-ideal of all military folk from Sicily to the Alps. And he had never suspected it! Dull-witted he did now account himself. Enough descriptions had he heard of that famous *condottiero*, that mirror of Italian chivalry. He might have known that there did not live two men of such commanding ways as he had seen instances at Roccaleone. What was his object there? Was it love of Valentina, or was it——? He paused, as in his mind he made swift a review of the politics of Babbiano. A sudden possibility occurred to him that made his eyes sparkle and his hands tremble with eagerness. Was this but a political scheme to undermine his cousin's throne, to which Gonzaga had heard of it rumoured that Francesco del Falco was an aspirant ? If it were so, what a vengeance would be his to unmask him ! How it must humble Valentina ! The letter lay before him. Within it the true facts would be disclosed. What did his friend Fafulla write him ?

He took the letter up and made a close inspection of the seal. Then softly, quietly, slowly he drew his dagger. If his suspicions were unfounded, his dagger heated in the taper should afford him the means to conceal the fact that he had tampered with that missive. He slipped his blade under the seal and worked it cautiously until it came up and set the letter open. He unfolded it, and as he read his eyes dilated. He seemed to crouch on his chair, and the hand that held the paper shook. He drew the candle nearer, and shading his eyes he read it again, word for word :

My dear Lord Count,

I have delayed writing until the time when the signs I observed should have become more definite, as they have now done, so that I may delay no longer. This, then, goes by the hand of Zaccaria, to tell you that to-day has word been sent Gian Maria giving him three days in which to return to Babbiano or to abandon all hope of his crown, of which the people will send the offer then to you at Aquila, where you are believed to be. So now, my dear Lord, you have the tyrant at your mercy, tossed between Scylla and Charybdis. Yours it is to resolve how you will act ; but I rejoice in being the one to send you word that your presence at Roccaleone and your stubborn defence of the fortress has not been vain and that presently you are to reap the well-earned reward of it. The people have been stirred to this extreme action by the confusion prevailing here.

News has reached us that Cæsar Borgia is arming at Rome a condotta to invade Babbiano, and the people are exasperated at Gian Maria's continued absence in such a season. They are short-sighted in this, for they overlook the results that must attend the alliance with Urbino. May God protect and prosper your Excellency, whose most devoted servant is

Tanfulla degli Arcipreti.

CHAPTER XXII

A REVELATION

" FRANCESCO," said Valentina, and the name came from her lips as if it were an endearment, " why that frowning, careworn look ? "

They were in the dining-room alone, where the other had left them, and they were still seated at the table at which they had supped. Francesco raised his dark, thoughtful eyes, and as they lighted now on Valentina the thoughtfulness that was in them gave place to tenderness.

" I am fretted by this lack of news," he acknowledged. " I would I knew what is being done in Babbiano. I had thought that ere now Cæsar Borgia had stirred Gian Maria's subjects into some manner of action. I would I knew ! "

She rose, and coming close to him, she stood with one hand resting upon his shoulder, her eyes smiling down upon his upturned face.

" And shall such a trifle fret you—you who professed a week ago that you would this siege might last for ever ? "

" Account me not fickle, *anima mia*," he answered her, and he kissed the ivory fingers that rested on his shoulder. " For that was before the world changed for me at the magic of your bidding. And so," he repeated, " I would I knew what is toward at Babbiano."

" But why sigh over a wish so idle ? " she exclaimed. " By what means can news reach you here of the happenings of the world without ? "

He pondered a moment, seeking words in which to answer her. A score of times during that week had he been on the point of disclosing himself, of telling her who and what he was. Yet ever had he hesitated, putting

off that disclosure until the season should appear more
fitting. This he now considered the present. She trusted
him, and there was no reason to remain silent longer.
Perhaps already he had delayed too long, and so he was
about to speak when she started from his side and crossed
hastily to the window, alarmed by the sound of approaching steps. A second later the door opened, and Gonzaga
appeared.

A moment he hesitated in the doorway, looking from
one to the other, and Francesco, lazily regarding him in his
turn, noted that his cheeks were pale and that his eyes
glittered like those of a man with the fever. Then he
stepped forward, and, leaving the door open behind him,
he advanced into the room.

" Monna Valentina, I have something to communicate
to you." His voice shook slightly. " Messer—Francesco, will you give us leave ? " And his feverish eyes moved
to the open door with an eloquence that asked no words.

Francesco rose slowly, endeavouring to repress his
surprise, and glanced across at Valentina, as if awaiting
her confirmation or refusal of this request that he should
leave them.

" A communication for me ? " she marvelled, a slight
frown drawing her brows together. "Of what nature, sir ?"

" Of a nature as important as it is private."

She raised her chin, and with a patient smile she seemed
to beg of Francesco that he would suffer her to humour
this mood of Gonzaga's. In quick obedience Francesco
inclined his head.

" I shall be in my chamber until the hour of my
rounds, Madonna," he announced, and with that took
his departure.

Gonzaga attended him to the door, which he closed
after him, and, composing his features to an expression of
sorrowing indignation, he came back and stood facing
Valentina across the table.

" Madonna," he said, " I would to Heaven this communication I have to make to you came from other lips.
In the light of what has passed—here at Roccaleone—
through my folly—you—you may think my mission
charged with vindictiveness.

Perplexity stared at him from her eyes.

"You fill me with alarm, my good Gonzaga," she answered him, though smiling.

"Alas! It has fallen to my unfortunate lot to do more than that. I have made the discovery of as foul a piece of treachery here in your fortress as ever traitor hatched."

She looked at him more seriously now. The vehemence of his tone, and the suggestion of sorrow that ran through it and gave it so frank an accent, commanded her attention.

"Treachery!" she echoed in a low voice, her eyes dilating. "And from whom?"

He hesitated a moment, then waving his hand:

"Will you not sit, Madonna?" he suggested nervously.

Mechanically she seated herself at the table, her eyes ever on his face, alarm spreading in her heart, born of suspense.

"Be seated too," she bade him, "and tell me."

He drew up a chair, sat down opposite to her, and taking a deep breath: "Heard you ever of the Count of Aquila?" he inquired.

"It were odd if I had not. The most valiant knight in Italy, fame dubs him."

His eyes were intently on her face, and what he saw there satisfied him.

"You know how he stands with the people of Babbiano?"

"I know that he is beloved of them."

"And do you know that he is a pretender to the throne of Babbiano? You will remember that he is cousin to Gian Maria?"

"His relationship to Gian Maria, I know. That he pretends to the throne of Babbiano, I was not aware. But whither are we straying?"

"We are not straying, Madonna," answered Gonzaga, "we are making a straight line for the very heart and soul of this treachery I spoke of. Would you believe me if I told you that here, in Roccaleone, we have an agent of the Count of Aquila, one who in the Count's interest is protracting this siege with the pretended aim of driving Gian Maria off."

"Gonzaga——" she began, more than half guessing

the drift of his explanation. But he interrupted her with unusual brusqueness."

"Wait, Madonna," he cried, his eyes upon her face, his face imperiously raised. "Hear me out in patience. I am not talking idly. Of what I tell you I am armed with proof and witness. Such an agent of—of the Count's interests we have among us, and his true object in protracting this siege and encouraging and aiding you in your resistance, is to outwear the patience of the people of Babbiano with Gian Maria and drive them in the hour of their approaching peril from Cæsar Borgia's armies to bestow the throne on Aquila."

"Where learnt you this foul lie?" she asked him, her cheeks crimson, her eyes on fire.

"Madonna," he said in a patient voice, "this that you call a lie is already an accomplished fact. I am not laying before you the fruits of idle speculation; I have upon me the most positive proof that such a result as was hoped for has already been reached. Gian Maria has received from his subjects a notification that unless he is in his capital within three days from this they will invest the Lord of Aquila with the ducal crown."

She rose, her anger well controlled, her voice calm.

"Where is this proof? No, no; I don't need to see it. Whatever it is, what shall it prove to me? That your words, in so far as the politics of Babbiano are concerned, may be true; our resistance of Gian Maria may indeed be losing him his throne and doing good service to the cause of the Count of Aquila; but how shall all this prove that lie of yours, that Messer Francesco—for it is clearly of him you speak—that Messer Francesco should be this agent of the Count's? It is a lie, Gonzaga, for which you shall be punished, as you deserve."

She ceased, and stood awaiting his reply, and as she watched him his calm demeanour struck a chill into her heart. He was confident, so full of assurance; and that, in Gonzaga, she had learnt to know, meant a strong bulwark 'twixt himself and danger. He sighed profoundly.

"Madonna, these cruel words of yours do not wound me, since they are no more than I expected. But it will wound me—and sorely—if when you shall have learnt the

rest you do not humbly acknowledge how you have
wronged me, how grossly you have misjudged me.   You
think 1 come to you with evil in my heart, urged by a
spirit of vindictiveness against Messer Francesco.   Instead, I come to you with nothing but a profound sorrow
that mine must be the voice to disillusion you and a
deep indignation against him that has so foully used you
to his own ends. Wait, Madonna ! In a measure you are
right.   It is not strictly true to say that this Messer
Francesco is the agent of the Count of Aquila.''

" Ah !   You are recanting already ? ''

" Only a little—an insignificant little.   He is no agent,
because——''   He hesitated, and glanced swiftly up.
Then he sighed, lowered his voice, and with consummately
simulated   sorrow   he   concluded :   " Because he is,
himself, Francesco del Falco, Count of Aquila.''

She swayed a moment, and the colour died from her
cheeks, leaving them ivory pale.   She leaned heavily
against the table, and turned over in her mind what she
had heard   And then, as suddenly as it had gone, the
blood rushed back into her face mounting to her very
temples

" It's a lie ! '' she blazed at him ; " a lie for which you
shall be whipped.''

He shrugged his shoulders and cast Francesco's letter
on to the table.

" There, Madonna, is something that will prove all that
I have said.''

She eyed the paper coldly.   Her first impulse was to
call Fortemani and carry out her threat of having Gonzaga whipped, refusing so much as to see this thing that
he confidently termed a proof ; but it may be that his
confidence wrought upon her, touching a chord of femin-
ine curiosity.   That he was wrong she never doubted ;
but that he believed himself right she was also assured,
and she wondered what this thing might be that had so
convinced him.   Still she did not touch it, but asked in
an indifferent voice :

" What is it ? ''

" A letter that was brought hither to-night by a man
who swam the moat and whom I have ordered to be
detained in the armoury tower.   It is from Fanfulla degli

Arcipreti to the Count of Aquila. If your memory will
bear back to a certain day at Acquasparta, you may recall
that Fanfulla was the name of a very gallant cavalier
who addressed this Messer Francesco with marked
respect."

She took that backward mental glance he bade her, and
remembered. Then she remembered, too, how that very
evening Francesco had said that he was fretting for news
of Babbiano and that when she had asked how he hoped
that news could reach him at Roccaleone, Gonzaga had
entered before he answered her. Indeed, he had seemed
to hesitate upon that answer. A sudden chill encompassed her at that reflection. Oh, it was impossible—
absurd! And yet she took the letter from the table.
With knit brows she read it, whilst Gonzaga watched
her, scarce able to keep the satisfaction from gleaming
in his eyes.

She read it slowly, and as she read her face grew
deathly pale. When she had finished she stood silent
for a long minute, her eyes upon the signature and her
mind harking back to what Gonzaga had said and
drawing comparison between that and such things as
had been done and uttered, and nowhere did she find
the slightest gleam of that discrepancy which so ardently
she sought.

It was as if a hand were crushing the heart in her
bosom. This man whom she trusted, this peerless champion of her cause, to be nothing but a self-seeker, an
intriguer, who, to advance his own ends, had made a pawn
of her. She thought of how for a moment he had held her
in his arms and kissed her, and at that her whole soul revolted against the notion that here was no more than
treachery.

" It's all a plot against him ! " she cried, her cheeks
scarlet again. " It's an infamous thing of your devising,
Messer Gonzaga, an odious lie ! "

" Madonna, the man that brought the letter is still
detained. Confront him with Messer Francesco, or apply
the question to him and learn his master's true name and
station. As for the rest, if that letter is insufficient proof
for you, I beg that you will look back at facts. Why
should he lie to you and say that his name was Francesco

Franceschi ? Why should he have urged you—against
all reason—to remain here, when he brought you news
that Gian Maria was advancing ? Surely had he but
sought to serve you he had better accomplished this by
placing his own castle at Aquila at your disposal and
leaving here an empty nest for Gian Maria, as I urged."

She sank to a chair, a fever in her mind.

" I tell you, Madonna, there is no mistake. What I
have said is true. Another three days would he have
held Gian Maria here, whilst if you gave him that letter
it is odds he would slip away in the night of to-morrow
that he might be in Babbiano on the third day to take
the throne his cousin treats so lightly. Sainted God ! "
he cried out. " I think this is the most diabolically
treacherous plot that ever mind of man conceived and
human heartlessness executed."

" But—but——" she faltered, " all this is presupposing
that Messer Francesco is indeed the Count of Aquila.
May there—may it not be that this letter was meant for
some other destination ? "

" Will you confront this messenger with the Count ? "

" With the Count ! " she inquired dully. " With
Messer Francesco, you mean ? " She shuddered, and
with strange inconsistence : " No," she said in a choking
voice, her lip twisting oddly at the corner. " I do not
wish to see his face again."

A light gleamed in Gonzaga's eye and was extinguished
on the instant.

" Best make certain," he suggested, rising. " I have
ordered Fortemani to bring Lanciotto here. He will be
waiting now, without. Shall I admit them ? "

She nodded without speaking, and Gonzaga opened the
door, and called Fortemani. A voice answered him from
the gloom of the banqueting-hall.

" Bring Lanciotto here," he commanded.

When Francesco's servant entered, a look of surprise
on his face at these mysterious proceedings, it was
Valentina who questioned him, and that in a voice as cold
as though the issue concerned her no whit.

" Tell me, sirrah," she said—" and as you value your
neck, see that you answer me truly—what is your
master's name ? "

Lanciotto looked from her to Gonzaga, who stood by, a cynical curl on his sensual lips.

" Answer Monna Valentina," the courtier urged him. " State your master's true name and station."

" But, lady," began Lanciotto, bewildered.

" Answer me ! " she stormed, her small clenched hands beating the table in harsh impatience. And Lanciotto, seeing no help for it, answered :

" Messer Francesco del Falco, Count of Aquila."

Something that began in a sob and ended in a laugh burst from the lips of Valentina. Ercole's eyes were wide at the news, and he might have gone the length of inter- posing a question, when Gonzaga curtly bade him go to the armoury tower and bring thence the soldier and the man Gonzaga had left in his care.

" I will leave no shadow of doubt in your mind, Madonna," he said in explanation.

They waited in silence—for Lanciotto's presence hin- dered conversation—until Ercole returned accompanied by the man-at-arms and Zaccaria, who had now changed his raiment. Before they could question the new-comer, such questions as they might have put were answered by the greeting that passed between them and his fellow- servant Lanciotto.

Gonzaga turned to Valentina. She sat very still, her tawny head bowed and in her eyes a look of sore distress. And in that instant a brisk step sounded without. The door was thrust open and Francesco himself stood upon the threshold, with Peppe's alarmed face showing behind him. Gonzaga instinctively drew back a pace, and his countenance lost some of its colour.

At sight of Francesco, Zaccaria rushed forward and bowed profoundly.

" My lord ! " he greeted him.

And if one little thing was wanting to complete the evidence against the Count, that thing, by an odd mis- chance, Francesco himself seemed to supply. The strange group in that dining-room claiming his attention, and the portentous air that hung about those present, confirmed the warning Peppe had brought him that something was amiss. He disregarded utterly his servant's greeting, and with eyes of a perplexity that may have worn the look of alarm he sought the face of Valentina.

She rose upon the instant, an angry red colouring her cheeks. His very glance, it seemed, was become an affront unbearable after what had passed—for the memory of his kiss bit like a poisoned fang into her brain. An odd laugh broke from her. She made a gesture towards Francesco.

"Fortemani, you will place the Count of Aquila under arrest," she commanded, in a stern, steady voice, "and as you value your life you will see that he does not elude you."

The great bully hesitated. His knowledge of Francesco's methods was not encouraging.

"Madonna!" gasped Francesco, his bewilderment. increasing.

"Did you hear me, Fortemani?" she demanded. "Remove him."

"My lord?" cried Lanciotto, laying hand to his sword, his eyes upon his master's, ready to draw and lay about him at a glance of bidding.

"Sh! Let be," answered Francesco coldly. "Here! Messer Fortemani." And he proffered his dagger, the only weapon that he carried.

Valentina, calling Gonzaga to attend her, made shift to quit the apartment. At that Francesco seemed to awaken to his position.

"Madonna, wait," he cried, and he stepped deliberately before her. "You must hear me. I have surrendered in earnest of my faith, and confident that once you have heard me——"

"Captain Fortemani," she cried almost angrily, "will you restrain your prisoner? I wish to pass."

Ercole, with visible reluctance, laid a hand on Francesco's shoulder; but it was unnecessary. Before her words, the Count recoiled as if he had been struck. He stood clear of her path with a gasp at once of unbelief and angry resignation. An instant his eyes rested on Gonzaga so fiercely that the faint smile withered on the courtier's lips and his knees trembled under him as he hastened from the room in Valentina's wake.

CHAPTER XXIII

IN THE ARMOURY TOWER

The rough stones of the inner courtyard shone clean and bright in the morning sun, still wet with the heavy rains that had washed them yesternight.

The fool sat on a rude stool within the porch of the long gallery, and, moodily eyeing that glistening pavement, ruminated. He was angry, which, saving where Fra Domenico was conecrned, was a rare thing with good-humoured Peppe. He had sought to reason with Monna Valentina touching the imprisonment in his chamber of Messer Francesco, and she had bidden him confine his attention to his capers with a harshness he had never known in her before. But he had braved her commands and astonished her with the information that the true identity of this Messer Francesco had been known to him since that day when they had first met him at Acquasparta. He had meant to say more. He had meant to add the announcement of Francesco's banishment from Babbiano and his notorious unwillingness to mount his cousin's throne. He had meant to make her understand that had Francesco been so minded he had no need to stoop to such an act as this that she imputed to him. But she had cut him short, and with angry words and angrier threats she had driven him from her presence.

And so she was gone to Mass, and the fool had taken shelter in the porch of the gallery, that there he might vent some of his ill-humour—or indeed indulge it—in pondering the obtuseness of woman and the incidiousness of Gonzaga, to whom he never doubted that this miserable state of things was due.

And as he sat there—a grotesque, misshapen figure in gaudy motley—an ungovernable rage possessed him.

What was to become of them now ?   Without the Count
of Aquila's stern support the garrison would have forced
her to capitulate a week ago.   What would betide now
that the restraint of his formidable command was withdrawn ?

" She will know her folly when it's too late.   It's the
way of women," he assured himself.   And, loving his
mistress as he did, his faithful soul was stricken at the
thought.   He would wait there until she returned from
Mass, and then she would hear him—all should hear him.
He would not permit himself to be driven away again so
easily.   He was intently turning over in his mind what
he would say, with what startling, pregnant sentence
he would compel attention, when he was startled by the
appearance of a figure on the chapel steps.   Sudden and
quietly as an apparition it came, but it bore the semblance
of Romeo Gonzaga.

At sight of him Peppe instinctively drew back into
the shadows of the porch, his eyes discerning the suspicious furtiveness of the courtier's movements and
watching them with a grim eagerness.   He saw Romeo
look carefully about him, and then descend the steps on
tiptoe, evidently so that no echo of his footfalls should
reach those within the chapel.   Then, never suspecting
the presence of Peppe, he sped briskly across the yard
and vanished through the archway that led to the outer
court.   And the fool, assured that some knowledge of the
courtier's purpose would not be amiss, set out to follow
him.

In his room under the Lion's Tower the Count of Aquila
had spent a restless night, exercised by those same fears
touching the fate of the castle that had beset the fool,
but less readily attributing his confinement to Gonzaga's
scheming.   Zaccaria's presence had told him that Fanfulla
must at last have written, and he could but assume that
the letter, falling into Monna Valentina's hands, should
have contained something that she construed into treason
on his part.

Bitterly he reproached himself now with not having
from the very outset been frank with her touching his
identity ; bitterly he reproached her with not so much as
giving a hearing to the man she had professed to love.

Had she but told him upon what grounds her suspicions against him had been founded, he was assured that he could have dispelled them at a word, making clear their baselessness and his own honesty of purpose towards her. Most of all was he fretted by the fact that Zaccaria's presence, after coming so long expected and so long delayed, argued that the news he bore was momentous. From this it might result that Gian Maria should move at any moment and that his action might be of a desperate character.

Now through the ranks of Fortemani's men there had run an inevitable dismay at Francesco's arrest and a resentment against Valentina who had encompassed it. His hand it was that had held them together, his judgment—of which they had unequivocal signs—that had given them courage. He was a leader who had shown himself capable of leading and out of confidence for whom they would have undertaken anything that he bade them. Whom had they now ? Fortemani was but one of themselves, placed in command over them by an event purely adventitious. Gonzaga was a fop whose capers they mimicked and whose wits they despised ; whilst Valentina, though brave enough and high-spirited, remained a girl of no worldly and less military knowledge, whose orders it might be suicidal to carry out.

Now by none were these opinions more strongly entertained than by Ercole Fortemani himself. Never had he performed anything with greater reluctance than the apprehension of Francesco, and when he thought of what was likely to follow his consternation knew no bounds. He had come to respect and, in his rough way, even to love their masterful Provost, and since learning his true identity in the hour of arresting him, his admiration had grown to something akin to reverence for the *condottiero* whose name to the men-at-arms of Italy was like the name of some patron saint.

To ensure the safe keeping of his captive, he had been ordered by Gonzaga, who now resumed command of Roccaleone, to spend the night in the anteroom of Francesco's chamber. These orders he had exceeded by spending a considerable portion of the night in the Count's very room.

"You have but to speak," the bully had sworn, by
way of showing Francesco the true nature of his feelings,
"and the castle is yours. At a word from you my men
will flock to obey you, and you may do your will at
Roccaleone."

"Foul traitor that you are," Francesco had laughed
at him. "Do you forget under whom you have taken
service? Let be what is, Ercole. But if a favour you
would do me, let me see Zaccaria—the man that came to
Roccaleone to-night."

This Ercole had done for him. Now Zacaria was
fully aware of the contents of the letter he had carried,
having been instructed by Fanfulla against the chance
arising of his being compelled for his safety to destroy it
—an expedient to which he now bitterly repented him
that he had not had recourse. From Zaccaria, then,
Francesco learnt all that there was to learn, and since the
knowledge but confirmed his fears that Gian Maria
would delay action no longer he fell a prey to the most
passsionate impatience at his own detention.

In the grey hours of the morning he grew calmer, and
by the light of the lamp that he had called Ercole to re-
plenish he sat down to write a letter to Valentina, which,
he thought, should carry conviction of his honesty to her
heart. Since she would not hear him, this was the only
course. At the end of an hour—his moribund light grown
yellow now that the sun was risen—his letter was accomplished, and he summoned Ercole again to charge him
to deliver it at once to Monna Valentina.

"I shall await her return from chapel," answered
Ercole.

He took the letter and departed. As he emerged into
the courtyard he was startled to see the fool dash towards
him gasping for breath and with excitement in every
line of his quaint face.

"Quickly, Ercole!" Peppe enjoined him. "Come
with me."

"Devil take you, spawn of Satan—whither?"
growled the soldier.

"I will tell you as we go. We have not a moment to
spare. There is treachery afoot—Gonzaga——" he
gasped, and ended desperately: "Will you come?"

Fortemani needed no second bidding. The chance of catching pretty Messer Romeo at a treachery was too sweet a lure. Snorting and puffing—for hard drinking had sorely impaired his wind—the great captain hurried the fool along, listening as they went to the gasps in which he brought out his story. It was not much, after all. Peppe had seen Messer Gonzaga repair to the armoury tower. Through an arrow-slit he had watched him take down and examine an arbalest, place it on the table and sit down to write.

"Well ? " demanded Ercole. "What else ? "

"Naught else. That is all," answered the hunchback.

"Heaven and hell ! " roared the swashbuckler, coming to a standstill and glowering down upon his impatient companion. "And you have made me run for this ? "

"And is it not enough ? " retorted Peppe testily. "Will you come on ? "

"Not a foot farther," returned the captain, getting very angry. "Is this a miserable jest ? What of the treachery you spoke of ? "

"A letter and an arbalest ! " panted the maddened Peppe, grimacing horribly at this delay. "God, was there ever such a fool ! Does this mean nothing to that thick empty thing you call a head ? Have you forgotten how Gian Maria's offer of a thousand florins came to Roccaleone ? On an arbalest quarrel, stupid ! Come on, I say, and afterward you shall have my motley, the only livery you have a right to wear."

In the shock of enlightenment Ercole forgot to cuff the jester for his insolence, and allowed himself once more to be hurried along, across the outer court and up the steps that led to the battlements.

"You think——" he began.

"I think you had best tread more softly," snapped the fool, under his breath, "and control that thunderous wheeze, if you would surprise Ser Romeo."

Ercole accepted the hint, meek as a lamb, and leaving the fool behind him on the steps, he went softly up and approached the armoury tower. Peering cautiously through the arrow-slit, and favoured by the fact that Gonzaga's back was towards him, he saw that he was no more than in time.

The courtier was bending down, and by the creaking sound that reached him Ercole guessed his occupation to be the winding of the arbalest string.   On the table at his side lay a quarrel swathed in a sheet of paper.

Swiftly and silently Ercole moved round the tower, and the next instant he had pushed open the unfastened door and entered.

A scream of terror greeted him, and a very startled face was turned upon him by Gonzaga, who instantly sprang upright.   Then, seeing who it was the courtier's face reassumed some of its normal composure, but his glance was uneasy and his cheek pale.

" *Sant Iddio* ! " he gasped.   " You startled me, Ercole. I did not hear you coming."

And now something in the bully's face heightened the alarm in Gonzaga.   He still made an effort at self-control, as, planting himself between Ercole and the table, so as to screen the tell-tale shaft, he asked him what he sought here.

" That letter you have written Gian Maria," was the bruff, uncompromising answer, for Ercole recked nothing of diplomatic issues.

Gonzaga's mouth jerked itself open and his upper lip shuddered against his teeth.

" What——   Wha——"

" Give me that letter," Ercole insisted, now advancing upon him and wearing an air of ferocity that drove back into Gonzaga's throat such resentful words as he bethought him of.   Then like an animal at bay—and even a rat will assert itself then—he swung aloft the heavy arbalest he held and stood barring Ercole's way.

" Stand back ! " he cried ; "or, by God and His saints, I'll beat your brains out."

There was a guttural laugh from the swashbuckler, and then his arms were round Gonzaga's shapely waist and the popinjay was lifted from his feet.   Viciously he brought down the cross-bows, as he had threatened ; but it smote the empty air.   The next instant Gonzaga was hurtled, bruised, into a corner of the tower.

In a rage so great that he felt it draining him of his very strength and choking the breath in his body, he made a movement to rise and fling himself again upon his aggressor. But Fortemani was down upon him, and for all his struggles contrived to turn him over on his face, twisting his arms behind him, and making them fast with a belt that lay at hand.

" Lie still, you scorpion ! " growled the ruffler, breathing hard from his exertions. He rose, took the shaft with the letter tied about it, read the superscription— " To the High and Mighty Lord Gian Maria Sforza "— and with a chuckle of mingled relish and scorn he was gone, locking the door.

Left alone, Gonzaga lay face downward where he had been flung, able to do little more than groan and sweat in the extremity of his despair, whilst he awaited the coming of those who would probably make an end of him. Not even from Valentina could he hope for mercy, so incriminating was the note he had penned. His letter was to enjoin the Duke to hold his men in readiness at the hour of the Angelus next morning and to wait until Gonzaga should wave a handkerchief from the battlements. At that he was to advance immediately to the postern, which he would find open, and the rest, Gonzaga promised him, would be easy. He should take the whole garrison at their prayers—and weaponless.

When Francesco read it a light leapt to his eye and an oath to his lips ; but neither glance nor oath were of execration, as Ercole stood expecting. A sudden idea flashed through the Count's mind, so strange and humorous and yet so full of promise of easy accomplishment, that he burst into a laugh.

" Now may God bless this fool for the most opportune of traitors ! " he exclaimed, in surprise at which Fortemani's mouth fell open and the eyes of Peppe grew very round. " Ercole, my friend, here is a bait to trap that lout my cousin such as I could never have devised myself."

" You mean——? "

" Take it back to him," cried the Count, holding out letter with a hand that trembled in the eagerness of his spirit. " Take it back and get him by fair means or foul to shoot it as he intended ; or if he refuses, why, then, do you seal it up and shoot it yourself. But see that it gets to Gian Maria."

" May I not know what you intend ? " quoth the bewildered Ercole.

" All in good time, my friend. First do my bidding with that letter. Listen ! It were best that, having read it, you agree to join him in his betrayal of Roccaleone, your own fears as to the ultimate fate awaiting you at Gian Maria's hands being aroused. Urge him to promise you money, immunity, what you will, as your reward ; but make him believe you sincere, and induce him to shoot his precious bolt. Now go ! Lose no time or they may be returning from chapel, and your opportunity will be lost. Come to me here afterwards and I will tell you what is in my mind. We shall have a busy night of it to-night, Ercole, and you must set me free when the others are abed. Now go ! "

Ercole went, and Peppe, remaining, plagued the Count with questions which he answered until in the end the fool caught the drift of his scheme and swore impudently that a greater jester than his Excellency did not live. Then Ercole returned.

" Is it done ? Has the letter gone ? " cried Francesco. Fortemani nodded.

" We are sworn brothers in this business, he and I. He added a line to his note to say that he had gained my co-operation, and that, therefore, immunity was expected for me too."

" You have done well, Ercole," Francesco applauded him. " Now return me the letter I gave you for Monna Valentina. There is no longer the need for it. But return to me to-night towards the fourth hour, when all are abed, and bring with you my men, Lanciotto and Zaccario."

CHAPTER XXIV

THE morning of that Wednesday of Corpus Christi, fateful to all concerned in this chronicle, dawned misty and grey, and the air was chilled by the wind that blew from the sea. The chapel bell tinkled out its summons, and the garrison trooped faithfully to Mass.

Presently came Monna Valentina, followed by her ladies, her pages, and, lastly, Peppe, wearing under his thin mask of piety an air of eager anxiety and unrest. Valentina was very pale, and round her eyes there were dark circles that told of sleeplessness; and as she bowed her head in prayer her ladies observed that tears were falling on the illuminated Mass-book over which she bent. And now came Fra Domenico from the sacristy in the white chasuble that the Church ordains for the Corpus Christi feast, followed by a page in a clerkly gown of black, and the Mass commenced.

There were absent only from the gathering Gonzaga and Fortemani, besides a sentry and the three prisoners, Francesco and his two followers.

Gonzaga had presented himself to Valentina with the plausible tale that, as the events of which Fanfulla's letter had given them knowledge might lead Gian Maria at any moment to desperate measures, it might be well that he should reinforce the single man-at-arms patrolling the walls. Valentina, little recking now whether the castle held or fell, and still less such trifles as Gonzaga's attendance at Mass, had assented w thout heeding the import of what he said

And so, his face drawn and his body quivering with the excitement of what he was about to do, Gonzaga had repaired to the ramparts so soon as he had seen them all safely into chapel. The sentinel was that same clerkly youth Aventano, who had read to the soldiers that letter Gian Maria had sent Gonzaga. This the courtier accepted as a good omen. If there was a man among the soldiery at Roccaleone with whom he deemed that he had an acccunt to settle, that man was Aventano.

The mist was rapidly lightening, and the country grew visible for miles around. In the camp of Gian Maria he observed a coming and going of men that argued an inordinate bustle for so early an hour. They awaited his signal.

He approached the young sentinel, growing more and more nervous as the time for action advanced. He cursed Fortemani, who had selfishly refused to take an active part in the admission of Gian Maria. Here was a task that Fortemani could perform more satisfactorily than he. He had urged this fact on Ercole's attention, but the swashbuckler had grinned and shook his head. To Gonzaga fell the greater reward, and so Gonzaga must do the greater work. It was only fair, the knave had urged ; and while Gonzaga was about it he would watch the chapel door against interruption. And so Gonzaga had been forced to come alone to try conclusions with the sentry.

He gave the young man a nervous but pleasant " Good morrow," and observed with satisfaction that he wore no body armour. His original intention had been to attempt to suborn him and render him pliable by bribery ; but now that the moment for action was arrived he dared not make the offer. He lacked for words in which to present his proposal, and he was afraid lest the man should resent it and in a fit of indignation attack him with his partisan. He little imagined that Aventano had been forewarned by Ercole that a bribe would be offered him and that he was to accept it promptly. Ercole had chosen this man because he was intelligent, and had made him understand enough of what was toward, besides offering a substantial reward if he played his part well, and Aventano waited. But Gonzaga, knowing naught of this, abandoned at the last moment the notion of bribing him—which Ercole had enjoined him, and which he in his turn had promised Ercole was the course he would pursue.

" You seem cold, Excellency," said the young man deferentially, for he had observed that Gonzaga shivered.

" A chill morning," Aventano, returned the gallant with a grin.

" True ; but the sun is breaking through yonder. It will be warmer soon."

" Why, yes," answered the other abstractedly, and still he remained by the sentinel, his hand, under the gay mantle of blue velvet, nervously fingering the hilt of a dagger that he dared not draw.   It came to him that moments were passing and that the thing must be done.   Yet Aventano was a sinewy youth, and if the sudden stab he meditated failed him he would be at the fellow's mercy.   At the thought he shivered again, and his face turned grey.   He moved away a step and then inspiration brought him a cruel ruse.   He uttered a cry.

" What is that ? " he exclaimed, his eyes on the ground.

In an instant Aventano was beside him, for his voice had sounded alarmed—a tone, in his present condition, not difficult to simulate.

" What, Excellency ? "

" Down there," cried Gonzaga excitedly. " There, from that fissure in the stone. Saw you nothing ? " And he pointed to the ground at a spot where two slabs met.

" I saw nothing, Illustrious."

" It was like a flash of yellow light below there. What is under us here ?   I'll swear there's treachery at work.   Get down on your knees and try if anything to be seen."

With a wondering glance at the courtier's white twitching face, the unfortunate young man went down on all fours to do his bidding.   After all—poor fellow !— he was hardly as intelligent as Fortemani opined.

" There is nothing, Excellency," he said. " The plaster is cracked.   But—— A-h ! "

In a panic of haste Gonzaga had whipped the dagger from its sheath and sunk it into the middle of Aventino's

broad back. The fellow's arms slid out, and with a
long-drawn gurgling sigh he sank down and stretched
himself horribly on the stones.

In that instant the clouds parted overhead and the
sun came out in a blaze of golden glory. High above
Gonzaga's head a lark burst into song.

For a moment the assassin remained standing above
the body of his victim with head sunk between the
shoulders like a man who expects a blow, his face grey,
his teeth chattering and his mouth twitching hideously.
A shudder shook him. It was the first life he had
taken, and that carrion at his feet filled him with sickly
horror. Not for a kingdom—not to save his vile soul
from the eternal damnation that act had earned—would
he have dared stoop to pluck the dagger from the back
of the wretch he had murdered. With something like
a scream he turned and fled in a panic from the spot.
Panting with horror, yet subconsciously aware of the
work he had to do, he paused a moment to wave a
kerchief, then dashed down the steps to the postern.

With trembling fingers he unlocked the door and
set it wide to Gian Maria's men, who, in answer to his
signal, were now hurrying forward with a bridge composed of pine trees, that they had hastily and roughly
put together during the previous day. This, with some
efforts and more noise than Gonzaga relished, was
thrust across the moat. One of the men crept across
and assisted Gonzaga to make fast his end.

A moment later Gian Maria and Guidobaldo stood
in the castle-yard, and after them came almost every
man of the five score that Gian Maria had brought to
that siege. This was what Francesco had confidently
expected, knowing that it was not his cousin's way to
run any risks.

The Duke of Babbiano, whose face was disfigured by
a bristling hedge of reddish stubble—for in obedience to
the vow he had made, he now carried a fortnight's growth
of beard on his round face—turned to Gonzaga.

" Is all well ? " he asked, in a friendly tone, whist
Guidobaldo contemptuously eyed the popinjay.

Gonzaga assured them that the whole thing had been
effected without disturbing the garrison at their prayers.

Now that he deemed himself well protected his usual serenity of manner returned.

"You may felicitate yourself, Highness," he ventured to say, with a grin, to Guidobaldo, "that you have reared your niece in devout ways."

"Did you address me?" quoth the Duke of Urbino coldly. "I trust it may not again be necessary."

Before the look of loathing in his handsome face Gonzaga cringed. Gian Maria laughed in his piping treble.

"Have I not served your Highness faithfully?" fawned the gallant.

"So has the meanest scullion in my kitchens, the lowliest groom in my stables—and with more honour to himself," answered the proud Duke. "Yet he does not go the length of jesting with me." His eye carried a menace so eloquent that Gonzaga drew back, afraid; but Gian Maria clapped him on the shoulder in a friendly manner.

"Be of good heart, Judas," he laughed, his pale face a-grin, "I shall find room for you in Babbiano, and work, too, if you do it as well as this. Come; the men are here now. Let us go forward whilst they are at their prayers. But we must not disturb them," he added, more seriously. "I will not be guilty of an impiety. We can lie in wait for them without."

He laughed gaily, for he seemed in a preposterously good humour, and bidding Gonzaga lead the way he followed with Guidobaldo at his side. They crossed the courtyard, where his men were ranged, armed to the teeth, and at the door of the archway leading to the inner court they paused for Gonzaga to open it.

A moment the gallant stood staring. Then he turned a face of consternation on the Dukes. His knees shook visibly.

"It is locked," he announced in a husky voice.

"We made too much noise in entering," suggested Guidobaldo, "and they have taken the alarm."

The explanation relieved the growing uneasiness in Gian Maria's mind. He turned with an oath to his men

"Here, some of you," his sharp voice commanded.

" Beat me down this door. By the Host ! Do the fools think to keep me out so easily ? "

The door was broken down and they advanced. But only some half-dozen paces, for at the end of that short gallery they found the second door barring their progress. Through this, too, they broke, Gian Maria fiercely blaspheming at the delay. Yet when it was done he was none so eager to lead the way.

In the second courtyard he deemed it extremely probable that they should find Valentina's soldiers awaiting them. So bidding his men pass on, he remained behind with Guidobaldo until he heard word that the inner court was likewise empty.

And now the entire hundred of his followers were assembled there to overpower the twenty that served Monna Valentina ; and Guidobaldo—despite Gian Maria's scruples—strode coolly forward to the chapel door.

. . . . .

Within the chapel Mass had started. Fra Domenico at the foot of the altar had pattered through the Confiteor, his deep voice responded to by the soprano of the ministering page. The Kyrie was being uttered when the attention of the congregation was attracted by the sound of steps approaching the chapel door to the accompaniment of an ominous clank of steel. The men rose in a body, fearing treachery, and cursing— despite the sanctity of the place—the circumstance that they were without weapons.

Then the door opened, and down the steps rang the armed heels of the newcomers, so that every eye was turned upon them including that of Fra Domenico, who had pronounced the last " Christe eleison " in a quavering voice.

A gasp of relief, followed by an angry cry from Valentina, went up when they recognised those that came. First stepped the Count of Aquila in full armour, sword at side and dagger on hip, carrying his head-piece on the crook of his left arm. Behind him towered the bulk of Fortemani, his great face flushed with a strange excitement, a leather hacketon over his steel cuirass, girt, too, with sword and dagger, and carrying his shining morion in his hand.   Last came Lanciotto and Zaccaria, both fully equipped and armed at all points.

" Who are you that come thus accoutred into God's House to interrupt the holy Mass ? " cried the bass voice of the friar.

" Patience, good father," answered Francesco calmly. " The occasion is our justification."

" What does this mean, Fortemani ? " demanded Valentina imperiously, her eyes angrily set upon her captain, utterly ignoring the Count.   " Do you betray me too ? "

" It means, Madonna," answered the giant bluntly " that your lap-dog, Messer Gonzaga, is at this very moment admitting Gian Maria and his forces to Roccaleone, by the postern."

There was a hoarse cry from the men, which Francesco silenced by a wave of his mailed hand.

Valentina looked wildly at Fortemani, and then, as if drawn by a greater will than her own, her eyes were forced to travel to the Count.   He instantly advanced and bowed his head before her.

" Madonna, this is no hour for explanations.   Action is needed, and that at once.   I was wrong in not disclosing my identity to you before you discovered it by such unfortunate means and with the assistance of the only traitor Roccaleone has harboured, Romeo Gonzaga —who, as Fortemani has just told you, is at this moment admitting my cousin and your uncle to the castle.   But that my object was ever other than to serve you, or that I sought, as was represented to you, to turn this siege to my own political profit, that, Madonna, I implore you in your own interests to believe untrue."

She sank on to her knees and with folded hands began to pray to the Mother of Mercy, deeming herself lost, for his tone carried conviction, and he had said that Gian Maria was entering the castle.

" Madonna," he cried, touching her lightly on the shoulder ; " let your prayers wait until they can be of thanksgiving. Listen. By the vigilance of Peppe there, who, good soul that he is, never lost faith in me or deemed me a dastard, we were informed last night—Fortemani and I—of this that Gonzaga was preparing. And we have made our plans and prepared the ground. When Gian Maria's soldiers enter they will find the outer doo s barred and locked, and we shall gain a little time while they break through them. My men, you will observe, are even now barring the door of the chapel to impose a further obstacle. Now while they are thus engaged we must act. Briefly, then, if you will trust us we will bear you out of this, for we four have worked through the night to some purpose."

She looked at him through a film of tears, her face drawn and startled. Then she put her hands to her brow in a gesture of bewildered helplessness.

" But they will follow us," she complained.

" Not so," he answered smiling. " For that, too, have we provided. Come, Madonna, time presses."

A long moment she looked at him. Then, brushing aside the tears that dimmed her sight, she set a hand on either of his shoulders and stood so, before them all, gazing up into his calm face.

" How shall I know that what you say is true—that I may trust you ? " she asked, but her voice was not the voice of one that demands an overwhelming proof ere she will believe.

" By my honour and my knighthood," he answered in a ringing voice, " I make oath here, at the foot of God's altar, that my purpose—my only purpose—has been, is, and shall be to serve you. Monna Valentina."

" I believe you," she cried ; to sob a moment later : " Forgive me, Francesco, and may God, too, forgive my lack of faith in you."

He softly breathed her name in such sweet accents that a happy peace pervaded her and the bright courage of yore shone in her brown eyes.

" Come, sirs ! " he cried now, with a sudden briskness that startled them into feverish obedience. " You, Fra Domenico, put off your sacerdotals, and gird high your habit. There is climbing for you. Here, a couple of you, move aside that altar-step. My men and I have spent the night in loosening its old hinges."

They raised the slab, and in the gap beneath it was disclosed a flight of steps leading down to the dungeons and cellar of Roccaleone.

Down this they went in haste but in good order, marshalled by Francesco, and when the last had passed down he and Lanciotto, aided by others below, who had seized a rope that he had lowered them, replaced the slab from underneath so that no trace should remain of the way by which they had come.

A postern had been unbarred below by Fortemanı, who had led the way with a half-dozen of the men ; and a huge scaling ladder that lay in readiness in that subterranean gallery was rushed out across the moat, which at this point was a roaring torrent.

Fortemani was the first to descend that sloping bridge, and upon reaching the ground he made fast the lower end.

Next went a dozen men at Francesco's bidding, armed with the pikes that had been left overnight in the gallery. At a word of command they slipped quietly away. Then came the women, and lastly the remainder of the men.

Of the enemy they caught no glimpse ; not so much as a sentry, for every one of Gian Maria's men had been pressed into the investment of the castle. Thus they emerged from Roccaleone and made their way down that rough bridge into the pleasant meadows to the south. Already Fortemani and his dozen men had disappeared at the trot, making for the front of the castle, when Francesco stepped last upon the bridge and closed the postern after him. Then he glided rapidly to the ground, and with the assistance of a dozen ready hands he dragged away the scaling ladder. They carried it some yards from the brink of the torrent and deposited it in the meadow. With a laugh of purest relish Francesco stepped to Valentina's side.

" It will exercise their minds to discover how we got out," he cried, " and they will be forced to the conclusion that we are angels all, with wings beneath our armour. We have not left them a single ladder or a strand of rope in Roccaleone by which to attempt to follow us, even if they discover how we came. But come, Valentina *mia*, the comedy is not finished yet. Already Fortemani will have removed the bridge by which they entered and engaged such few men as may have been left behind, and we have the High and Mighty Gian Maria in the tightest trap that was ever fashioned.''

IN the sunshine of that bright May morning Francesco and his men went merrily to work to possess themselves of the ducal camp, and the first business of the day was to arm those soldiers who had come out unarmed. Of weapons there was no lack, and to these they helped themselves in liberal fashion, whilst here and there a man would pause to don a haubergeon or press a steel cap on his head.

Three sentries only had been left to guard the tents and these Fortemani and a couple of his men had made prisoners, whilst the others were removing the bridge by which the invaders had entered. And now beneath the open postern by the drawbridge gaped a surging torrent that no man would have the hardihood to attempt to swim.

In that opening, presently, appeared Gian Maria his face red for once, and behind a clamouring crowd of men-at-arms who shared their master's rage at the manner in which they had been trapped.

At the rear of the tents Valentina and her ladies awaited the issue of the parley that now seemed toward. The bulk of the men were busy at Gian Maria's cannons, and under Francesco's supervision they were training them upon the drawbridge.

From the castle a mighty shout went up. The men disappeared from the postern to reappear a moment later on the ramparts, and Francesco laughed deep down in his throat as he perceived the purpose of this. They had bethought them of the guns that were mounted there and were gone to use them against Valentina's little army. Gun after gun they tried, and a fierce

cry of rage burst forth when they realised by what
dummies they had been held in check during the past
week. This was followed by a silence of some moments,
terminated at last by the sound of a bugle.

Answering that summons to a parley, and with a last
word of injunction to Fortemani, who was left in charge
of the men at the guns, Francesco rode forward on one
of Gian Maria's horses, escorted by Lanciotto and
Zaccaria similarly mounted, and each armed with a
loaded arquebuse.

Under the walls of Roccaleone he drew rein, laughing
to himself at this monstrous change of sides. As he
halted—helmet on head, but beaver open—a body
came hurtling over the battlements and splashed into the
foaming waters below. It was the corpse of Aventano,
which Gian Maria had peremptorily bidden them to
remove from his sight.

" I desire to speak with Monna Valentina della
Rovere," cried the furious Duke.

" You may speak with me, Gian Maria," answered
Francesco's voice, clear and metallic. " I am her
representative, her sometime Provost of Roccaleone."

" Who are you ? " quoth the Duke, struck by a
familiar note in that mocking voice.

" Francesco del Falco, Count of Aquila."

" By God ! You ! "

" An age of marvels, is it not ? " laughed Francesco.
" Which will you lose, my cousin—a wife or a duchy ? "

Rage struck Gian Maria speechless for a moment.
Then he turned to Guidobaldo and whispered something ; but Guidobaldo, who seemed vastly interested
now in this knight below, merely shrugged his shoulders.

" I will lose neither, Messer Francesco," roared the
Duke. " Neither, by God ! " he screamed. " Neither,
do you hear me ? "

" I should be deaf else," was the easy answer. " But
you are gravely at fault. One or the other you must
relinquish, and it is yours to make a choice between
them. The game has gone against you, Gian Maria,
and you must pay."

" But have I no voice in the bartering of my niece ? "
asked Guidobaldo with cold dignity. " Is it for you,

Lord Count, to say whether your cousin shall wed her or not ? ''

" Why, no. He may wed her if he will, but he will be a duke no longer. In fact, he will be an outcast with no title to lay claim to, if indeed the Babbianians will leave him a head at all ; whilst I, at least, though not a duke with a tottering throne, am a count with lands, small but securely held, and shall become a duke if Gian Maria refuses to relinquish me your niece. So that if he be disposed to marry her will you be disposed to let her marry a homeless vagrant or a headless corpse ? ''

Guidobaldo's face seemed to change, and his eyes looked curiously at the white-faced Duke beside him.

" So you are the other pretender to my niece's hand, Lord Count ? '' he asked in his coldest voice.

" I am, Highness,'' answered Francesco quietly. " The matter stands thus : Unless Gian Maria is in Babbiano by morning, he forfeits his crown, and it passes to me by the voice of the people ; but if he will relinquish his claim to Monna Valentina in my favour then I shall journey straight to Aquila and I shall trouble Babbiano no more. If he refuses, and insists upon this wedding, abhorrent to Monna Valentina, why, then, my men shall hold him captive behind those walls until it be too late for him to reach his duchy in time to save the crown. In the meantime I will ride to Babbiano in his stead, and—reluctant though I be to play the duke—I shall accept the throne and silence the people's importunities. He can then endeavour to win your Highness's consent to the union.''

For perhaps the first time in his life Guidobaldo was guilty of an act of positive discourtesy. He broke into a laugh—a boisterous, amused laugh that cut into Gian Maria's heart like a knife.

" Why, Lord Count,'' he said, " I confess that you have us very much in your hands to mould us as you will. Now, you are such a soldier and such a strategist, as it would pleasure me to have about my person in Urbino. What says your Highness ? '' he continued, turning now to the almost speechless Gian Maria. " I

have yet another niece with whom we might cement
the union of the two duchies; and she might prove
more willing. Women, it seems, will insist upon being
women. Do you not think that Monna Valentina and
this your valiant cousin——"

"Heed him not!" screamed Gian Maria, now in
a white-heat of passion. "He is a smooth-tongued
dog that would argue the very devil out of hell. Make
no terms with the hind! I have a hundred men,
and——" He swung suddenly round. "Let down
that drawbridge, cowards!" he bawled at them,
"and sweep me those animals from my tents."

"Gian Maria, I give you warning," cried Francesco
loudly and firmly. "I have trained your own guns on
to that bridge, and at the first attempt to lower it
I'll blow it into splinters. You come not out of Roccaleone save to my pleasure and upon my terms, and if you
lose your duchy by your obstinacy it will be your own
work; but answer me now, that I may take my course."

Guidobaldo, too, restrained Gian Maria, and counter-
manded his order for the lowering of the bridge. And
now on his other side Gonzaga crept up to him and
whispered into his ear the suggestion that he should
wait until night had fallen.

"Wait until night, fool!" blazed the Duke, turning
on him in a fierce joy at finding one whom he might
rend. "If I wait until then my throne is lost to me.
This comes of sorting with traitors. It is your fault, you
Judas!" he cried more fiercely still—his face distorted;
"but you at least shall pay for what you have done."

Gonzaga saw a sudden flash of steel before his eyes,
and a piercing scream broke from him as Gian Maria's
dagger buried itself in his breast. Too late Guidobaldo
put forward a hand to stay the Duke.

And so by a strangely avenging justice the magnificent
Gonzaga sank dead on the very spot on which he had
so cravenly and dastardly poniarded Aventano.

"Throw me that carrion into the moat," growled
Gian Maria, still quivering with rage that had prompted
his ferocious act.

He was obeyed, and thus murdered and murderer
were united in a common grave.

After the first attempt to restrain Gian Maria, Guido-baldo had looked on in unconcern, deeming the act a very fitting punishment of a man with whose treachery he, at least, had never been in sympathy.

As he saw the body vanish in the torrent below, Gian Maria seemed to realise what he had done. His anger fell from him, and with bent head he piously crossed himself. Then turning to an attendant who stood at his elbow :

" See that a Mass is said for his soul to-morrow," he solemnly bade him.

As if the act had served to pacify him and restore him to his senses, Gian Maria now stepped forward and asked his cousin, in calmer tones than he had hitherto employed, to make clear the terms on which he would permit him to return to Babbiano within the time to which his people limited him.

" They are no more than that you relinquish your claim to Monna Valentina and that you find consola-tion—as I think his Highness of Urbino has himself suggested—in the Lord Guidobaldo's younger niece."

Before he could reply Guidobaldo was urging him in a low voice to accept the terms.

" What else is there for you ? " Montefeltro ended pregnantly.

" And this other niece of yours——? " quoth Gian Maria lamely.

" I have already passed my word," answered Guidobaldo.

" And Monna Valentina ? " the other almost whined.

" May wed this headstrong *condottiero* of hers. I'll not withstand them. Come ; I am your friend in this. I am even sacrificing Valentina to your interests. For if you persist, he will ruin you. The game is his, my lord. Acknowledge your defeat, as I acknowledge mine, and pay."

" But what is your defeat to mine ? " cried Gian Maria, who saw through Guidobaldo's appreciation of the fact that such a nephew-in-law as Francesco del Falco was far from undesirable in the troublous times that threatened.

" It is at least as absolute," returned Guidobaldo

with a shrug. And in this vein the Duke of Urbino continued for some moments, till, in the end, Gian Maria found himself not only deserted by his ally, but having this ally now combating on his cousin's side and pressing him to accept his cousin's terms, distasteful though they were. Thus urged, Gian Maria lamely acknowledged his defeat and his willingness to pay the forfeit. With that he asked how soon he might be permitted to leave the castle.

" Why, at once, now that I have your word," answered Francesco readily, whereat treachery gleamed from Gian Maria's eye, to be swiftly quenched by Francesco's next words. " But lest your men and mine should come to trouble with one another, you will order yours to come forth without arms or armour, and you will depose your own. His Highness Guidobaldo is the only man in whose favour I can make an exception to this condition. Let it be broken, and I promise you that you will very bitterly regret it. At sight of the first armed man issuing from those gates I'll give the word to fire on you, and your own guns shall work your destruction."

Thus was the second siege of Roccaleone ended almost as soon as it was begun, and thus did Gian Maria capitulate to the conqueror. The Duke of Babbiano and his men marched out sheepishly and silently and took their way to Babbiano, no word—not even so much as a glance—passing between Gian Maria and the lady who had been the cause of his discomfiture, and who blithely looked on at his departure.

Guidobaldo and his few attendants lingered after his late ally had gone. Then he bade Francesco lead him to his niece, in which Francesco readily obeyed him.

The Duke embraced her coldly—still that he embraced her at all after what was passed augured well.

" You will come with me to Urbino, Lord Count ? " he said suddenly to Francesco. " It were best to celebrate the nuptials there. Everything is in readiness —for all had been prepared for Gian Maria."

A great joy came into Valentina's eyes ; her cheeks flushed and her glance fell ; but Francesco scanned the Duke's face with the keen eye of one who is incredulous of so much good fortune.

" Your Highness means me well ? " he made bold to ask.

Guidobaldo stiffened, and a frown broke the serenity of his lofty brow.

" You have my princely word," he answered solemnly, at which, with bended knee, Francesco stooped to kiss his ducal hand.

And so they departed on the horses that they kept as the spoils of war. They made a goodly show, Guidobaldo riding at their head, with Francesco and Valentina, whilst the rear was brought up by Peppe and Fra Domenico, who, touched by this epidemic of goodwill, were at last fraternising with each other.

And as they rode it chanced that presently Guidobaldo fell behind, so that for a moment Francesco and Valentina found themselves alone a little ahead of the others. She turned to him, a shyness in her brown eyes, a tremble at the corners of her red lips :

" You have not yet said that you forgive me, Francesco," she complained, in a timorous whisper " Were it not seemly that you did since we are to be wed so soon ? "

THE END

PRINTED BY THE ANCHOR PRESS, LTD., TIPTREE, ESSEX, ENGLAND.